# The Uncollected Stories by Edgar Wallace

## Volume I

Richard Horatio Edgar Wallace was born on the 1st April 1875 in Greenwich, London. Leaving school at 12 because of truancy, by the age of fifteen he had experience; selling newspapers, as a worker in a rubber factory, as a shoe shop assistant, as a milk delivery boy and as a ship's cook.

By 1894 he was engaged but broke it off to join the Infantry being posted to South Africa. He also changed his name to Edgar Wallace which he took from Lew Wallace, the author of Ben-Hur.

In Cape Town in 1898 he met Rudyard Kipling and was inspired to begin writing. His first collection of ballads, The Mission that Failed! was enough of a success that in 1899 he paid his way out of the armed forces in order to turn to writing full time.

By 1904 he had completed his first thriller, The Four Just Men. Since nobody would publish it he resorted to setting up his own publishing company which he called Tallis Press.

In 1911 his Congolese stories were published in a collection called Sanders of the River, which became a bestseller. He also started his own racing papers, Bibury's and R. E. Walton's Weekly, eventually buying his own racehorses and losing thousands gambling. A life of exceptionally high income was also mirrored with exceptionally large spending and debts.

Wallace now began to take his career as a fiction writer more seriously, signing with Hodder and Stoughton in 1921. He was marketed as the 'King of Thrillers' and they gave him the trademark image of a trilby, a cigarette holder and a yellow Rolls Royce. He was truly prolific, capable not only of producing a 70,000 word novel in three days but of doing three novels in a row in such a manner. It was estimated that by 1928 one in four books being read was written by Wallace, for alongside his famous thrillers he wrote variously in other genres, including science fiction, non-fiction accounts of WWI which amounted to ten volumes and screen plays. Eventually he would reach the remarkable total of 170 novels, 18 stage plays and 957 short stories.

Wallace became chairman of the Press Club which to this day holds an annual Edgar Wallace Award, rewarding 'excellence in writing'.

Diagnosed with diabetes his health deteriorated and he soon entered a coma and died of his condition and double pneumonia on the 7th of February 1932 in North Maple Drive, Beverly Hills. He was buried near his home in England at Chalklands, Bourne End, in Buckinghamshire.

## Index of Contents

Richard Bruce, Burglar

Sunset in Angel Gardens! If there could be a sunset where the sun had never risen. At all events, it was the time when the sun usually sets everywhere else but at Angel Gardens—since, except for a few hours daily when, by eluding a forest of chimney stacks and dodging the obstruction caused by an immense and ugly structure which in ghastly satire had been named Palace Mansions, the sun, as an Angel Gardener put it, "hadn't a look in."

If there were few palatial tendencies in the Mansions, there was certainly nothing either Arcadian or "angelic" about the Gardens.

A long, narrow street, with the regulation allowance of street lamps; the usual general shop on one side, and the invariable beer shop at the corner; the houses, bearing a dreary resemblance to each other; the groups of children playing in various stages of dirtiness, happy in the blissful ignorance of their abject poverty; above their cries, the coarse laughter of the many bare-armed women, who seemed to spend one half of their time hanging out of their windows or sitting on their doorsteps, and the other half making pilgrimages to the ever-handy beer shop. To the lively strains of a street-organ, a couple of slatternly girl-women with frowsy, unkempt locks and heavy fringes were dancing, their fishy eyes sparkling from their unwonted exertions. Everywhere the same signs of misery and want.

From the oft-opened door of the "Cow and Meadow" (even in naming their public houses they sought the pastoral) came discordant snatches of tuneless songs, mingled with the din caused by half-a-dozen people speaking at once.

No. 14 differed in very little respect from the remainder of the Gardens. If possible, it was just a trifle more dirty. Such windows as remained intact still bore the marks of the glazier's thumb, even though they had been in for over a year. Where glass was not, a small piece of brown paper made an excellent substitute!

The fastidious were not tolerated in Angel Gardens. The Gardeners' motto was "Keep your nose out of other people's business." Not that I would dare for one moment to assert that the Gardeners were at all reticent concerning their family histories; as a matter of fact, everybody knew everybody, and even an outsider might hear for the asking the pedigrees as far as they were known of anyone from No. 1 up to the little shop at the corner (which, owing to its being a supplementary addition, was numbered 41a). But to ask a woman what her husband did for a living, or a man where he worked, was neither policy or sense, and was likely to get the enquiring one into serious trouble. And quite right, too. What did it matter to anybody if Mr. Jigger disappeared for periods of six, nine, and twelve months at a stretch, re-appearing at the end of that time with a generally run-down look and wearing his hair cut suspiciously close? Whose business was it if Mr. Boozy (better known as Ginger) never left home till dusk and always carried his tools in ingeniously designed pockets?

A periodical house-to-house search by the police, if inconvenient, was seldom resented, although the virtuous wrath of the "lady of the house" when the missing criminal remained undiscovered, or her pretended amazement and whining protestations of innocence and ignorance when the sought one was found underneath a bed or hiding in a convenient cupboard, was a sore trial for the patience and tempers of the "X" Division!

Mr. Richard Bruce, who was responsible to the owners of No. 14 for the rent, rates, and taxes, and who paid the same when he had the money and owed it when he hadn't, was not at all fastidious, and as he sat in the first floor front of No. 14, in front of a fire that was trying hard to die a natural death, he had not the look of a person who would go into ecstacies over the drape of a mantle or the symmetry of a Grecian vase. He was by no means a handsome man, and yet there was a strength about the square-cut chin and broad forehead that made him anything but repulsive, and his clean-shaven face and shaggy eyebrows gave him an air of distinction

Dick Bruce was, in his way, a celebrity. His photograph occupied a prominent position in the Rogues' Gallery, he was known to the police as a man to be knocked on the head first and argued with afterwards, and the head of the C.I.D. himself had condescended to study him, and had written a long analysis of the man's character, for the benefit of a scientific man who was preparing a book on "Crime and Criminals."

Dick paid very little attention to the state of the fire: the poverty of his surroundings did not seem to affect him much. A man who had spent a third of his life in prison could afford to overlook such trifles.

His head was sunk on his breast, and a worried, hunted look was on his face.

To be hunted or "wanted" was quite an ordinary state of affairs, but to be worried was for a man of his temperament an unusual thing. The turning of the door-handle made him start and look round. The newcomer was a little girl scarcely eight years old, yet wearing on her small, sharp face that look so common to children, old in worldly wisdom; the average observer would have called her unusually plain, but to Dick's eye she was all that was clever and beautiful. For a child of eight to be so far advanced as to read and write was to him nothing short of marvellous, and Aggie's accomplishments were continually being "trotted out" for the benefit of admiring friends. The child closed the door after her, and then, seeing that the ricketty box that served for a table still bore the remains of the evening meal, she asked, "'Ave you 'ad your tea, daddy?"

Dick, who had resumed his former attitude of abstraction, made no reply, and the question was repeated. He raised his head and, answering in the affirmative, resumed his study of the fire. After hanging her tattered cloak up, the girl drew a little stool up to her father's feet, and getting as close as possible to the feeble fire, began warming her hands. Rousing himself with an effort he asked, "'Ow did you get on at school to-day?"

"Pretty well," was the reply. "Miss Boyd says I shall soon be put in a 'igher standard."

"That's right," said Dick in a tone of approval. "That's right, matey, make 'ay while the sun shines, I only wish I'd a 'ad your chance when I was a boy, but I 'ad to pick up my learning in the streets."

"I was thinkin', daddy," said the girl thoughtfully, "'Ow ard it must be not to be able to read and write, 'specially when you 'ave to go away in the train to work—like you did last week—an' p'r'aps don't know the stations."

Dick nodded acquiescence. It was very awkward when he went away to "work" not to be able to tell whether he was breaking into the house of a parson or a banker, when a mere glance at the door-plate would have put him in possession of the necessary information had he been able to read it.

Talking of work brought a new train of thought into the child's mind, and she added, "But you wasn't away very long last time, was you, daddy, wasn't there any bells to hang?"

(Dick was usually described on the charge-sheet as a plumber, although his tools were used for a less legitimate purpose than for mending broken pipes).

"No," was his somewhat gruff reply.

"I always think of you," she went on, "when you are away an' I pray, same as they do at school, for my daddy who is away workin' for me."

Dick's lips tightened as she spoke, and in the ash-strangled fire he could all but see the scene of his recent labours. The old oak-pannelled hall, with the moonbeams tinted in their passage through the stained glass, bathing in their mellow light the stately mail-clad figures that formed a lifeless guard; he lived again the awful moment when he had heard that faint footfall behind him and had turned with uplifted "jimmy" to silence the intruder. Again he seemed to see, as he had seen, not once, but a thousand times since, the silent motionless figure lying on the polished floor, the moonlight playing round the silver hair of the old servant who had been faithful unto death. He had told himself again and again that he had to do it. To have been caught red- handed meant a "lifer" for him, and better the gallows than an eternal prison. For life! He shuddered, then meeting the girl's wondering eyes, and thinking some explanation was due to her—for after her reference to his work he had subsided into a morose reverie, he said not unkindly, "You mustn't talk about my work; you see, matey, I ain't a union man—an'—an'—the plumbers are on strike an' I ain't supposed to work, they might call me a blackleg, and you wouldn't like your father to be called that, would you, matey?"

"Not tell anyone," faltered Aggie, disregarding the question. "Not tell anyone about your work! Oh daddy, I didn't know you wanted it kept quiet, an'—an'—"

"An' what?" he asked roughly. "You 'avn't been blabbing about what I've been doin', 'ave yer?" Then seeing the tears that had risen to her eyes, he added in a kindlier tone, "There, there, matey, I didn't mean to frighten yer, but who was it yer told?"

"A gentleman," was the tearful answer.

"A gentleman!" repeated Dick, his face darkening again.

"Yes," she went on, trying hard to stop a sob. "'E said 'e wanted a plumber to do a bit o' work, an' 'e asked me if you did much, an' whether you'd care to go into the country to do some work; an' I said you wouldn't mind goin' 'cos only last week you went down to do a job at Hazley—"

Dick started up with an oath, his face an ashen grey, his eyes blazing with the terror of death. "Who told, you?" he said hoarsely. "Who said I was at Hazley?"

"I found the railway ticket on the floor," cried the child, beginning to whimper again.

Dick remembered seeking to evade observation at the station. He had dropped on to the metals as the train slowed up before reaching the terminus.

There was a silence outside, a drunken loafer homeward-bound was warbling a doleful ditty; and the cries of a couple of beldames engaged in a slanging match rose shrilly above the shouts of an encouraging crowd.

Composing himself with a mighty effort, Dick asked quietly, "What sort of a gentleman was 'e?"

The little one was now thoroughly frightened; child though she was she knew that this cross-examination was for no idle purpose, and between her sobs she answered, "He was a nice gentleman with a dark moustache and a red mark on 'is cheek."

Dick nodded, he knew the man, it was Fowler of Scotland Yard, the cutest "tec" in the force, they were old acquaintances. The red mark referred to was Dick's handiwork, for which that worthy had retired for five years. Yes, the evil had been done! Fowler, he knew would strain every nerve to bring him to grief. The man pondered for a little while and then asked, "How long ago was it?"

"Just before I came in," was the reply. "He stopped me at the corner of the Mansions and asked me if I was Mr. Bruce's little girl."

"The sneakin' cur," Dick muttered. "To make the kid give me away," and then leaning forward, and with a touch of tenderness that seemed foreign to him, he drew the child gently towards him, and laying her head upon his shoulder, he commenced to gently stroke her hair. "You ain't got no mother," he said huskily, "an' I—well I ain't been as good as I might a' been—but there's pals o' mine who are on the straight who'll look arter you for Dick Bruce's sake—'cos—I—I'm goin' away."

"Goin' away!" cried the child. "Oh no daddy, not goin' to leave me?"

"Yes, matey, yes," and a lump stood in his throat; "I've remembered a job that's to be done—there, there! don't cry little 'un. 'Ere," putting his hand in his pocket, "Take this quid to Mrs. Brown in Commercial Road an' say 'For old time's sake Dick Bruce sent me.' I saved her kid's life once, an' now she can save mine."

There was a sound of heavy footsteps on the stairs and a vigorous protestation on the part of somebody below, and putting the child gently from him, Dick said, "'Ere comes the gentlemen as I'm goin' away with—to work for; now stay 'ere while I go out an' see 'em.' He paused at the door and hesitated, for the words seemed to stick in his throat, "Be a good girl," he said with a quaver in his voice, "an' may Gawd bless yer an' keep yer."

Through the half-opened door she heard her father conversing in a low tone with the men outside. Somebody said something that sounded like "Wilful murder." There was a snap of steel, and Dick Bruce and his "friends" went down the stairs together. The girl was sobbing bitterly, but obedient to her father's command she remained on the stool before the dead fire, her head resting on her arms, still clutching in her hand the gold for which Dick Bruce had sold his soul.

## Good-bye

In view of the evident unrest among the hill tribes, the Officer Commanding the 90th Sikhs will detail an officer and sixty men to proceed by march-route to Mangoon. They will take with them preserved rations sufficient to last 20 days, and 200 rounds of ammunition a man."

As he finished reading, Colonel Burton, of the 90th Sikhs, laid down the document he had been reading aloud with a gesture of impatience.

"Sixty men!" he said, looking across the flower-laden vases, that gave his writing-table the appearance of a small garden, to his daughter, who, seated in a comfortable basket-chair, was busily engaged in her lace work. "Sixty fiddlesticks! Why don't they put, 'Will proceed to Mangoon for the purpose of affording the hillsmen target practice'?"

"Is it really so bad, father?" asked Gladys, looking up from her work.

"Bad?" answered the Colonel. "It's worse. It's murder pure and simple—that is as far as murder can be pure and simple, but there are the orders," picking the paper up again and running his eye over it. "What chance, I should like to know, will sixty have against a possible six thousand? If they escape the fever—and you know, dear, the country between here and Mangoon is one long swamp, they can never hope to hold their own against these men. Don't I know; haven't I had a substantial token of their fighting quality?" And the long scar that extended from his temple to his jaw grew an angry red as the blood of the choleric old Colonel began to warm at the recollection of his fighting days.

"No, Gladys, my girl," he said, "to send sixty men against a hundred times their number may be a great compliment to the 90th, but it's hard lines on the men who are sent."

Gladys was silent, for awhile, and then she asked, "Did you say Captain Henniker is going?"

"Yes," was the reply; I must send a captain. Boyd's on leave, so is Grier. Hayton's down, with fever. I can't send Hinge, the poor fellow is only just married. I confess that I was in a dilemma when Henniker, who is awaiting leave, helped me out by volunteering."

"Poor fellow," said Gladys softly.

"A brave man," replied the Colonel, in that snappy fashion he adopted when he wanted to be unusually impressive. "I wonder," he went on, gazing meditatively at the Burmese idol that served as a paper-weight, "I wonder if the people at Home ever realise the number of men who die here in India, unrewarded, unrecognised, and unknown, for their country's cause. I'm afraid that they are apt to look upon a brilliant cavalry charge as the highest type of valour, and fail to remember that the officer and man who fight one long, running, tiring fight, harassed by bush skirmishing, overcome by heat and thirst, and weakened by fever, are entitled to just a little hero worship. I speak feelingly, dear, for I've had as much of that kind of thing as will last me a lifetime."

The girl rose from her seat as the Colonel was speaking, and crossing the room, leant lovingly over her father's shoulder. They made a pretty picture, and the half-darkened bungalow, with its skins and screens, its bamboo walls covered by trophies of many a frontier fight, made a splendid setting for the tough old soldier and his fair young daughter, and as he ran his fingers through the gold-brown tresses that hung over her shoulder, and saw the sympathetic tears that glistened in her sweet grey eyes at the recital of her father's past troubles, the old man said, "You have a kind heart, darling, you are a true soldier's daughter. It is the dearest wish of my heart to see you a soldier's wife."

"A soldier's wife, dad?" she repeated.

"Yes, clear," said the Colonel kindly, "a soldier's wife. You know that I have no desire to pry into your love affairs, but I am rather curious to know how matters stand with Boyd and yourself."

For a time she did not answer, but walked to her table, and commenced to tidy her work.

"Captain Boyd," she said after awhile, a faint flush rising to her cheek, "is a—friend."

The Colonel, who was fitting on his helmet and trying to make her believe that he did not notice her very evident confusion, stopped short as the last word fell in incisive tone from her lips.

"A friend? Why, Gladys, I thought—"

"Yes, yes, I know," the girl said hastily, almost tearfully. "I don't want you to think any more about it. Captain Boyd and I are friends, very good friends, but nothing more."

This was, indeed, news for the Colonel. Everybody who was anybody from Tugabad to Simla knew, or thought that they knew, that the affair of Boyd and "Burton's little girl" was as good as settled.

Probably had Colonel Burton been anybody else but Colonel Burton he would have seen the change; as it was, he had thought it strange that Boyd, who had applied for leave for sporting purposes, should prefer the solitude of the tiger-run jungle to the company of Gladys; but this he had put down to the fact that all men require a little change. He was just a trifle angry that he had not been made acquainted with the change of affairs, for although there had been no engagement, things drifting along in a free-and-easy style characteristic to Anglo-Indian society, yet like everybody else, he had thought that it was merely a matter of time for Boyd to speak. Boyd was a great favourite of his, and had been ever since he had come to the regiment a white- faced boy, straight from his mother's apron strings.

The Colonel had been struck by the youngster's grit, and when in an affair on the Afghan border, "Burton's Boy," as he had been nicknamed, saved his commanding officer's life by the simple expedient of jumping in front of him, and receiving a half-arm jab from an Afridi's knife, the friendship was cemented more firmly than ever.

When he had seen the evident pleasure the society of his daughter had given his protégé, the old man had felt that his cup of happiness was full. There was no one to whom he would have sooner given her, and now to hear that all his cherished plans were tumbling to the ground like a card-house, was, to say the least, annoying. "What has Boyd said or done?" he asked as mildly as was possible—for him. "Some silly lovers' quarrel, I'll be bound. Now look here, Gladys, my girl, I've set my heart on you're marrying Boyd, and—"

He got no further, for with an air of queenly dignity she had risen.

"And I, dad," she said, "have set my heart on marrying whom I please."

Further altercation was prevented by the arrival of a native orderly, who saluted his chief.

"The Doctor sahib wishes to see you at the Hospital," he said.

"What's wrong?" asked the Colonel, tartly; the little encounter had not improved his temper.

"And the Boyd sahib wishes to see you at the orderly room," went on the impassive Oriental, quietly ignoring the question.

"Boyd?" said the Colonel, quickly. "Boyd? Why his leave doesn't expire for another week. I wonder why he's back." Then turning to follow the soldier, he said half abashed, "I'm sorry I got so peppery, dear, but you know how I feel, and how much I have this at heart."

"I know, dad, dear," said Gladys, putting her arms round the old man's neck, and kissing him. "I know, it will be hard for you; but—"

"Well, well," he answered with a sigh. "I suppose you will have to decide for yourself; after all you are entitled to choose the man who is to make life all or nothing to you."

"Arthur back," mused the girl, watching her father's figure disappearing across the palm-bordered square, "His leave doesn't expire for an awful long time yet. I wonder what has brought him back. Poor dad! how I wish—" with a long-drawn sigh, as she seated herself and resumed her work, "but there, it's all over now, and wishes are vain and useless."

The Colonel had unconsciously described the estrangement very accurately when he called it "a silly lovers' quarrel."

It had been such a quarrel as none but lovers would have indulged in, and as such was, of course, absurdly childish.

How well she remembered that night when in the cool of sun-down they had sat together in one big chair and watched the young moon rise over the rice plantations, making in the black waters of the lagoon a glittering silvery background for the motionless giant rushes and jungle grass that fringed the waters.

How happy they were then, and how beautiful the world had seemed.

It all came back to her as she worked, the sweet scent of the jessamine, the strange weird calls from the distant jungle, the sing-song drawl with its tom-tom accompaniment that came from the road-side temple where the devotees of Shiva were holding "high-jinks," as Arthur had irreverently put it.

How handsome he had looked as he sat there with a cigarette between his lips. As a matter of fact he wasn't—few men are—but the light favoured him, and in its mysterious fashion adjusted the shape of his features to something like proportion, and converted the sun-tan and freckles into a complexion.

Gladys had said something trivial, it might have been anything from an opinion of a book or a description of a dinner, with which he did not agree, a little innocent bantering evolved into rather plain-speaking personalities: "Don't be a fool, Gladys!" and thus the quarrel. Had it ended by her leaving him in tears, it would have been the usual comedy of a lovers' tiff, but unfortunately she did not; choosing to remain and say all the nasty things that occurred to her—and they were not a few.

In return he had driven her almost to desperation by telling her with a laugh that she would be only too pleased to ask his forgiveness in the morning.

He had a powerful imagination, and he sketched out the form the reconciliation would take, even going as far into details as to describe how they would gaze into one another's eyes, and such little things as lovers do, and the un-loved world know nothing about.

This wounded her pride more deeply than he could ever have known. Even love cannot stand against ridicule; he thought that he was being unusually smart, but he was a man—and a fool; He had sent imploring letters since, asking, nay imploring forgiveness, but had received no answer. Once she had felt inclined to forgive him, but there rose before her the scene he had sketched so graphically, and he had lost his chance. A shadow fell across the doorstep, and there stood the object of her thoughts.

The colour left her cheeks; it was the first time they had met since that night.

He was in uniform; she did not stop to wonder why, she remembered he looked his best in khaki.

"Won't you come in?" she faltered.

"Thanks," he answered rather huskily (he had not noticed any particular hoarseness until that moment). "I shan't keep you long, but I—I—" He looked helplessly round for something inspiring. Gladys with downcast eyes had resumed her work. For a time neither spoke, he was thinking of something to say that would give him an opening, some trivial remark that would lead up to the point in view.

"I've come," he said, nervously twisting his sword-knot into a spiral, "to ask you—whether you—that is—whether you will be as we were before. I know," he added hastily, seeing she had risen with a heightened colour. "I know I have no right to ask, particularly as you have as good—or as bad—as refused; but now that I—"

"Exactly," put in Gladys with a scornful smile. "Now that you have returned, after so long an absence, I, having fretted myself into a state of lachrymose collapse, will instantly fall into your arms, and confess my faults. That is as you have already pictured, is it not? Unfortunately, Captain Boyd, that melodramatic situation does not appeal to me. I'm afraid I have no histrionic soul!"

He was not an emotional man, and as deeply as he felt her stinging words, not a muscle of his bronzed face moved. They stood facing one another in the dim light of the bungalow.

"You did not give me time," he said quietly. She had never heard that tone before, and the anger died within her, and the intuitive knowledge of some approaching calamity came upon her.

"You did not give me a chance to finish the sentence, but perhaps it doesn't matter."

A bugle sounded the "Fall in," and they could see a crowd of men leaving the shade of bungalows, and form into an orderly line.

"The men for the front," said the girl, temporarily forgetting the quarrel. "Henniker's men, poor fellow!"

"Poor fellow," repeated Boyd absently; then changing his tone he pointed with a reckless laugh to the distant horizon, where, shimmering in the heat, the first of the Mangoon heights frowned down upon the purple swamp that stretched as far as eye could see.

"Do you see that?" he asked, almost rudely. "Do you see those hills ? Do you know that Khas Khan is waiting with a thousand men to cut up this little force, not one of which will probably return? The Government knows, the General knows, but as in theory Khas Khan is a loyal and faithful servant to the Queen, and has made no declaration of war, they dare not send more for fear of exciting the country, and bringing down upon the head of the British Government, the abuse of every fire-side critic from John O'Groat's to Hong Kong."

"And do you mean," said Gladys in horror, as the awfulness of the thing dawned upon her, "Do you mean that these men are to be used as a bait, a human, living bait, to be sacrificed so that a secret enemy may be made an open foe? Oh, surely not!"

"That's about the size of it," said Boyd, with a mirthless laugh. "See! your father is addressing the men."

"I can't see Captain Henniker anywhere," said the girl. In the last few minutes they had unconsciously returned to old familiarity of manner.

"It isn't likely you will," said Boyd grimly, "considering that at present he is lying in a very hopeless condition in the hospital."

"In hospital?" repeated Gladys, in bewilderment. "In hospital? How? When?"

"About an hour ago, poor old chap, he took a touch of sun, and went down in the middle of the parade ground."

This was why her father had been sent for, and then a thought striking her, she asked,

"But who is going with the men? Not—not—" The colour died from her cheeks as she began to realise the truth.

"Yes," he said quietly, "you have guessed rightly. I am. I heard that a detachment was going up, and returned to volunteer my services. As it happened, I returned at the very moment I was required."

For a moment she stood as if dazed, then catching both his hands in hers, and looking beseechingly in his face she said, almost in a whisper, "No, no, not you, Arthur! Say you are joking. You must be, you cannot mean that. Why, you yourself have said it is certain death!"

Even as she spoke she knew that it was the truth he had told her.

She noticed for the first time he was dressed in Field Service order.

A bugle drawled from the parade ground.

"Officers come and be damned," said Boyd bitterly. He was repeating the words that soldiers have put to the "officers' call."

They seemed just then so very à propos.

He slipped his arm round the girl's waist, and drawing down the brown head to his breast, tried to soothe her, for she was weeping softly.

"Don't cry, darling," he said, with a quaver in his voice. "It's all my fault, all mine. I was a fool, don't make it harder for me than it already is."

She did not answer, but raised her tear-stained face to his, and their lips met.

"Good-bye," she whispered between her sobs. "Good-bye," he muttered, and putting her gently from him, he left her.

A little aloof from the other officers, the Colonel was waiting his arrival.

"Here's your instructions," he said roughly. He was trying to hide the man under the martinet. "And you're a young fool, and—God bless you—a brave man; and now don't forget if you have the slightest excuse for returning do so. If Khas shows any signs of armed resistance—I know the devil won't till you're hemmed in on all sides—but if, by God's mercy, he does, you are to retire at once, do you understand? And now good-bye!"

Boyd wrung the extended hands, and turned to his company who were standing at ease.

"Slope arms!" he called.

Sixty butts crashed to "Attention," and then with a rattle came up together.

An orderly had left the telegraph office and was running towards the Colonel, who, surrounded by his officers, was waiting to see the company march off.

"'Fours—right!" said Boyd, casting one look towards the white figure that stood in the doorway of the Colonel's quarters. "By the left—quick march."

With a quick step the little body of men wheeled round the group of officers, towards the gate that led to the Mangoon road. "Goodbye," he said between his set teeth; "Good-bye to all that makes life worth living."

They had crossed the square and were nearing the main guard-room.

The guard composed of men of a British Infantry regiment had turned out with shouldered arms, ready to salute their dusky comrades. The regular footfalls of the little party reverberated through the stone archway that formed the entrance to the cantonments and the straggling street that led to the bazaars, beyond which the torturous swamp road lay before them.

"Halt!"

Mechanically the troop came to a standstill, and Boyd looked round in astonishment, for he had recognised the Colonel's voice.

"What is it, sir?" he asked wearily, he was not in the humour for further instructions or fresh farewells.

Colonel Burton did not answer, but handed the telegram he had just received to him. Like a man in a dream, Boyd read:

"FROM GENERAL OFFICER COMMANDING THE FORCES IN TUGABAD TO THE O.C. 90TH SIKHS. STOP OR RECALL DETACHMENT PROCEEDING TO MANGOON. TRIBE HAS RISEN. A BRIGADE IS BEING ORGANISED FOR DESPATCH TO THE AFFECTED DISTRICT."

He handed the orange-coloured form back, and for a moment could not believe his senses; at last he found his voice:

"Fall out, men," he said. "Go back to your quarters." Then turning to the Colonel, who was watching him rather closely, he said, "If you don't mind, sir, I should like to see Gladys?"

The elder man laughed and rubbed his hands.

"I haven't the slightest objection to offer," he said.

Phalaenopsis Gloriosa

Two men sat over their liquor and cigars in the big library of Driscoll's country place. It was a chilly evening in April, and the great pine logs which blazed on the hearth before them and threw tremendous lightings over the books, paintings, and heavy ebony furnishings of the apartment scarcely served to dissipate the chill of the unused room.

To the right, three long French windows looked westward over acres of lawn sweeping down to the broad river, while to the south the view was shut off by dense masses of evergreen shrubbery, supplemented by vines and creepers which had flung their festoons of delicate leafage in every direction across the windows. A great elm standing guard at this corner of the house tossed its branches to and fro in the spring wind and tapped nervously on the nearest window.

The house, in spite of its wealth and beauty, impressed one with a sense of loneliness. A dwelling reflects the daily life of its tenants in the same intangible way that a man carries the reflection of his life writ large in face and person; and this stately room had the air of one who has looked on his dead and stands appalled and desolate. From the more distant parts of the house came the occasional creak of a board or the slam of a shutter in the wind, and at each fresh noise the elder of the two men turned a face full of ill-concealed uneasiness in the direction of the sound. At last the other tossed the ash of his cigar in the fire and turned to his host.

"Bob, old fellow, what's the matter with you? You're as nervous as my grandmother! Is it a ghost or delirium tremens that is freezing your young soul? Speak out man, what is it?"

Driscoll, thus addressed, rose, and going almost stealthily to the two doors leading out of the room, slipped the massive bolts across into their, sockets; then he came back to the fire, poured out some liquor, drank it, and pulled his chair near to Larcher.

"Larcher, you and I have been out together for big game. The tiger skin there tells one story, this leopard's skin beneath our feet another, but I have brought you here to-night to help me kill or capture the most devilish thing that ever walked the earth. You, because you are the one man whose brain and nerve and muscle I can trust."

"Good!" said Larcher. "Is it man or beast?"

"Not beast, yet scarcely human," replied the other, "but I must go back and tell you the story of this accursed thing that has come upon the place. You know what a hobby my orchid houses have long been to me, and you have heard me speak of the difficulty I have had in getting a capable foreman to minister to my favorites. The run of these fellows know merely the few common commercial varieties, and my interest has always centred in the rarer species. Six months ago I was in such despair over my collection that I had almost decided to give up their culture entirely rather than suffer the constant disappointment of having successive importations die on my hands, when, in response to my advertisement in the Herald, there walked into my office one morning a fellow who seemed exactly the one for the place. I couldn't tell his nationality exactly, but his bronzed face bore out his statement that he had spent many years in the tropics, collecting orchids for one of the big English importing houses. Details were soon adjusted between us, and it was arranged that he was to come down here and begin work at once. I inquired if he had a family, and he replied that he had a wife, who would come down here with him the next day.

"As he rose to leave the office, I said: 'One thing more, Hearston. I hope you are up in growing Phalaenopsis Gloriosa. They are my favorite orchid, and I have a special house of them out there.' Larcher, at mention of the orchid's name I could have sworn that the fellow turned green under his tan. He caught at the chair back as though to steady himself, and answered oddly that he thought he could do nothing with them, and then added, as though he had said more than he had meant to: 'They are the most difficult orchids in the world to bloom in captivity, sir.' I smiled at the conceit of the orchids as imprisoned wild things, bade him good morning, and forgot the incident for the time.

"Well, they went down the next day, and were soon established in the pretty little cottage on the slope of the hill near the greenhouses. I went down some weeks later, found everything running smoothly, and Hearston introduced me to his wife. You know that since Mollie died, women have rather gone out of my life, and I am not easily impressed with a pretty face, but I shall never forget the exotic beauty of that woman.

"Whatever doubt there might be about his nationality, hers was unmistakable. She was pure, high-caste East Indian; you know the type, tall, slim, with exquisite features and eyes of midnight witchery. I thought as I looked at her that she had the same subtle atmosphere of mingled spirituality and splendor that my orchid blooms possess. She spoke no word of English, and stood beside Hearston as we talked, eyeing him with a world of pathos in her dark, unfathomable eyes. It was plain to see that she adored her husband from his footprints upward. You remember the handsome collie dog I had here, a beautiful fellow, who lived up to his ideals in a way to shame most humans. He had always been slow to make friends with strangers, though devoted to the old servants on the place. He came bounding up to us as we stood there, and to my surprise, ignored me to fawn at Mrs. Hearston's feet, leaping upon her with the utmost affection. 'Your wife has made a friend worth having,' I remarked to Hearston. The man smiled and assented, and the subject passed.

"We spent the rest of the day going through the greenhouses together, and I found that I had made no mistake in my man. Such a knowledge of orchids, of their native conditions of growth and climate, and such a stock of East Indian lore was a revelation to me.

"The greenhouses have been altered and enlarged considerably since you saw them last; the chief addition being an immense circular house at the foot of the range. Here I have gathered thousands of fine plants of Phalaenopsis Gloriosa. Instead of the usual equipment of benches I had a number of trees on the place cut down and sunk in the ground at irregular intervals from each other, on all sides of the house, and the orchid plants were then wired to them from the ground up, interspersed with ferns imbedded in moss. Great palms were planted thickly round the trees, and hundreds of orchids were suspended by wire from the roof. The whole effect was that of a bit of tropical jungle. In spite of all my care they had never done well, and I was anxious to have, my new foreman's advice on the subject.

"Rather to my surprise, Hearston's wife accompanied us on our rounds, but when she came to the floor of the Phalaenopsis house, she drew back pale and shuddering. He spoke some rapid words in what I suppose was her native tongue to her, and she turned and sat on a stool in the shed outside. He murmured some apology to me about her being tired, and followed me into the house. Before communicative, the man grew oddly quiet and nervous. We were there some five minutes, and in that time he never took his eyes off the slim little figure in the shed beyond. I could get nothing out of him about the culture of the Gloriosas, and attributing his evident embarrassment to his ignorance on the subject, we returned to the other houses. That night I went back to town.

"I am going into all this wearisome detail, Larcher, in the hope that you, with your years of experience in India, and your knowledge of the Oriental character, may be able to see some glimmer of dawn in the darkness of the mystery that followed."

Larcher nodded, eagerly, and Driscoll continued:

"Six weeks passed, and Hearston's reports were uniformly satisfactory. At the end of that time I received a curious letter from him. It was a request for a couple of private police to patrol the place night and day, and the man urged haste as though oppressed with terror. We are too far off the turnpike here to be often troubled with tramps. Still I felt that my new foreman had deserved my confidence so far, and I took steps that afternoon to engage a couple of men for watchman's duty. The next day was Sunday, and still a bit worried by the unusual tenor of Hearston's letter, I took the afternoon train and came out here. I had neglected to wire anyone of my coming, so there was no trap at the station to meet me, and I walked the mile to the place in a bleak February twilight that seemed to deepen in perceptible gradations.

"As I came down the curve of the drive and round the southern corner of the house, I paused, struck by the beauty of the view. Great crimson clouds were banked up on the horizon as though rolled up by a stupendous fire, while streaks of sullen red shooting almost to the zenith flung their sinister reflection on the river and the lawns. I had never seen the place take on such a lurid unearthly beauty, fit setting for the tragedy to come. The group of dwarf Norwegian pines at this corner of the house stood out against the angry sky like some exquisite tracery, and while I stood admiring their symmetry and grace, a branch not twenty feet away from me swung back and—a face looked out.

"A hideous face, such as one might conjure up in the nightmares of a fever, a yellow, square Mongolian face, seamed with a thousand wrinkles, and every seam a sin. Larcher, I saw that face as plain as I see you now. For the space of three seconds I stood still, looking straight at that grinning mask, hypnotised, perhaps, by those beady glittering eyes gazing into mine. Then the branch dropped back into place, and I, released from the spell cast over me, darted forward to the spot where it had been. It had vanished like a dream. I searched among the bushes for half-an-hour or more, but finally gave up in despair, and went into the house.

"I took occasion, while old Mrs. Mayhew was serving my dinner, to question her guardedly on the subject of tramps or strangers on the place. She told me there hadn't been a stranger seen on the place all the winter. That some of the servants had been commenting on the fact only the night before. This made Hearston's letter more inexplicable than ever, and after dinner I sent for him, intending to have a plain talk with him on the subject. He came in answer to my summons, and I jumped at sight of the man's face. White and haggard, with a certain hunted fierceness in his eyes and a restlessness in his manner which changed him utterly. I felt that the situation rose to its feet, and explained itself as a bad combination of man and whisky. I never strike a man when he's down, or preach temperance to a convalescent drunkard, so I ignored Hearston's apparent condition, told him of my receipt of his letter and the arrangements I had made for the patrolling of the place.

"'They must be quick, Mr. Driscoll,' Hearston broke in. 'They, must be quick. For God's sake, sir, get them over here at once!' He came up to me in his excitement and laid his hand on mine. I shivered at his touch; it was so cold. His eyes blazed into mine in passionate eagerness, and then I saw my mistake. It wasn't drink that had changed the man; it was sheer, clear, cold, blue terror!

"'Hearston,' I said, 'there is something wrong here on the place; I want you to tell me frankly what you fear.'

"Before the fellow had a chance to reply the night was broken by a succession of sharp yelps like an animal in pain, followed by a shrill scream, and on the sound the man beside me dashed through the door and out over the verandah. I followed him almost instantly and ran out of doors. There, ahead of me, Hearston was running over the lawn to his cottage, as though he had been shot from a bow. I followed him as rapidly as possible, marvelling at the speed with which he crossed the ground, and a second later I came up to him bending over his wife lying in a dead faint on the verandah of his cottage. A shadow lay at the woman's feet, and as I bent to see what it was, a pitiful little moan came up from the darkness.

"Someone brought a lantern, and by its light I saw, my collie Donald lying there, his bright fur all matted with blood from a murderous knife-wound in his side. His beautiful, faithful eyes turned up to mine as I knelt beside him, then glazed as the little life went out. Together we lifted Mrs. Hearston, and, carrying her into the house, laid her upon the bed. Hearston, wild with excitement, bent over her, begging me to do something—anything. In a few minutes she recovered her consciousness, but relapsed at sight of us into a state of helpless hysteria. They both seemed too near the verge of collapse to give me any information as to what had occurred.

"Hearston was walking to and fro like a crazy man, wringing his hands, while his wife lay laughing and sobbing uncontrolledly. The dog's death showed me that something serious was on foot on the place, and, feeling that they were probably not safe in the cottage by themselves, I proposed to Hearston that he and his wife come up here for the night. He assented with eagerness, and they came up to the house with me. Mayhew put them in a room on the ground-floor which had at one time been used as a sort of spare room when the house was crowded. It was in this wing, but on the other side and facing the greenhouses. I saw them comfortably installed, told Mayhew to see that Mrs. Hearston had everything she needed, and bade them good-night.

"I sat long over the fire that evening, trying in vain to puzzle out Hearston's behavior, and the cause of my dog's death. It all depressed me more than I can tell you, and I was filled with a miserable, presentiment of evil, try as I might to shake it off. I must have sunk into a sort of a doze before the fire, for I dreamed a curiously vivid dream. I was out on the lawn in the moonlight, pursuing a baffling shape which fled from me, eluding me ever as I gained on it, and which kept giving out yelps like the dying cry of the dog.

"Faster it fled, and I faster, with that curious rapid increase of momentum peculiar to dreams, till at last I had him by the shoulder. He turned in my grasp, and I saw again the hideous yellow face outlined against the shrubbery, and an appalling scream shot through my brain and brought me to my feet. I knew that I had dreamt the rest, but I could have sworn that the scream was real. I rushed to the door and flung it open. The hall lay dark and silent. I threw open a window thinking the sound might have come from without, but the grave could not be quieter; and cursing my nervous imagination for the fright that it had given me, I turned in and went to bed.

"The next morning I woke early, and eager to clear up in the daylight the wretched business of the night before, I sent Hendricks over to Hearston's room to tell him I wished to see him as soon as possible. The fellow came back and said he had knocked repeatedly on Hearston's door, but couldn't rouse him, and in that instant all the vague horror of the night before returned to me. The room had two long French windows in it like these, opening out on the north verandah, so I sent Hendricks out on the porch to reconnoiter from the outside. He returned, almost immediately this time, to say that one of the windows was wide open, and he had looked in. The room was in confusion, Hearston and his wife were gone. It came to me that they might have risen early and gone back to the cottage, so I sent Hendricks for the third time to deliver my message. A third time he came back to say that they were not there. I went myself to the cottage. It was just as we had left it the night before. I hailed one of the gardeners on his way to work. 'Have you seen Hearston?' 'No,' he answered; 'perhaps he is in the greenhouses.'

"'Perhaps he is,' I said; 'we must find him. You and Hendricks take the first house and I'll take the second, and we'll go through alternating.' I started on my tour of the houses, calling Hearston's name aloud in my eagerness to find him safe, and shake off the deepening conviction that I should find him otherwise.

I reached the Phalaenopsis house at the foot of the range, still calling, opened the door and started to go in. The masses of greenery made the interior seem dim to me after the morning sunlight; but as I closed the door I saw something coming towards me out of the forest twilight of the place. At first I thought that it was Broughton's Great Dane—the dog is over here half the time—but it rose upright, upright and gibbering, lunged at me through the shadows of the green! I leaped to the door and crashed it behind me, and the thing fell against it heavily, and rolled over on the floor. It was Hearston; Hearston with snow-white hair and eyes of flame! Hearston, and he was mad—mad!"

"And the woman?"

"No trace! If the earth had opened and swallowed her she could not have disappeared more utterly. We captured Hearston after a terrible struggle; there was nothing to be elicited from him. Every inch of this place has been searched and searched again, and still, no trace! And, Larcher, It seems a trivial thing, a weak and empty fancy, and yet—"

"Tell!"

"Since that night when that mysterious horror happened, those Gloriosas seem to have taken a new lease, of life! Great sprays have started from every plant and hang laced and interlaced like some strange web on every side. Buds developed, but they do not bloom! A month ago I said to the man in charge—'To-morrow will see this house white with blossoms.'

"He looked at me curiously. 'So I thought, sir, a week ago.'

"'They were not sufficiently developed, then,' I answered.

"'Yes, sir, just as they are now.'

"'Why, man, they couldn't be,' I cried! 'look at them, they are just ready to burst open.'

"'As you say, sir,' he answered; reservedly.

"'But you don't agree with me?' I asked.

"'No, sir, they were just like this ten days ago; one would say, sir, they were all ready to bloom, but—that they were waiting for something!'

"It is true! I have watched them ever since. The whole place is full of a dismal, haunting oppression that I cannot shake off or banish. An indescribable terror hangs over it, and I never want to see it again.'

Larcher rose to his feet, his face alight with excitement, and stood with his back to the fire looking down at Driscoll.

"And the motive, the clue, the explanation to it all? What do people say? What do they think?"

"Everything and nothing! A woman is made away with—by whom? By Hearston, himself, some say: Bah! The man loved her. She had no fear of him. There was a third person whom they both feared—the face in the pines."

"The other men on the place?"

"Are above suspicion! They all room together in quarters over the carriage-house, and were all there that night. They say that Hearston was a good fellow and devoted to his wife; that she was with him in the green-houses every day, and that he never seemed content unless she was close beside him. Further, it was brought out that in the ten days preceding the occurrence Hearston had seemed strangely excited and nervous, but perfectly sober and sane, and, note this, that there had been no tramp nor suspicious character seen on the place since Hearston had come on it."

"Did you tell the police of the face you had seen?"

"I did. But no one else had seen it; I had no tangible proof that I had, and the consensus of opinion seemed to be that it was the result of overstrained nerves."

"What has become of Hearston?"

"He is, or rather was, till two days ago, in the lunatic asylum, the tower of which you can see just over the trees, to the west of the place. It's about three miles distant. They said from the first that his condition was quite hopeless. When they took him there he was almost uncontrollable; then he sank into a sullen silence difficult to break. Two days ago I received word from the superintendent that Hearston had burst the heavy iron bars at his window and escaped. They begged me, if I had any knowledge of his whereabouts, to inform them at once, and added that they were watching my place, as it was likely that he would seek his home.

"I came down here immediately, but so far, have had no sight of him. Yesterday afternoon I grew lonely and nervous. I had been in the house all day, and, thinking a little exercise would do me good, I strolled up the drive to the gate. It was almost dark when I turned to come back, and I couldn't help glancing sharply through the shrubbery as I passed along. I had on an old pair of tennis shoes I found in my room here, and the soft soles were almost noiseless on the gravel roadway. And as I walked it seemed to me I heard a sort of swish, swish, as of someone moving through the bushes to my right. I drew my revolver, and gradually slackened my speed, that whatever it was might pass me.

"The movement in the bushes slackened, too, and I knew that I was being watched. I walked on till we came to a place where the shrubbery lining the road was thinner than usual, and, wheeling suddenly, I plunged through the bushes in the direction of the sound. As I wheeled, so did the intruder, and put such distance between us that I could but faintly make out a tall supple figure in the robe of some dark stuff, wound round the waist with a scarf. I had hoped to find it Hearston. But it wasn't he, for the man glanced around just before he disappeared, and I saw again the villainous yellow face, and the beady eyes! I ran after him, discharging my revolver as I ran, but the shots went wild in the gathering night, and for a second time he eluded me. This morning I sent you a wire. You are here. That is all."

"Driscoll, you say the face you saw in the shrubbery was grinning? Did you notice anything, peculiar, about the teeth?"

Driscoll sprang to his feet with a smothered oath. "Larcher, you have seen it! Where?"

"I haven't seen it, Bob, upon my word!"

"Then how did you know that it hadn't any teeth? At least, just the two incisors, at the angle of the jaw, long and yellow like a wolf's fangs! How did you know the one thing I omitted to tell you?"

"Sit down, and I'll tell you. It's a bit of a story I haven't thought of for years," answered Larcher, lighting a fresh cigar. "By the way, since you confess so frankly to carrying a gun, I may as well unload myself of my armoury. I never stay in civilisation long enough at a time to accustom myself to going without a weapon. I'll lay it here on the table, if you don't mind. Well, you remember that I went out with the British East India Geographical Commission some seven years ago, and you will remember, further, perhaps, that our chief mission at that time was the exploration of some of the tributaries of the Mekhong River. The British Government has ploughed India with its army, and harrowed it with its civil service, till it is surprising that there should be a wild spot left; but there are still great stretches of territory unknown and almost impenetrable, where the weeds of native custom flourish in rank luxuriance. There is probably no place on the habitable globe, under the nominal control of the civilised nation, concerning which so little is known as the valley of the Mekhong River. Immense forests, centuries o]d, stretch unbroken for hundreds of miles, hiding in dank, impenetrable morass and jungle, the wild, fierce people who inhabit them.

"We struck the Lam-nam-si River at its junction with the Mekhong, and started off to follow it to its source. We had not been out more than three days' march when we began to hear of tigers, and I determined to leave the party at Menatkong and browse round the neighborhood a bit to see if I could get a tiger skin or two. I expected to join the others about a week later at a point agreed upon. They protested that my life wouldn't be worth a farthing, alone in that country; so I compromised by taking Haranya Vatani, a native, who accompanied the party as guide and godmother. The first day we were disappointed in our game, and found ourselves at dusk, with a tropical storm on our track, near an isolated native village.

"It was the only place for miles around that offered human habitation and a shelter from the storm, but in spite of that Haranya tried to steer me past it. This only made me curious to see it, so I took the rudder in my own hands, and we stayed over night there. We were civilly received, for Vatani's fat face is a sort of general ticket of admission to that part of the universe; but the next day, the worst of the storm being over, one of the inhabitants tipped Vatani the wink that it would be more tactful if we would move on, and we, accordingly, did so. After we left the place, Vatani told me the cause of our scant entertainment. The name of the village is Kong-Satru. You know, doubtless, that practically all the Gloriosas come from there."

"No, I thought they came from Panom-Pehn; that is the place mentioned in the invoices."

"That is the river-port where they are packed for shipment. They are stolen from the forests around Kong-Satru by sturdy adventurers, who evidently have little love of life, and shipped by stealth and night down the Mekhong to the sea. The forests on the hills around Kong-Satru are the most magnificgnt imaginable, and teeming with this variety of orchid. A native, Haranya said, would much sooner think of selling his children than a plant of the Gloriosas, which are indescribably sacred to them. These people mix their religion with the culture of the plants in a manner at once horrible and grotesque. The flowers are cared for by a band of native priests, who to the thousand other Oriental ideas, add one more, the most gruesome of them all.

"They say," and Larcher leaned across the table towards Driscoll and gazed meditatively out into the night as he continued: "They say that the orchids must have blood, human blood, and so it happens just before the plants' blooming season, the priests select a victim from among the inhabitants of the village for this sacrifice."

"And then?" asked Driscoll, as Larcher paused, still gazing past him out of the window, sunk in reminiscence.

"I was thinking of the night Haranya told me this tale, sitting in a little tent in the midst of the jungle, not 30 miles from Kong-Satru, with the tail of the storm lashing round us, and Vatani shivering with fright lest he be overheard in the telling; in India it is neither polite nor healthy to discuss your neighbor's religion."

"And then?"

"And then, on the day of the feast of the flowers, which was the festival our presence interrupted, on that full moon of April, when I unwittingly grazed Death, there is high carnival in Kong-Satru, and the priests take the victim to the forests above the town—and feed the flowers!"

"And then?"

"'And then they bloom!' said Haranya, 'and not until then!' The priests are a vile-looking lot, with yellow skin like parchment, their teeth not gone as you describe, it, but the four front teeth blackened so that at a distance they are invisible. There is a large Chinese element in these priests, if they are not indeed full-blooded Mongolians, which marks them off from the rest of the Aryan population."

"And you think that Hearston's wife—"

"Was doomed to the sacrifice! That Hearston was in the neighborhood gathering Phalaenopsis, and either had seen her before, or met her while she was trying to escape; that by his knowledge of the country he succeeded in getting her to some sea-coast town where they shipped for England. Then they came here and lived content, till the fanatic face rose up at her elbow, inexorable as fate. I think myself that those priests must have some hypnotic influence over the people; you heard the girl's cry when he came to her that night? How else did he awe them to the submission and silence that followed?"

"I see it now. It must have been the priest, too, who killed my poor collie."

"Do not lament the dog, Bob; he died trying to defend the gentle soul who had been kind to him, and no death could be nobler. I think that the priest has the girl in hiding, hypnotised; he is waiting for, the hour. It has struck! This is the full moon of April, the day of the feast of the flowers. If the girl is to be saved, it must be now. We shall have an able ally."

Driscoll sprang to, his feet. "Who?"

"Hearston! He is tracking the priest; I have been watching him at it the last half-hour."

"Where?"

"There! See! The gaunt figure crouching in the shadow of the pillar on the porch! At first I thought he was the priest; and laid my gun handy; then he moved a bit, and the moonlight fell on the white hair and asylum garb. Depend upon it, Driscoll, Hearston, too, has seen that face from his prison windows and the iron bent like tin beneath the maniac strength that gathered itself and passed out to slay. See! He is watching something that is moving across the lawn from south to north. I can tell that, from his movements. It can be nothing else but the priest. Look, he is rising! Are you armed? Then come."

Leading the way, Larcher noiselessly unlatched the window and passed out on the verandah, Driscoll following. The man in front of them crept cautiously forward from the shadow of one tree to the next till he reached a clump of shrubs commanding a view of the great stone staircase which terraced the hill beside the greenhouses. He paused here, watching the stairs intently. Larcher and Driscoll at a little distance did the same.

"He's lost him," whispered Driscoll; but Larcher shook his head. A moment later the priest glided out of the bushes fringing the stairway, almost at the bottom of the hill. For an instant the supple figure stood out in the full moonlight, black against the whiteness of the stonework, listening; then, apparently satisfied, he beckoned, and a slender white figure crept out and after him as he opened a door and disappeared. In an instant Hearston was making his way down the steps, the others following as before. There was no hesitation or undue haste in his movements; as silently and relentlessly as the tide laps up the shore, so did he cover the space between himself and the priest. He reached the door of the Phalaenopsis house and melted into the blackness of the wall. As the door opened a low monotonous sing-song chant struck the ears of the two outside.

"Chinese, by all that's holy? Bob, he is worshipping the flowers!"

A second later they had reached the door and looked in.

It was a weird scene! Lofty trees towered sheer to the height of forty feet or more, covered with the delicate green of ferns among the darker shades of the orchid plants, while thousands of sprays of half-open flowers filled the house with a subtle and exquisite odor.

The priest stood in the centre of the house, his back to the door. He had cast off his robe, and, naked save for a loin cloth, was swaying to and fro in a sort of religious ecstasy, his arms extended towards the flowers above him, and chanting as he swayed. At his feet knelt the woman, white, unseeing, tranced!

Behind him, mute and terrible, crouched Hearston, waiting for the instant of his spring.

"Hearston's unarmed!" breathed Driscoll.

"Yes, like a gorilla! Let be! The quarry's his."

At last the priest paused in his chant and the moment came. Hearston reached out with his left hand, caught the bolt of the door, and shot it home with a crash that shook the house. It was challenge and ultimatum in one, and at the noise the priest swung round and faced his death!

He flung one arm aloft, in what almost seemed like a gesture of command; but, as he did so, Hearston's embrace went round him like a hoop of steel, crushing him in with slow, resistless force. The Mongol would have been a match for a heavier man in a poorer cause, and he writhed in Hearston's grasp, making frantic efforts to release himself, till the mighty muscles rolled under the yellow skin like the coiling and uncoiling of a cobra. A frantic tug at the loin cloth and his free arm flung upward, a curved knife in his grasp, and twice it fell in abortive strokes which glanced off Hearston harmlessly.

The men outside flung themselves against the barred door with a force that splintered the glass in the upper half, but the bolt held. Larcher reached, in through the splinters that remained, pushed back the bolt, and the two rushed in.

Suddenly, in one last supreme effort, the priest raised himself to his full height, almost lifting Hearston off his feet. Again the light quivered along the knife as it rose and fell, and as the priest sank backward, dead, he carried Hearston with him, the knife lodged in his back.

Driscoll bent over the prostrate forms, trying in vain to unlock Hearston's fingers still knotted round the priest. A cry broke from the lips of the girl beside them, and the men both turned and looked at her. She was standing gazing at Hearston in pathos unutterable; the cry that had escaped her was the long, low Indian wail for the dead. Larcher stooped, and with practised hand drew out the knife, then turned.

"Do not mourn," he said to the girl in her own tongue. "He will live, since you have come back to him."

And as he spoke Hearston released his hold on the priest, and turned and held out his arms to the girl. The flame had died out of his eyes—the man was sane!

"Driscoll," cried Larcher, in a curious toneless voice, "look up, look up at your orchids, they think they are going to be fed!"

Driscoll straightened himself from surveying the priest and looked about him. He went white as he gazed and threw a steadying hand against the nearest tree.

Multitudes of great white flowers swayed on every stalk, crisp, new blown! Wide open, each petal distended and with eager stems, as happier flowers turn to the sun, they craned their faces towards the dead priest on the floor.

I

Two men sat at one of the little tables at Garriani's in Soho, London.

Garriani's spelt soiled tablecloths, vin ordinaire, and the smell of yesterday's cooking. If you ask at Garriani's for the daily paper, they will bring you the 'Petit Parisien,' and if you complain, Antonio, the head waiter, suave and unshaven, will apologise, and bring in exchange 'El Imparcial.'

But it was an English newspaper that was spread before the elder of the two men. It was the foreign page that lay under his impatiently drumming fingers, and heavy black headlines, that stood out from the sheet that overstood the matter that filled his mind.

Leonine of head, Paul Kressler had never been a handsome man. His was the face that men call 'striking.' He had the eyes of the dreamer, and the square jaw of the tyrant, as befits the Nihilist who seeks the idyllic through ways of violence. His companion, squat of figure, fat of face, puffy of eye, yet comfortable withal, was of the class that sees in Nihilism, Anarchism, Socialism, and any -ism that is opposed to established law and constitutional practice a means to personal end. Such men have no cause—they have only a purpose.

'You're mad, my friend,' he was saying; and his tone was almost jovial. 'There is nothing to be gained, unless you see in this a means of regaining your position.'

Paul Kressler gave a bitter laugh.

'Something for something, eh? That's your creed, Von Masteich.* Have I not given sufficient proof of my disinterestedness?'

[* Spelling conjectural. Poor quality of digital source makes name difficult to decipher.]

'Your pardon, baron. I did not mean—' muttered the other, averting his eyes.

'Five years ago, what was I?' continued Kressler. 'Captain of the Petroski, with an admiral's flag for the reaching. To-day I am what I am-exile, suspect, Anarchist, what you will!'

'You have made great sacrifices,' cooed the German, flicking the grey ash from his cigar.

'And you think, having made the surrender, I want to go back on the principles that are so dear to me—'

'To us,' corrected his companion comfortably.

'It is because I love Russia, as I hate its Government—because I love the land as I hate its lords!'

'But the Czar will never—'

Kressler waved an impatient hand.

'That remains to be seen; I can but try. Look at this—look at this!' He brought down his great fist with a crash on the table, and Antonio, dozing at the servery, woke with a jump. 'Can I read day by day such things as these? Can I see the glory of Russia pass away before my eyes, and never lift my hand to strike a blow?'

The German rose, and the other followed suit.

'Then you persist?'

There was a sneer in the question.

'Yes'—quietly. Then, with an outburst of that fiery passion that had made him at once the joy and terror of the Brotherhood, he cried: 'Not for the Czar, I tell you—not for the cursed bureaucracy—not for the cruel little devils that sit behind desks, and send innocents to damnation; but for Russia, the land, and the people-for the Fatherland!'

The German bit the end from a fresh cigar, and balanced a silver matchbox on two fingers.

'Some will call you patriotic,' he said slowly—'some may call you quixotic. As for me—'

'You think I am a fool,' rejoined the other quickly.

'Ach, Gott!' said the little man admiringly. 'You are the occult!'

They stepped out into the thin drizzle that fell on the London streets, and the German went to his club, and Paul to the dark little room on the third floor of a back street off the Tottenham Court Road.

A week after this meeting, the Imperial Secretary at St. Petersburg sent a telephone message to the Grand Master of the Police, in response to which that high official came post haste to the palace.

'Who is Kressler?' asked the Secretary, without any preliminary.

'Paul Kressler—Naval officer; flag captain '88; author of the 'Torpedo Boat Tactics,' and,' added the chief of police, with a certain grim emphasis, 'a most excellent brochure, 'God and the Czar'; a member of the society known as the Little Brethren of Russia; a revolutionary of the most dangerous type. Present address—'

'I know—I know!' said the great Secretary, impatiently tapping an open letter that lay before him. 'But what plot, conspiracy, assassination if you like, was he associated with?'

The other shrugged his shoulders.

'None that I know about; but he is a dangerous man. He has even spoken against—'

And the head of the police lowered his voice to an awestruck whisper.

The Secretary bit the end of his pen thoughtfully.

'As a naval officer, what sort of a man was he?' he asked.

The police chief threw out protesting hands.

'I am no judge of a naval officer's abilities. If he was as thorough an officer as he is a revolutionist, he deserves to control the navy!'

The Secretary stretched back in his chair.

'If half he says is true,' he muttered, partly to himself, 'if he is sincere, such a man might work wonders. We want good men.'

His brows knit in a perplexed frown, and he sat for a moment silent; then he started forward, as though on some sudden impulse, and, seizing a pen, wrote a few words on a printed slip.

He read it over carefully, and fixed a tiny red seal to the corner of the document.

'Take this,' he said tersely.

The chief took the paper and glanced at it. He expressed no surprise, nor anything more than a casual interest.

'You understand, monsieur?' said the Secretary, pointing his remarks with a white forefinger. 'Paul Kressler is to be allowed to return to Russia. He is to go on his way unmolested. You will arrange that he is watched carefully?'

The policeman smiled, as at an unnecessary question.

'You intend that he should remain in Russia?' asked the official carelessly.

'I intend that he shall receive his commission as a naval captain, and leave immediately for Vladivostok,' was the quiet reply.

And even the policeman, hardened as he was to the eccentricities of his Government, raised his eyebrows as he left the room.


II


So it came about that when Paul Kressler called at the little shop to which his letters were directed, a square official envelope was handed to him.

He clutched it eagerly, and walked rapidly back to his lodging. He reached home, and with trembling hands struck a match and lit the tiny lamp. Eagerly he ripped open the flap of the envelope, and extracted two documents. He read the first in silence, but there was eloquence in the glow of his cheek and the dancing light in his eyes.

It was a formal notification of his liberty to return to Russia. It bore the official stamp of the Chief of Police, and the counter-seal of the Imperial Secretary. The other document he unfolded with a puzzled face. His bewilderment was only momentary, however, for he started up from his seat with a great cry of joy, as he read the words that gave him back his old rank and his old profession. A slip of paper fell to the ground. He picked it up.

'You will proceed by the shortest route to Dalny, and take over the command of the torpedo vessel Riga,' it ran briefly, and was followed by the signature of the Secretary to the Admiralty.

That night Captain Paul Kressler left Charing Cross by the nine o'clock mail train, travelling third-class, and carrying, carefully folded in a bundle by his side, a uniform which, according to no less than three distinct Admiralty orders, was obsolete of pattern.

It was a tired-looking man that stepped down on to the platform at Vladivostok a month later. The train had brought him from Dalny, in response to an urgent telegram from the commandant of the naval port. A dapper young officer met him, and saluted, eyeing him curiously.

'Captain Kressler?' asked the officer, with his hand to his cap.

Kressler nodded awkwardly. Before the stripling, resplendent in his well-fitting uniform, he felt shabby and mean.

Something of his thoughts was reflected in the face of his junior.

'If it would please you,' said the young man urbanely,'you will come at once to the office of the commandant.'

Paul bowed, and followed his conductor.

In a large, bare room near the docks sat the naval chief of the ill-fated port.

A grey-haired man, sallow of face and stout of build, he sat at the side of, rather than behind, the table.

He rose as Paul entered, and adjusted a pair of pince-nez.

Without unnecessary introduction, he plunged into the subject that filled Paul's mind.

'The enemy's fleet are ten miles out,' he said, speaking rapidly; 'the destroyer Riga is laying in the inner harbour. You wrote to the Czar, saying you wished to strike a blow for our Holy Master—'

'For Russia,' corrected Kressler.

'It is the same,' said the commandant haughtily. 'For the Czar or for Russia, you are willing to take great risks—to make great sacrifices?'

'I have already made great sacrifices for Russia,' said Kressler, speaking slowly.

'The enemy is brave, with a reckless courage that is past all understanding. Officers and men deem it a delight to die in the service of their barbarous country. The damage our fleet has sustained is mainly due to the extraordinary disregard they have for their personal safety.

'I have not noticed,' he added, with some bitterness, 'the same qualities displayed amongst my officers.' He rose to his feet, and walked to where Kressler, who had also risen, was standing, and laid a big hand upon the other's shoulder. 'When a Japanese officer takes his torpedo-boats out,' he said, and he dropped his voice,' he does so with the full intention of never returning alive. You understand, my child?'

Paul nodded.

'He goes forth,' the admiral went on, 'with one desire, and that is to do as much damage as he can before he himself is killed. I make myself clear?'

'Perfectly, admiral,' said Paul quietly.

The admiral tightened his grip on Paul's shoulder.

'At ten o'clock to-night you will take the Riga out of harbour, and set a course for the enemy's fleet.'

And the elder man dropped his hand suddenly, and returned to his place by the table.

'You may go,' he said shortly.

Paul saluted and went to the door.

As he opened the door, he turned to the man at the table.

'I shall not return,' he said, with simple directness.

The admiral nodded.

'It will be better so,' he said gravely.

When the stars were struggling through the mist that lay on the waters the Riga slipped from her mooring and, passing between two cruisers aflare with the naked lights of working engineers, glided silently to sea. As he felt the throb of the engines beneath his feet and swayed with the motion of the little vessel, a wild joy filled the heart of its captain.

The smell of the engine room, the scent of the sea, the taste of the first errant drop of the flying spray, filled him with a mad delight. There were no other officers on board but himself. His second-in-command was a petty officer, who, by the masked light of a lantern, was picking a course clear of the mine field that guarded the harbour's entrance. Under quarter speed the destroyer zig-zigged a path through the floating engines of death, until with a sigh of relief, the petty officer looked up.

'We are clear now, little Father,' he said.

Paul's hand was on the telegraph. He threw over the lever, and there was a muffled tinkle between his feet.

The thin steel hull of the destroyer trembled for a second; then came such a sudden leap ahead as to well-nigh throw the captain off his feet. From her three funnels poured a rain of red-hot cinders, sizzling down to her soddened decks. High-flung clouds of spray broke over her bows, and great waves smashed against her.

In the conning-tower Paul set his course. According to the instructions he had received, the enemy's fleet lay sixty miles off. In a little over two hours he could come up with his quarry at the speed he had set, but he knew that the last twenty miles must be run dead-slow, lest the flame from the funnels betray him.

Shuddering, trembling, leaping like a thing of life, the torpedo-boat threshed through the tumbled seas.

Paul looked at his watch.

'An hour and a half out,' he muttered, and laid his hand on the telegraph.

The pace of the Riga slackened; the convulsive shudders that had shaken the little ship died away to a tremble.

The second officer clutched his arms.

'Look-look!' he whispered, as though fearful that he would be overheard.

They had run out of the mist, and the night was perfect. The sky was all a smother of winking stars, and on the horizon blazed one bright comet. A comet, with a straight white tail stretched upward, that moved uneasily from left to right.


III

Paul's hand sought the telegraph, and the boat stopped.

'They've got their searchlights working,' he said.

And his subordinate's perplexed face reminded him that unconsciously he was speaking in English,

'Go ahead dead slow!' he ordered in Russian.

And the destroyer crawled ahead.

And now, at various points on the horizon, other comets came into life, and soon the ocean's rim bristled with swaying spokes of white light.

Paul frowned.

'We shall never get near them—never get near them!' be said bitterly.

An hour passed in helpless contemplation of the foe. At the speed she was moving, and with a strong current running against her, the destroyer had progressed less than five miles.

With rage in his heart, Paul watched the wheeling searchlights play on the sea, lacing the black waters with a fret of silver. He had no fear of discovery. He was too far away to be observed.

'I shall not come back,' he repealed to himself. And the admiral's grave voice, 'It, will be better so,' rang in his ears.

It wanted an hour to the dawn, when the searchlights of the fleet grew strangely blurred. Each ray shone in a strange nimbus that softened and diffused the fierce white light.

The captain of the Riga took one long, eager observation through his glasses, and a smile broke the hard lines of his face.

'Half speed ahead!' he signalled; and the sea hissed under the stripped hull of the destroyer.

The searchlights were now but a white, steamy glow on the horizon.

'Sea fog!' said Paul, in fierce exultation. 'Every man to his post! Man the quickfirers; stand by to torpedo!'

The lights were now blotted out, and Paul threw over the indicator to full speed. Again the Riga leaped forward. Paul, peering ahead through the spray-washed outlook of the conning-tower, saw the white banks of of the sea fog rolling towards him. In a moment the ship had plunged into the mist.

For twenty minutes the little craft raced onward; then, out of the thinning mist, ahead loomed the huge hull of a battleship.

In a minute they were abreast. Paul pressed a button, and something white and long and slender leapt into the water abeam. Then came a burst of white flame, and a deafening roar, and the fog lifted. There was a flash of a searchlight. By its rays Paul saw a great vessel sinking astern of his milky wake.

'Hit!' he cried, dropping on his knees. 'Merciful Heaven, I thank thee!'

Then a dozen searchlights focussed fierce on the destroyer. It seemed that a regular inferno had been let loose round the gallant ship. Torn and racked with shell, Paul Kressler felt his ship sinking rapidly beneath him.

What Paul died without knowing was that the blow he had struck for Russia was at Russia herself. For the ships he had come upon in the mist belonged to the long waited Auxiliary Russian Fleet.


The Calm Chauffeur

"Do you do much motoring?"

I made a flippant reference to the Arrow and Vanguard services.

"But have you done much motoring—have you owned a car?" Once upon a time, as I related, I bought a German car with French engines. I also acquired a serious chauffeur and two acetylene lamps.

The car suffered from many ailments, most of which the serious chauffeur—he is a policeman now, poor fellow—was able to diagnose with accuracy, but none of which he was able to cure.

It was a nice-looking car, with a beautiful leather hood, and ran easily with two persons, or without the hood, three.

When I drove down-hill I got up terrific speed, especially if the hood was on, but when it came to climbing hills I used to get out and walk ahead, pretending that the labouring machine behind and the red-faced chauffeur—more serious than ever—had nothing to do with me.

It was a nice car for the winter, because the works were under the seat, and they kept one's feet warm. Also in the summer the scent of petrol banished the moths from one's clothes.

I used to drive about in motor-goggles, and as people always associate goggles with speed I deceived a man into making me an offer for the car.

The letter containing the offer came by the night post, and I took a cab and drove to his house to accept. I did not take the car, because I wanted to reach him before he changed his mind.

As to motoring...

"But," persisted the inquiring enthusiast, "have you any idea of speed—have you ever travelled in a racing car, in a car that doesn't stop to think...."

I cited the cars I had known—the 24-hp Coliseum, the 12-hp Little Wanderer, the 6- or 8- (as the case may be) hp Runaway.

"Very good," said the enthusiast, "I will call for you at ten tomorrow morning."

So he came.

He brought a machine. None of your rough-finished, soap-box seated racing cars painted like a dirty warship, but a sleek green Mercedes "60" touring-car, all varnish and polished brass and silver fittings, with a fur-coated chauffeur lolling back in an armchair seat, and taking no interest in the proceedings.

"Are we going to a wedding?" I asked, and regretted that I had not put on a tie to match the car.

Then we started....

The car was purring like a tame cat, as we played musical chairs with the traffic of Ealing; it made no protest when asked to spring between a brewer's dray and a tramway-car in Brentford High Street. It stopped dead before a nervous lady pedestrian who was standing in the middle of the street debating whether to scream or faint, and reached Hounslow before we—the enthusiast and I—had finished saying what we had to say about nervous pedestrians.

Outside Hounslow we met the Blue Car, and the young man who drove the Blue Car sat without cap or goggles, his hair streaming out behind and a black smut on his nose. His expression was the expression common to all hardened chauffeurs—a reflective, thinking-of-mother expression.

The Blue Car was just ahead of us when we saw It. We did not know it was blue because it trailed a skirt of dust behind it that obscured the landscape. Later we leapt up to it and got ahead. I think our dust must have annoyed the Blue Car very much, for between Hounslow and Basingstoke it sneaked past us at a level crossing.

Then we came to a great stretch of country inhabited by furze bushes and telegraph poles, and the fur-coated young man who sat by my side pulled down his goggles and slowly shifted a small lever on the steering wheel. Then for the first time I was conscious that a high wind blew. A wind that hammered my face and filled my lungs, a wind that roared about my ears till I was deafened. The Blue Car was ahead. Surely it had stopped. As we passed it I got one fleeting glimpse of the smutty-faced young man— supremely indifferent and still thinking of his mother. At the same time I noticed to my amazement that the Blue Car really was in motion, and that the telegraph poles that lined the road were passing with remarkable rapidity. The enthusiast leant over. "Sixty-five miles an hour," said his lips.

There was a village ahead, and we slowed down. Three little boys standing on the pavement displayed an inclination to 'run across', and the chauffeur lifted an admonitory finger. The little boys stopped abashed, and we passed. The little boys who were the pioneers of the 'running across' game are no longer with us to encourage the present generation. We passed the outskirts of Basingstoke before we realised that we had left London. On the side path as innocent old gentleman lifted a stick... We stopped in twenty yards, and the chauffeur descended and made an inspection of all his gauges—an earnest inspection that took him several minutes. Not so the chauffeur of the Blue Car who streaked past triumphantly—and was stopped twenty yards further on by a policeman.

The innocent old gentleman with the stick, was one end of a 'trap'—the waiting policeman the other. Alas! for the vanity of Blue Cars we passed the group at a funeral pace—a policemen, a notebook, and a chauffeur with a smut on his nose.

Into the open country again. Long, long stretches of white road, a wild deserted world, and a slender spire on the skyline.

Again the high wind, and the buffeting and breathlessness and the whizzing telegraph poles and the throb, throb, throb of the engine as the car flew across Salisbury Plain. A solitary cyclist ahead waved a hand and we slowed.

He came up to us at a tremendous pace, and the tiny engine of his cycle working pipity-pipity-pipity-pip.

He passed like a flash, but the waving hand said 'trap' quite plainly so we crawled. This time it was an innocent-looking agricultural labourer—with a walking stick—and his pal was lying on the grass a mile further on—a measured mile. And so the day passed, a procession of long roads, of fresh green hedges, quaint cottages, gardens ablaze with blossom, rivers and wet meadows, gloomy stretches of plain, crooked, narrow streets of country towns, till night came.

By then we were moving towards London, two white beams of light thrown ahead showing the road. Ghostly figures rose from the road and passed; invisible cyclists came into the circle of light and vanished. Lumbering wagons filling up the road—with no light to show their presence—appeared, and were circumvented.

The blasé chauffeur, touching a handle here and a lever there, working with both hands and both feet, sends us along through the darkness—accurately, carefully, unswervingly. Isn't it a little dangerous perhaps for the cyclist, for the pedestrian?

A nervous young man wheeling ahead lost his presence of mind, wobbled, slipped and fell in our track... but the car stopped almost in its own length, and the young man, dazed but voluble, called himself all kinds of a fool, and explained that he was a nervous idiot—hoped he hadn't alarmed us. We expressed our thankfulness that we had been able to pull up in time.

The chauffeur yawned.


The King's Birthday and Mickey's

Gordon Douglas had a grievance; so also had Millicent Gilbraithe. And the grievance they held in common was no ordinary one.

Eight years before, by a remarkable coincidence, both Gordon—christened Mickey by the Fleet—and Millicent— yclept Midge by the Station—had entered the world simultaneously. Mickey at first had thought it rather wonderful, and it bad caused him many hours of troubled meditation. Eventually he found a solution in the first column of the Times newspaper. It was quite by accident that he had happed upon the column headed births; his spelling was somewhat erratic, but mother had helped to elucidate the inscrutable. So it was quite an ordinary thing for lots of people to be born on the same day, and Mickey sighed a sigh of relief. For he had no desire to be out of the ordinary; what was good enough for other people Satisfactorily suited him. He wanted neither more—nor less. And therein lay his grievance.

Midge's attitude was one of sympathetic acquiescence. She was the most loyal subject in Mickey's kingdom, and Mickey had many, be it understood. Not for nothing was his father the captain of the flagship. They knew him well on board the Contentious, as they knew him on every man-o'-war on the station. In spite of his eight short years of life, Mickey had established a record in recklessness that would be difficult to excel. There still exists in the archives of Mintique Dockyard a letter from the secretary of a certain humane society in which that official regrets his committee's inability to bestow the medal for saving life upon Private William Jagger, owing to the fact that "the Society has already awarded at different times four bronze medals and three parchment certificates to various persons for saving from drowning Master Gordon Douglas."

All the greater hero was Mickey for these exploits, as Midge would tell you. His scrapes were phenomenal in their frequency. His comments on his escapes had the charm of piquancy, and his attitude to the world in general was one of insatiable curiosity. The fleet rode at anchor in the bay. Two long white dazzling lines they were, sitting stately on the sunlit waters. To-day they had more than usual interest for the two children who, regardless of all admonition, warning, and oft-repeated prayers, sat swinging their legs over the sheer face of a little cliff that fell straight as a plumb-line to the water fifty feet below.

"What's the flags for?" asked Midge, extending a chubby finger to the gaily dressed ships, decorated from bow to stern with lines of fluttering bunting.

"Father says it's King's birthday," said Mickey importantly.

"Is he on the ship?"

"You're silly," said Mickey frankly. "How can he be on his ship when he's on his throne in Windsor Castle—hey?"

The solution of this problem did not occur to Midge.

"They put flags on the ship every year," continued the youthful authority, "and they shoot their guns off—when it's the King's birthday."

"Why?" asked Midge, somewhat overpowered by the knowledge of her friend.

"Why?—oh, 'cos he's the King and—and—'cos they like him very much. My birthday's to-morrow, too."

"So's mine. Will they put up flags for me and you?" asked the girl eagerly.

This gave Mickey pause. As a matter of fact the possibility of an official recognition of his natal day had occurred to him during the morning, and he had determined to question his father on the subject that very day. In his own mind he had little doubt that even if it was an unusual proceeding, a point could be stretched in his favour.

"I think so," he replied confidently; "they'll put flags Up for me—but not for you, because you're a girl, and your father's only a soldier."

(Mickey had a profound contempt for all services outside the navy, a contempt which rather unjustly embraced the Royal Marine Light Infantry, of which gallant corps Major Gilbraithe was by no means an unimportant number.)

"But," added Mickey generously, "my flags will do for you as well."

And so it was settled. And after the Royal salute had been fired, a proceeding which filled Midge with considerable apprehension, the two descended the winding path that led to the little tropical town that serves as the headquarters of the Mauritius squadron.

That night, before the Creole nurse piloted him to bed, Mickey put a leading question to his father.

The flag-captain laughed, long and heartily, and Mickey's mother, ever the most sympathetic friend Mickey had, had hard work to stop herself joining in the mirth.

"Some day, Mickey," said his father, wiping the tears of merriment from his eyes, "you shall have a salute, I promise you. You shall have a big gold band round your arm and your own flag, and guns shall be fired for you—but not yet."

So Mickey went to sleep under the swaying punkahs with a grieved feeling, and awoke on his birthday morn with a heart full of resentment toward a disobliging world. Nor did the mechanical submarine that went by clockwork, which the captain of the Disconsolate had sent for from Paris, appease him, nor the model of the Victory donated by the Master-at-Arms of the Hydrangea, nor the telescope from the marine sergeant of the Impossible, nor the book of mother's, nor yet the musical box of father's—none of these things, in fact, lifted the cloud from his soul.

Soon after breakfast he went out to talk the matter over with Midge.

Midge, he regretted to find, had almost forgotten the honour that he had half promised her. She was displaying a foolish and unnatural exultation at the possession of an abnormal thing in dolls. A great kid-bodied monstrosity with a perpetual and wearisome expression of pained surprise on its highly coloured waxen face.

"There ain't going to be no flags," blurted Mickey ruefully.

"What flags?" asked Midge undiplomatically.

"Why, my flags!" cried the indignant Mickey, "the flags for my birthday—our birthday," he corrected cunningly. "Haven't you got some flags we can put up?"

Midge pondered.

"Where can we put them up?" she demanded.

This was a poser, for flagstaffs in Mintique were few, and jealously watched.

"You get 'em," said Mickey, after a pause, "I'll find some place to put 'em."

Midge thought awhile and then said—"We haven't got any at home, but I know where there are lots."

"Where?" demanded the eager Mickey.

The girl shaded her eyes from the hot sun, and looked upward to where, perched on an eyrie, the little white hut of the port signal-man looked forward to the rim of the horizon, and backward to the great range that walled the mysterious hinterland from the strip of land which H.M. Commissioners had chosen as a suitable site for the naval station.

"Peter," she said slowly, "Peter will give us flags."

Peter, retired Yeoman of Signals, kept house on the Peak. His duty it was, by day, to report the incoming vessels, visible to him an hour before the fleet below; to transmit directions for anchorage, to ask pertinent questions through the medium of his big black-armed semaphore, and, not least of all, to keep watch for the sign—the little blue-black cloud that sprung from out of the ocean's edge—that foretold the coming of the typhoon, which the sailors of these seas so dreaded. Sometimes, but not very frequently— indeed, it had only happened once during the last fifteen years—instead of the black cloud came a long strip of red haze. Higher and higher it mounted to the skies, changing from rose to red, from red to purple, and so to a deep violet, and then—black—black—black. A chaos of howling winds, winds that snatched at roof and wall, that lifted with giant clutches the stout limes, and made desolate in an hour the cultivation of a score of years.

Woe to the ship riding between the long jagged arms of rock that stretched out from the horns of the bay, when the "devil-wind" came.

Peter had seen one such storm, and hoped never to see another.

He was getting an old man now; his application for relief from his post was already before the Admiralty, and his successor had already sailed from England.

And Peter was glad. Rubicund of visage and unpleasantly stout was Peter. The summer, early as it was, was unusually trying for him; his breathing had grown more and more laborious, the slightest movement had come to be an almost painful exertion.

Even as the children below had commenced their hot and dusty climb, Peter, returning from a scrutiny of the horizon to the little inner room which served as sleeping quarters, had noticed a lace of his shoe that bad become untied.

Now, an untied shoe-lace is a very ordinary object, and one not calculated to intrude on daydreams of Devonshire, of shady lanes, of white, green-topped cliffs, and of friends of other days; but somehow, in a vague way, old Peter noticed the untidiness of his shoe, and stopped to tie it tight....

Midge and Mickey reached the signal-house, but there was no response to Mickey's yell or Midge's timid knock.

"I wonder where he is?" asked the astonished Mickey.

Such an event as Peter being absent from his post had not been for one moment anticipated. Peter was as much a part of the signal-house as the big white flagstaff, or the uncanny semaphore with its grim black arms—as the very hill itself.

"Perhap's he's in the garden," suggested Midge.

The little patch of garden, that lay in a hollow behind the house, produced no Peter, however.

"Shout!" said Midge, and Mickey gave a howl which scared the gulls on a ledge of rock a hundred feet below; but still Peter was not forthcoming.

"Perhaps he's asleep" was Mickey's suggestion, as he cautiously pushed open the door of the outer room.

There was no sign of Peter here. The floor was as white as milk; the brass telescope hanging on brackets over the window shone like silver, a little clock ticked loudly from the ledge of a sloping desk that ran the length of one wall. On the other side of the room, a nest of pigeon-holes labelled in alphabetical order was filled with rolls of parti-coloured bunting. Here and there a stray toggle hung down ready to hand; for these were the coveted flags.

Mickey eyed them favourably, and, greatly daring, pulled one half out.

"That's G for Gordon," he said admiringly. Midge looked on in fearful admiration.

"Hadn't we better see if Peter's in the other room?" she asked in a whisper.

Mickey, somewhat loth to relinquish the means of celebration, nodded his reluctant assent. Midge knocked at the door of the inner room.

"Mr. Peter," she called; another and louder "Mr. Peter!"

There was no response, and Midge, turning the handle gently, essayed to open the door. The door gave a little, but there was evidently a bundle of some weight lying against the other side which rendered ingress impossible.

The children looked at one another, and then Mickey, strolling nonchalantly toward the flag locker, twisted yet another flag half way from its abiding place.

"D's for Douglas," he said absently.

"Do you think Peter will mind?" asked the nervous Midge.

"Not if we don't keep them long," replied the tempter in knickerbockers, tapping off the letters with a grimy forefinger. "J, K, L, M—M's for Midge."

"Millicent," corrected the girl.

In her anxiety to assert her claim to something superior to a nickname, she overlooked the questionable nature of the proceedings.

"Same thing," said the unscrupulous Mickey, unfolding a square blue flag with a white St. Andrew's Cross. "They're not much to look at, are they?" he added.

G and D were not even flags, but triangular pennants; the first with a yellow base and a blue apex, and the second a plain blue ground, in the middle of which was a round white spot.

"There's another G for Gilbraithe; what a stunning idea!"

Mickey was growing ecstatic in his delight.

"Surely old Peter won't mind our taking 'em," said he.

They were out again in the sunlight now, and conscience, awakened by fear of detection, directed another half-hearted search for the missing signalman. He was nowhere in sight, and Mickey, with feverish haste, began to loosen the signal-whips, which hung without motion from the flagstaff.

Had he looked seaward, the gauzy, blood-like mist that hung on the horizon might have excited his curiosity.

"Me first," he demanded, snatching up two of the flags. "I'll keep 'em up a minute, and then I'll hoist yours."

On board the flagship, Captain Gordon was giving a few instructions to the Commander before returning to the shore. Under the awning of the quarter-deck the officer on duty paced slowly to and fro, stopping now and then to mop a very red face with his handkerchief. That evening the fleet were leaving for manoeuvres, and below the men were washing the grime of coal dust from their faces, or stowing away the stores and ammunition that had been arriving since daybreak.

"Hot?" queried the Captain, pausing on his way to the gangway.

"Yes, sir," replied the officer of the watch. "It's about the hottest day I remember, even in these latitudes; feels like a storm, don't you think, sir?"

The Captain nodded.

"The glass is going down very little, but one never gets much warning; at any rate there's no signal from the Peak."

He turned to go, when a cry from the officer on duty arrested him.

"Signal from the hill, sir."

Half a dozen paces brought them to the signalling-bridge.

"What is it?" asked the skipper of the petty officer, who, with a telescope glued to his eye, was watching the little specks that fluttered from the staff on the hill.

"They're only hoisted half-mast, sir, and old Peter seems to be in a hurry; he's hauling 'em down before we've answered!—G D," he continued.

The Captain turned sharply.

"G D?" he asked. "Isn't that—?"

The signalman consulted his book.

"Yes, sir—'Prepare for a hurricane.' He's making another signal, M G—what's that?"

But the Captain had read the message, "Stand off—put to sea at once."

"A devil-wind," he said quietly. "Make a signal to the fleet—K W," hastily turning the leaves of the code; and the two flags that instructed all and sundry to "weigh, cut or slip, wait for nothing—get an offing," received the acknowledgment of the other men-o'-war with an alacrity which indicated a common knowledge of the danger menacing.

It seemed hours, although it was not many minutes before one by one the great ships swung their bows round to the rapidly darkening east. The last ship had scarcely drawn clear of the bay before the first blast of the storm smote her. For a moment a deafening rush of wind—then an ominous silence. Another tremendous gust which carried away awning and boat-cover, and then the men-of-war were in the thick of the typhoon.

None too soon had they got away; huge seas washed their decks, a furious hurricane of wind kept them almost at a standstill. In vain raced the threshing screws. Now in the air, now shaking the shuddering ships with the violence of their half-submerged revolutions. It seemed almost as if the fleet would be driven back on the coast.

Hour followed hour, and no abatement of the storm was noticeable, and not until the afternoon had all but passed did the last fringe of inky cloud race out of sight beyond the Mintique Range, and the young moon look down upon a mountainous sea.

It was at daybreak next morning when the fleet dropped anchor in the bay. The havoc wrought on land was plainly visible. Everywhere roofless houses and uprooted trees met the eye, great masses of wreckage strewed the shore. Indeed, the only place which seemed to have escaped the fury of the hurricane was the signal-house on the hill, in the first room of which two tired, frightened children lay asleep on the floor, blissfully unconscious that behind the door of the next room lay a dead man, holding in stiffened fingers a broken bootlace.

## The Angel Child

The well-drilled organist waited with his fingers lightly resting on the keys; the admirably disciplined bell-ringer pulled with monotonous regularity at the furry rope, his eye glued to the American watch hanging on a nail. Exactly at the hour the ringer steadied the bell and the organist pressed forth the notes of his voluntary.

With the coming of the white-clad choir came also the newcomers—father, mother, and Angel Child. They tip-toed along the aisle, the mother leading, the boy in black, with a deep white Eton collar and new gloves, following, and the alert father bringing up the rear. They sidled noiselessly into a pew. Father and mother prayed conventionally; the boy surveyed the interior of the old church with approval.

He was a pleasant-faced boy with wide, unwinking blue eyes; and Mr. Stebbing, our respected fellow-townsman and grocer, marked him down for the Band of Hope, and a prominent position in Mrs. Stebbing's Bible-class for Small Boys.

Above the shrill cadences of the choir one sweet young voice rose dominant:

O come, let us sing unto the Lord;
Let us heartily rejoice
In the strength of our salvation,

and Mr. Stebbing silently and reluctantly surrendered the new boy to the choirmaster.

In the little churchyard, all red and golden with the glory of departing summer, the churchgoers lingered to gossip, before dispersing to the serious function of Sunday dinner. Broad-cloth convincingly creased, and best silks faintly perfumed with the preservative sachets that keep at bay the week-a-day corruption, silk hats immaculate, and squeaky boots advertising their newness and within, under and above all these, souls refreshed and minds relieved by a duty well discharged.

The Vicar held his reception in the porch.

"Yes", he said, answering Mr. Stebbing, "beautiful voice, I was particularly struck by it. I think we shall be able to do something with that boy—they are the new people at the End House."

Mr. Stebbing shook his head gloomily. "Can't understand people of that class taking the End House." he said, severely, "They are not gentlefolk, and they are not—er—"

He almost said "trades people", but stopped himself. He was too near his own retirement from trade to wish to unduly emphasise the distinction.

"I'm making nearly a thousand a year," he added complacently, "and I couldn't afford the upkeep of the End House."

Later in the week the Vicar called on the new tenants, and was received by the lady of the house. He duly reported Mrs. Houghton to be a quiet, charming lady, who skilfully fenced questions, the answering of which might have enlightened the small town.

"An educated woman with a keen sense of humour," said the Vicar, remembering with some appreciation the ripple of laughter that greeted the repetition of his only joke. "The boy? No, he's away. Attends a day-school, I should imagine, somewhere in London. At any rate, his father takes him to town on Mondays, and brings him home on Saturdays. I'm afraid that upsets our idea of bringing him into the choir."

Little Malsey is not of sufficient size to warrant a daily newspaper. It shares with four other villages a weekly sheet, which is comprehensively called The Westlawn Chronicle and Orkley Gazette (with which is incorporated The High Malsey Courier and Tingburn Despatch). Once upon a time little Malsey boasted a weekly, in which, it is currently reported, Mr. Stebbing sunk no less than a hundred pounds. It lasted three weeks, and was worth every penny of the hundred pounds that Mr. Stebbing invested.

This was fourteen years ago, and Mr Stebbing still speaks about it

"Newspapers! Don't tell me anything about newspapers! Did I ever tell you about my newspaper venture? ... Leading article on the High Church Ritualism of the Vicar ... positively disgraceful ... I said, 'Look here, when I asked you to edit this paper ...' He said, 'But ...' I said, 'Never mind, you are well paid for your work, and you write scandalous things about my friends ...' He said, 'Thirty shillings a week ...' I said, 'And very good pay too; when I was your age ...' So I sent him to the right-about, sir ... dictate to me?"

There is really no need for a newspaper at Little Malsey, because everybody knows. And a newspaper would not dare to print the things that people say over tea-tables. There is of course no slander in saying that the End House people had a big brand new motor car, but I am of the opinion that the doubts, crudely expressed as to how they came by it are distinctly actionable.

So far as could be gathered, the Angel Child was the idol of his parents, and in the great garden that surrounded the End House there was a dear little toy railway that ran from the kitchen garden to the orchard via the rosary. And there were real little points and signals and tunnels and stations, and our small boy who was invited to play with Frankie came home in that state of ecstatic misery which poets associate with naughty angels excluded from Paradise.

Frankie did not always go to London on Mondays. Sometimes he was seen quite late in the week, a self-possessed, demure little man in knickerbocker suit and bowler hat and the inevitable Eton collar, sauntering along the High Street, gazing in shop windows. He had a bright smile for everybody, but was singularly uncommunicative for one so young.

"Good morning, Frankie," said Mr. Stebbing, "How is your father?"

"He's very well, sir," said Frankie, respectfully.

"Doesn't he find his work very trying?" asked Mr. Stebbing, artfully.

"No, sir," said Frankie with his innocent smile.

After which Mr. Stebbing could not well pursue the subject. Later, in the bosom of his family, our respected fellow townsman expressed his displeasure.

"Why on earth he" (meaning Frankie's father) "doesn't say out right what he does for a living, I cannot think. I must confess I do not like those mysterious people with motor cars. I was saying to Hackett at the Borough Council meeting yesterday, 'he might be a kind of up-to-date burglar for all I know. Look at Charles Peace! He used to drive about in a trap or something, and played the fiddle too!'"

But none the less the Houghtons, with all their reserve, were popular, and people came from miles around to hear Frankie's one solo.

For the Vicar had persuaded the father to allow the Angel Child to don the surplice for Harvest Thanksgiving, and Frankie had come down specially from one London day to rehearse.

"You ought to allow the boy to take up singing," said the Vicar.

Frankie's father smiled enigmatically.

"My boy has special gifts which I am helping him develop," he said quietly. "Frankie is a good boy and a sensible boy, although he's only eleven. So far, his education has cost me four thousand pounds."

The Vicar permitted himself to gasp.

"I beg your pardon?" he said, striving to hide his incredulity.

"Four thousand pounds," said the other with a grim smile, "and on one occasion at the rate of a thousand pounds a minute."

The Vicar spoke the truth when he afterwards remarked to his wife that the Houghtons were altogether beyond his understanding.

It was at a concert given in aid of the new School Harmonium Fund that the Vicar made a discovery.

Frankie had been asked to sing. It was on a Monday night, and Mr. Houghton signified his willingness. So Frankie came, looking more angelic than ever in his boyish evening dress. He sang his song in a sweet sympathetic treble, and received a vociferous encore. Also he was made a great deal of by charming young ladies, who brought him milk and pastries.

"It has been a most successful and pleasant evening," beamed the Vicar at the close. "Thanks in no small measure to you, Frankie." And he held out his hand to the boy.

As he took it he experienced a shock.

The childish hand that rested in his was unusually large and, what is more, it was hard and muscular, and the clasp that the boy returned was a grip like steel.

"Good gracious!" cried the astonished Vicar, and turned the palm of the boy's hand to the light.

It was as red and rough as that of a labouring man's.

The inspection was short, for the boy pulled his hand away, and the Vicar saw a red flush rise to his cheek.

The Vicar was a discreet man, but his wife was not so discreet, and Frankie's hands were the topic of the hour in Little Malsey the following week.

What was the secret of this strange disfigurement? A theory generally accepted was that the hardened palms were eloquent of excessive punishment with Frankie's father playing Sikes to his Oliver.

Mr. Stebbing did not take part in the discussion. He, poor man, was conscious of the horrible certainty that before another week had passed Little Malsey would have yet a greater subject to debate.

For Mr. Stebbing was insolvent. It came as much a surprise to Mr. Stebbing as it must to the reader. There was a son of Mr. Stebbing's who does not come into this story. The son is now in Canada, having been sent there by Mr. Stebbing, who in common with other foolish Britons, imagines that thrift and honesty is a matter for propinquity, and that there is something in the moral atmosphere of Canada that immediately makes thieves honest, idlers energetic, and the wastrels of the world suddenly useful members of society. This son, with a facile pen and a supply of blank cheques, brought a solid pillar of Little Malsey commerce crumbling to earth in so short a space of time that the victim was dazed and hypnotised by the magnitude of his misfortune.

From his wife he kept the dreadful news, and yet his poor old heart craved a confidant. What extraordinary inclination took him to the Houghton's we shall never know. Subconsciously he may have regarded himself as a criminal and sought the sympathy of what he believed to be a fellow, but to Houghton he went and poured forth the incoherent story of his terrible plight.

He remained with Frankie's father an hour, and came back more dazed than ever.

Next morning he journeyed to High Halsey and interviewed the bank manager; then he went to London, where Frankie s father met him. He returned home the same night alone.

The next day he was like a man demented.

Mr. Hackett, fellow councillor, who called in at the little office to discuss the remarkable problem of Frankie's hands, found a singularly erratic listener.

"...The extraordinary thing is," said Mr. Hackett impressively, "that the boy has got great corns on his palms, as if he were—"

Mr. Stebbing interrupted him with a burst of semi-hysterical laughter.

"Corns!" he cried, "Oh, Hackett, what dunderheaded babies you and I are by the side of that child! What innocent old fellows—"

Mr. Hackett left the office alarmed and puzzled.

He might well have been more perturbed had he watched the antics of Mr. Stebbing throughout that day.

How he walked aimlessly up and down the street and in and out the shop. How he haunted the telegraph-office, and how, when the telegram came, he shut himself up in his room to read it, and came out after a time looking ten years younger.

Little Halsey never knew of the big cheque that came to swell Mr. Stebbing's account and avert bankruptcy.

Little Halsey learnt all about Frankie later, but for many years before the discovery was made Mr. Stebbing carried in his pocket book a newspaper cutting which ran:—

"...at the Bushes, Whitelock was beaten, and Monna went on clear of St. Fax and Constance, but the winning post only a few strides away, Ambrosia came with a rush, and, magnificently ridden by little Frankie Houghton, our crack light-weight, snatched a victory by a short head."

Chapter I

The Promise That Haunted

The Livingstone came threshing down the Lulanga River, tacking from bank to bank to avoid the shoals.

With a hand on the telegraph, and the other free to signal the native steersman, the young skipper watched with anxious eyes the ever-changing shades of the treacherous water.

"Loba-ko-lo-kal!"

The sing-song warning of the boy at the bow sent the telegraph over to "astern" with a jangle.

Of its own accord the big stern-wheeler slowed down as the water shallowed.

Again the boy at the bow stabbed the water with his long, pliant sounding rod.

"Loba-ko-lete-anane," he sang reassuringly.

And with a fathom and a-half under her, Mac rung the engines full ahead.

He had come straight down from Baringa, stopping only for fuel; he had contravened the unwritten regulations, and had run his boat through the night with only starlight to show him his course, he had stopped at Basankusu to tell his news, whilst the sweating natives piled logs aboard till there was scarcely room to move. He had not stopped at Bonginda, the headquarters of the mission, but had bawled a message through the megaphone.

Now, as he swung the vessel round into deep water, a young man dressed in white, with the marks of sorrow on his tanned face, walked along the narrow gangway and joined him.

"I heard the engine-bell ring," he said, as if to explain his presence.

The youthful captain removed his big sun-hat, and wiped his streaming forehead.

"A sand bank," he said briefly; "the river's lower than I have ever known it to be before. There is Lulanga"—Mac pointed ahead as the Livingstone swept round a bend of the river.

"And the waters beyond?" asked the other.

"The Congo," said Mac. He interpreted the question in the younger man's eyes, and answered him: "We shall be there to-night, heaven willing," he said soberly. "How is your friend?"

The other shook his head sadly.

"He's sinking fast," he said shortly, and turned away abruptly.

In the big hospital cabin at the stern a man fought for an hour of life. Clean-shaven, grey, and hollow-cheeked, he lay beneath the furled mosquito net, licking his dry lips.

From time to time he shot a glance at the young man who sat by his side waving a palm-leaf fan.

He might have been a man of sixty-five, and there was something in his appearance that was curiously suggestive of the English body-servant. It may have been the little grey side-whiskers that ran down his face, the length of the ears; it may have been the intangible stamp with which Nature classifies humanity.

That Simon Leatherdale was, indeed, of that class of domestic which the fashionable world calls "man" was true. Trusted servant and friend of the seventh Stanmore baronet—that erratic genius whose adventures and eccentricities were the talk of London in the eighties—Simon Leatherdale had been nurse, tutor, and companion of the boy who had inherited the Stanmore title.

The thud of the Livingstone's engines shook the little room as the boat raced down the broad stream.

The old man beckoned his nurse.

"Tell the captain to slow down." He spoke with long pauses between his words, and he reached for the young man's hand.

"But, Simon," said the boy earnestly, "we must go as fast as this, if we are to reach Bolengi to-night."

Simon shook his head wearily. "I shall not reach Bolengi," he said faintly, "I know it. Do not deceive yourself, Charles; you know it also. I must have quiet now—for now I have something to tell you."

There was something in the old man's face that sent a numb, aching pain to the other's heart, and he left the cabin quietly.

The thunder of the wheel died down a little when he returned and took his place by the old servant's side.

"Something you've promised to tell me," said the other painfully. "You—you told me, Simon," the young man said gently, "the day you were so ill."

"Did I?" The sick man closed his eyes, and muttered: "You will live to hate me."

"No, no, no!" cried the boy. "I shall always love you, and think of you as though you were my father."

"Heaven forgive me!" muttered the old man; "it was my vanity—my wicked pride. If I had only told Sir George!"

Then the great cloud came to his mind. The cloud that is blacker than night, and is fringed with a wondrous radiance. And he was with the old baronet again. "Old" baronet he had been, but not in years.

Old in sorrow for the young wife he had passionately loved, and whom death had taken in the glory of her youth and beauty. Old in his care for the child—his boy and hers.

"I'll look after the boy," Simon muttered. "Yes, Sir George—French and German, and the sciences. Myself, myself—I will teach him everything myself, Sir George. Heaven, what have I done?"

He tossed from side to side in his delirium.

On the deck forward Mac kept his vigil. They were running at full speed again, and the water foamed under her bows. One eye for the chart, and one for the shifting shoals; his ear alert for the warning of the boy with the sounding-stick revolving incessantly. An anxious eye, too, for the sun that was moving with what seemed incredible swiftness to the west—Mac was racing for a life.

The sun went down, and tropical night came swiftly. Strange night birds flapped across the deck, and the lights of the cabins attracted a million, winged creatures. The stars showed him the river, and the keen-sighted steersman helped him with the shallows. He snatched a hasty dinner—with one hand at the telegraph.

They passed strange fires on the bank, and saw, in the fitful red light, naked bodies squatting about them, and heard the shrill laughter of native woman, and the hoarse guffaws of the men. And they heard the "tic-tac" of the lokoli—the wonderful drum that beat messages from village to village—and once heard a tom-tom drumming out a native dance, and caught a glimpse of swaying bodies in the forest. Then, ahead of them, there appeared a twinkle of lights that came nearer and near, till Equatorville was abreast and past, and their goal was almost in sight.

Then Mac felt a hand on his shoulder, and turned. He could not see the face of the young man in the darkness, but he heard the pain in his voice.

"Stop, please!" it said huskily, and Mac's hand pulled the telegraph over. "My—my friend is—is—gone!"

The young baronet felt Mac's strong grip on his arm.

"You are a missionary," said the voice again. "I would like you—to—to say something."

With the steamer drifting slowly down the dark stream, Mac knelt beside the body of the dead man and prayed.

So, to the prayers of a mechanic, turned missionary, on the broad, mysterious bosom of this great African river passed Simon Leatherdale, sometime valet to the seventh baronet Stanmore, and under the great white stars of the African night they buried him at Bolengi; and the young man who had learnt his secret went home to face the world in terror of its discovery.

At Boma the British Consul bade him good-bye, then noticed the bandages. "You've hurt your hand," he said, and the baronet's muttered reply was incoherent.

Chapter II

## The Unjust Steward

Linsay Hastings examined his half-sister with a speculative eye. He wondered how far this tall, slim girl, with the smiling grey eyes and delicate mouth, might be cajoled or bullied into supporting his great plan.

He stretched his hand lazily without turning his head, and groped for the cigarette box.

One might, at first glance, describe Linsay Hastings as a handsome young man of the effeminate type, and as bearing some slight resemblance to his sister. But a closer and more searching examination revealed unsuspected weaknesses of chin that a cold straight line of lip did little to compensate. His eyes were too closely set, and there was something lacking in the shape of head that his smoothly brushed hair revealed.

"Is the enemy in sight, Sister Anne?" he bantered.

She smiled indulgently. "Isn't that from Bluebeard, and wasn't it succour rather than an enemy that Sister Anne sought?"

The opening was too good to be lost "Well, succour let it be," he drawled lazily, then he suddenly sat up, "and by Jove, succour it is, Agatha, if it is Sir Charles Stanmore you're looking for so anxiously."

She turned from the absent-minded contemplation of the road that was visible from the terrace of High Knoll House, and a faint flush overspread her cheek.

"I was thinking of Sir Charles," she said, steadily, "but I was not looking for him, and—and I do not quite understand your allusion to 'succour,' Linsay."

His laugh did not sound as easy as usual. "Oh, I was speakin' parabolically," he said, "our friend is a very rich man." He read the cold enquiry in her eyes, and threw away his cigarette with a frown. "Look here, Agatha," he said sharply, "you and I are not exactly rich. Our dear parents made very little provision for you, and less for me—Oh, yes, I know," he interrupted her, "I get a fairly decent income from the Stanmore estates, and it will probably go on, for Charles is mad enough to chuck away the only life that's worth living to go away again into the wilds."

He paused to select another cigarette. "If he goes away pretty soon," he went on slowly, "nothing matters, and I've no desire to alter existing conditions, but if he stays long enough to go into things—do you see what I mean?"

He had taken the plunge, he was half way to the greater confession, and he stopped a little breathlessly to note the effect of his words. The girl looked at him with a wrinkled brow and a gathering look of wonder in her eyes. "If he stays long enough to—look into things?" she breathed. "Why, what do you mean, Linsay?"

He sprang up impatiently. "Don't be a fool!" he said, roughly, "what do you think I mean? I've had a devil of a lot of bad luck since I've been managing my amiable cousin's property. Nothing has gone right."

"But," said the bewildered girl, "but surely that isn't correct. The crops have been good, the farms have been paying, and rents have gone up. Mr. Tyrwhitt was saying—"

"Crops, rents, farms!" he cried, angrily, "I'm not referring to those. I've had bad luck in other ways. There was 'Claudian Cæsar' in the Middle Park Plate, I lost a pot of money over him. I dropped two thousand over the Cambridgeshire."

The girl's face was white, and she held on to the stone balustrade for support. "The money!" she gasped, with her eyes wide open, "it was your money—oh, say it was your own money, Linsay."

He dropped his mask of geniality. "My money!" he said with a harsh laugh. "Where do you imagine I could get three or four thousand pounds to lose, eh?" He met her eyes, and read the pain and the scorn that shone so clearly, and he dropped his insolent stare before them.

"So you stole." She said it quietly enough, but the contempt in her voice stung him like a whip. "I do not know what means you devised to accomplish your end," she went on, "but this I know, that placed in a position of trust by your cousin to manage his estate during his long absence—"

"Let's have no heroics," he said, roughly. He paced the marble-paved terrace with quick, nervous strides. "Charles need know nothing about this. He has no lawyer, no banker, no men of business, as far as I can gather. When he wants money he comes to me and asks for it, and keeps no check on his expenditure. He has never asked me to give an account of my stewardship."

"He trusts you," she flamed.

Linsay Hastings smiled unpleasantly. "Say rather it was old Simon Leatherdale who trusted me," he sneered, "with his mysterious letters from abroad. Look here, Agatha," he schooled his voice to a gentle pleading, "it's no good crying over spilt milk. The money can be replaced—that's one solution, but there's a better way." He paused, and then went on deliberately: "Charles has only been home three weeks, and in those three weeks he has made it very evident that his susceptible heart—"

"Stop!" she cried, with flaming cheeks, "before I say something to you for which I may be sorry. There is no solution that way, not even to save you from the punishment you deserve would I throw myself at Sir Charles Stanmore's head."

His hand grasped her wrist, and the latent devil in him glittered in his eyes. "You won't, you won't," he muttered, "you fool, you must; I have promised you!"

"You dared!"

"This moony youth, with his nice notions of honour, has thought it necessary to ask the consent of your brother," he said, with a laugh, "and I—"

"Oh, hush!"

A figure turned on to the terrace and came towards them. The young baronet greeted the girl half shyly, and for the first time in her life she found it impossible to meet a pair of honest grey eyes.

"Admiring the view?" he asked.

He had the quiet voice that comes to men who have lived over-long in solitary places, and the far-away look peculiar to the dwellers in the wilderness.

She collected herself with an effort and gave him her hand.

"Going, Hastings?" he asked in surprise and with some inward feeling of alarm.

"I've an appointment at the house farm," mumbled the other, and reached awkwardly for his cigarette.

"Your brother looks worried, Miss Hastings; he's been overworking," Sir Charles said when they were alone. "I wish I could persuade him to come with me to Uganda next month; he wants a holiday."

She looked up. "So you are going?"

The hand that filled the well-worn briar shook a little. "I think so," he hesitated, "unless I have reason for staying, a reason I hardly dare hope for."

With a quickly beating heart, she changed the conversation. "You are very fond of the wilds, Sir Charles?"

He smiled grimly and sadly. "I know no other world," he said, "I was with my poor father from the age of four, and when he died, my wanderings were continued with Simon—it was my education."

"I wonder you managed to get any education at all."

He stooped to pick up his fallen tobacco pouch. "Oh, I don't know," he said slowly, "poor Simon was a genius, an extraordinary linguist, with a surprising knowledge of the classics, ancient and modern—he knew Shakespeare by heart—would you like to hear me recite the trial scene from the Merchant of Venice?" he asked, with his rare smile, "or the quarrel scene between Cassius and Brutus?"

"Spare me!" she replied laughingly.

He rose to his feet and stood opposite her.

"Miss Hastings," he said abruptly, "I want to ask you something."

She met his eyes unfalteringly now. "Perhaps it would be better if you did not," she said in a low voice.

"Suppose," he said quietly, "you had a secret—a dreadful secret, that oppressed you day and night— that seemed to come into every action of your daily life—-not a disgraceful secret but, none the less, unbearable, how would you seek relief?"

She breathed more freely. "The simplest way would be to confide it to somebody."

She stopped short, seeing the innocent trap he had set her.

"That is what I want to do," he said gravely. "I have wanted to find that somebody, and I have found her."

She was silent.

"I do not know enough of this world of yours, this great, mysterious social world to realise what dreadful blunder I may be committing, or what conventional laws I may he outraging, but I love you, Agatha, and I want you to be my wife."

She felt the world spinning, and, trying to rise, would have fallen, had not his strong arm caught her.

"I'm sorry—oh, I'm so sorry!"

His distress was so evident that even in her dazed condition she could not but notice it.

"You have done me a great honour," she murmured. She was trembling in every limb; "but—"

A wrangle of angry voices startled her. She heard Linsay's voice saying hotly: "You cannot go! I tell you, Rothstein, you mustn't—for heaven's sake—"

There was a scuffle, and through the open French window that led on to the terrace came a big, thick-set man, purple with rage, his hat on the back of his head, and beads of perspiration standing on his broad face. Linsay, white as death, followed him, and stood biting his lips as the stout man spoke.

"Sir Charles Stanmore, eh?" roared the stranger; "you're 'im, are yer? Eh? I'm Rothstein, of Charles Street, an'—"

The young baronet's face was stern, and his smouldering rage at the interruption showed in the compressed mouth and narrowed eyes.

"Will you be so good, Mr. Rothstein, of Charles Street, as to inform me by what right you break in upon my privacy?"

"I'm a man of business," said the other, a little cowed. "Fair and above-board's my motto. When I lend money I expect to be paid back—read that."

He thrust a slip of paper into Sir Charles's hand.

The girl, with a sickening premonition of what was to come, saw that he did not even so much as look at the paper.

"Well?" he asked.

"Read it!" stormed Rothstein.

"Well?" He kept his eyes on the moneylender.

"To the order of Charles Stanmore," recited Rothstein, "an' signed by you. Is that your signature?"

Agatha held her breath as the baronet's eyes fell upon the paper.

"Yes," he answered quietly, and the reply staggered the moneylender.

"But—but," he stammered, "I know it ain't. I could guess the man who signed that bill in two guesses. It was—"

"You are mistaken," said the baronet coldly, "this is my signature. What do you want?"

The moneylender floundered and stammered.

"If it's yours—-if you say it's yours," he spluttered.

Sir Charles turned to the pallid steward. "Pay this man—whatever it is," he said curtly.

"I don't want payin'!" almost shouted the bewildered usurer. "If it's your signature—"

"Pay him—and then throw him out."

The man turned with a snarl of fury. "Throw me out! Why, you whipper-snapper, there ain't two men in this house that could—"

So far he got when a lean, sinewy arm shot out and gripped him by the collar. He struck out scientifically, for Mr. Rothstein had not attained to the dignity of Charles Street, W., without acquiring some necessary accomplishments en route. But the man that held him, young as he was, had handled men before.

The drop from the terrace to the lawn below was little more than five feet, but Mr. Rothstein fell heavily. He got up painfully, and turned an inflamed countenance to the calm young man who was watching him with an unsympathetic smile.

"I'll be even with you, master bloomin' baronet!" he bellowed. "You took me unawares."

Sir Charles watched the slowly-retreating figure, that stopped every now and then to hurl imprecations and threats, then he turned to the girl. Linsay, nervously rubbing his hands, he ignored.

"I'm sorry this happened before you," he said with a faint smile. "Our friend came here without warning. I never had the pleasure of meeting him before."

"And yet—" Despite the angry glare from her brother she could not restrain the exclamation, which was half a question.

"And yet I admitted the signature?" he laughed. "Yes, I suppose it is all right. Poor Simon never consulted me in these matters!"

Linsay choked back an oath. The signature on the forged bill was little more than three weeks old, as he knew. Indeed, it had been given on the very eve of Sir Charles Stanmore's unexpected return to England. The baronet could not have failed to see the date. What object had he in shielding him?

Then his eyes fell upon his sister, and he saw more clearly.

"I had better settle this matter," he said coolly. "When you have a moment, Sir Charles, you will find me in my office."

Chapter III

Husband and Wife

Husband and wife, Sir Charles and Agatha faced one another in the deserted library. He had closed the door as he entered, but the hum of talk and the light laughter of the wedding guests penetrated even there.

The baronet's right hand was heavily bandaged. Two days before the wedding he had returned from London with a story of having met with a street accident. It had earned him no little inconvenience, for there were marriage settlements and registers to be signed, but the scrawl that stood for his name in the parish register proclaimed Agatha Margaret Hastings to be his wife.

"You want me, Agatha?"

She nodded; she could not trust herself to speak.

"I—I," she began, falteringly, then came towards him with appealing arms. "Charles—can't you see? Don't you understand?"

"I understand you are worried, dearest!" he said, in a troubled voice, "the ceremony—"

"If I had had the courage to tell you last night," she began, breathing quickly, "if I could have only told you!"

"Told me what?" His face was tense and his voice sharp.

She waited with her head bowed. "I do not love you—I have never loved anyone."

He staggered as though she had struck him. "Do not love me!" he repeated, "then in heaven's name, why did you marry me?"

"Because—oh, you know, Charles. Why do you torture me? Was not my marriage the price of Linsay's freedom? Did you not press me again after you had discovered Linsay had forged your name? Could I consider your action in shielding my brother in any other way?"

"I—shielded—your—brother," he repeated the words like a child repeating a lesson.

He leant against the heavy table, and for a while neither spoke. His face seemed to grow older, and lines, such lines as suffering men take on, appeared about his eyes.

"You have done me a cruel wrong," he said, and there was no bitterness in his voice. Then only an infinite sadness, "this mad quixotic sacrifice of yours has walled up hope." Then he flung out his arms in an excess of passion, and the appearance of imperturbability fell away. "You have married me! You have faced the danger-point for this brother of yours, and now with the purchase accomplished you fear to pay the price! You thought I knew that Linsay Hastings had robbed me—it was his handiwork, the moneylender's bill, was it? You thought I used my knowledge as a lever to force my life on yours." He lowered his voice. Between them was the polished table, with its litter of books. He clutched its edge, the better to control himself, and leant his body forward as he almost hissed the words: "I did not know! Before heaven I did not know that signature was forged; I believed you loved me as I love you!"

She made no answer, and he seemed to expect none.

"I had hoped to find in you—" he stopped with a weary gesture. His head sank forward on his chest, and his nervous fingers beat a soft tattoo on the table. Then: "I shall go abroad to-night," he said, quietly. "You may travel with me as far as the Canaries—then we can part. People need not know. When I have gone on, you may telegraph to your brother to come to you."

She looked at him for a moment with a strange light in her face. "You will go to Africa?" she asked, slowly.

He nodded. "It cannot matter much where I am," he said, bitterly, "not all the thousands of miles of land and sea that come between us can make us further apart than we are at present."

In Clubland, where the idlest excuse for gossip is seized upon with avidity, the departure of Sir Charles and Lady Stanmore on their strange honeymoon tour was discussed with relish.

"He's rather a strange chap, eccentric, isn't he?" asked a major of the Imperial Guard. "Enormously wealthy, keeps thousands of pounds in gold about the house, never gives cheques for anything."

"Rummest thing I know about him," replied the Colonel, "was over the Vermont case—you remember a couple of weeks ago all London was talking about the Vermont divorce. Harry Vermont was a brute, swore his wife had been married before and his marriage wasn't legal—you know. Well, I met Stanmore in Pall Mall, and after we'd talked a little about big game (he'd had a nasty accident with a gun, by the way, and his hand was bandaged out of all resemblance), I happened to mention the Vermont case. 'Haven't you read this evidence?' I said, and he got quite annoyed. My word, his behaviour was so suspicions that I quite expected to hear he was called to give evidence—eh, general?"

It was not one of General Tolmache's happiest days, and he replied, testily, "Don't talk rot, my good fellow, the boy hasn't been home a month, and previous to that hadn't been in England for fourteen years."

The colonel tactfully selected a new audience. "I heard from a man, who's keen on the poor heathen and all that sort of thing, that Stanmore's bought a fine boat on the upper Congo," he said. "It was the property of a Belgian Protestant mission that went broke. It was on the market and was under offer to a London mission when Stanmore heard of it, and bought it over their heads."

At that very moment Sir Charles Stanmore's honeymoon was under discussion elsewhere.

The steamer that bore him and his bride was rounding the high cliffs that hide Santa Cruz from the north. Agatha sat in her deck chair, drinking in the beauty of the scene. The vast green uplands, dotted with little white houses, the chequer squares of vineyards and cultivated gardens, and towering above all, the delicate pinnacle point of Teneriffe, tipped with its mantle of everlasting snow. About the point hovered the faintest gossamer of cloud, and over its steep slopes stretched here and there a filmy veil of mist.

A step sounded at her side, and she looked up to meet the grave eyes of her husband.

"We shall be in Santa Cruz in half-an-hour," he said, "but you will have ample time to get your trunks ashore—we coal here."

She made no reply, but took up the book that lay on her lap.

He waited a moment as though expecting some answer, then turned on his heel and strode along the deck towards the saloon. It was the first time he had spoken to her regarding her plans since the voyage had begun. Commonplace conversations they had had; talks of books and of people and places, maintaining, that convention might not be outraged, the polite fiction of companionship. That this pretence succeeded, you might gather from the kindly smiles of their fellow passengers, who, seeing no further than the surface, were ignorant of the blank misery that sat a guest in the breast of the one, or the despair that clouded all thought in the other.

The ship had been in port an hour, when Sir Charles came back to the almost deserted deck to find his wife as he had left her.

"You have very little time," he said, slowly.

She laid aside the book and raised her head. "I have all the time I require," she answered quickly. "I am not going ashore."

Had a bombshell exploded, the simple pronouncement could not have shocked him any more.

"Not going ashore? Agatha, are you mad?" he said, almost angrily.

She shook her head slowly. "On the contrary, I was never so sane."

"But you cannot come any farther—our next port is, Sierra Leone, and—"

"I am going with you—I could not give you love—I cannot give you less than service."

"But I will not have it!" he cried almost savagely. "We have made sufficiently great a blunder without adding to the sum of our folly. You must go ashore."

Something in the situation appealed to her sense of humour, for she suddenly laughed, and her amusement was so genuine that, against his will, his lips twitched sympathetically.

"Can't you see," she said coolly, "how completely you are at the mercy of a girl, on whom your 'musts' and 'shall' have no more effect than the whistle of that little steam launch?" The spirit of fun still sparkled in her eyes, and he felt, a little resentfully, that into his tragedy had crept an element of comedy which loosened his grip of the situation. "After all," she went on demurely, "you can't very well call a gendarme on board and have me removed—we must observe the decencies."

"But you don't realise where I am going," he said earnestly. "I am going into the wilderness, into fever-stricken countries, where white women are unknown, and where it would be murder to take you."

"Then you had better alter your itinerary," she replied with amazing self-assurance, "because I am going with you. I have thought it out on board."

She stopped his expostulations with a gesture, and there was a hint of mischief in her quiet smile. "Our marriage was a mistake; but then, so are ninety per cent. of marriages, only I made this discovery at an inconveniently early hour. Linsay deceived me, as he deceived you, and because I am possessed of a stronger sense of honesty than—than some, I confessed to you, what I might well have kept hidden. But I want to know you—I want"—she faltered, and a faint colour came to her cheeks—"I want to love you. Ah, a woman may say that to her husband? I want to share your secret—that secret"—she watched him closely as she went on—"that causes such a strange injury to your hand at all the critical periods of your life."

He stepped back a pace, a curious pallor on his face.

She nodded wisely. "Ah, I know," she said quietly. "When you came to England you had an injured wrist; when you went to London to settle your affairs the wrist, which had been well the day before, went into hospital again. When we were married you had cut your thumb—though I have looked in vain for the scar since—when we sailed your hand was still injured."

She spoke with deliberation, for her object was twofold—one to gain time, and this ruse he saw through.

"Agatha, I beg of you to go!" There was no mistaking his earnestness. "Some other day I may explain what mystery there is about my unfortunate hand. Some day, perhaps, you will know me better, and—and love me better, when all the pain and disappointment has vanished from my memory. But you must give up this plan—I implore you! No, I command you!"

She laughed frankly and undisguisedly into the stern, young face.

"You will not dare to quote the marriage service," she taunted. "Not the banal and commonplace reference to 'obedience.'"

"Agatha, for heaven's sake—" he began.

"You have time to go ashore," she went on calmly, "and to send a cable to my brother, telling him I have changed my plans."

He leant over her in a torment of exasperation.

"I feel that I could shake you," he said.

"I wish you would," she answered truthfully.

Ten minutes later he went ashore. Over her book she caught a glimpse of him at the gangway, and her pretty forehead was wrinkled in a troubled frown, for his right hand was thrust into the breast of his light Norfolk jacket, and she could see that it was bandaged.

Chapter IV

'Mid Savage Foes

There came from the forest the rhythmical "clop-clop" of the woodmen's axes.

Agatha, grateful for the shade that the interlaced branches of the high trees afforded, sat contentedly on a little mound, fanning her pink cheeks with her light helmet. She was in a little clearing near the river bank, and through the tangle of creepers she could see the two white funnels of the N'kema, and to her ears, above the ceaseless chatter of the forest, came the never-ending gurgle of the swift black river.

Charles was in the wood; she had heard the far-away "cloc" of his rifle. She had got past the stage of nervous apprehension and foreboding that came to her with his first disappearance into the forest. On that, the first occasion, she had spent five terrible hours staring into the solemn gloom of the wilderness—five hours, and every hour of sixty minutes and every minute overloaded with imaginations of disasters.

She had sat nervously tense, bolt upright on her canvas chair, with Elbo, the taciturn Kano boy, at her side, wondering, wondering, wondering. And when he had returned, swinging through the undergrowth ahead of his bearers, she had grown hysterical at the sight of his white helmet showing through the trees.

He had found her in a state bordering on collapse, and that had ended what promised to be a magnificent month of shooting.

So the prow of the boat had been turned farther up stream. There had been three weeks of dolce far niente, ceremonial calls at government posts, quiet Sundays amidst the soothing homeliness of mission stations.

That was past, the shooting excursions had begun again, and, as she grew familiar with the wilds, the mysterious forest had lost its terrors.

He had been a revelation to her, this husband of hers. She found him a constant source of interest. The depths of his resourcefulness were unplumbed. He was a doctor, an engineer, a cook, and a leader of men. He had alarming attacks of fever that drove her frantic, but which he treated with outrageous indifference. But one hot night when she lay in her roomy cabin in a vain pursuit of sleep—his form had filled the doorway, and she had sat up in bed with a fluttering heart.

He made no apology for his intrusion.

"I thought you'd be asleep," he said gruffly. "Where is your mosquito curtain?"

"It was so hot," she began.

"Have them put up at once," he said sternly. "Do you think I want you down with the fever. Call your woman," and he left her.

As a result of her escapade fever came, a mild attack, but sufficiently unpleasant. She woke one morning with a bad headache and a disinclination for food.

For three days he tended her, sitting by the side of her bed, dosing her with quinine, forcing food upon her, surprisingly palatable broths, wonderful light dishes, the composition of which she could not even guess. And in the days of her convalescence when the awful depression came, he it was who cheered her with a fund of dry humour, with stories of his life in wild places, and anecdotes of travellers he had met.

When she was well he had relapsed into his polite, distant self. She could have wished for the fever to continue.

She had seen the primitive man in him manifest. The fifty raw natives who comprised the crew needed careful handling. He was, like most Britons, admirable in his treatment of them. Just to a nicety, neither encouraging their confidence, nor repelling it. Once there had been a "woman palaver" on board and a general fight, and with two leaps he had been in the midst of it, striking right and left. The ringleader he discovered, and incontinently threw overboard.

"He can swim," was his cool answer to her agonised appeal.

She thought of all this as she sat in the clearing, and smiled gently.

A dark shadow fell across the ground before her. Elbo, the Kano boy, six feet in height, and as straight as a young tree, stood waiting, hat in hand.

"You fit for go on ship?" he asked.

She looked at him sharply, but his face was expressionless.

"Why should I go to the ship yet?" she demanded; "the master will return soon."

He looked over her head. "Them master he done go into N'gombi country; they chop him one time."

She rose quickly with her hand at her throat. She knew enough coast talk to understand him.

"But the N'gombi people are at peace," she faltered, "my—the master told me."

Elbo turned and spoke rapidly in the Bomongo tongue to some invisible person. A woman came through the undergrowth, shyly and hesitatingly. Her eyes were leaden, and about her shoulders she wore a stained cloth. There were rags about her ankles, and she walked as if in pain.

"Them woman she come by canoe from Lokobangi. N'gombi. He come fighting, burning. Plainty light, savvy?"

The danger came upon her without warning. Had she a more extended acquaintance with savage countries, she would have known that thus danger invariably came in a land where formal ultimatums were unknown, and war was little more than organised murder.

"Let us get back to the boat," she said, with compressed lips, and they crossed the narrow plank to the steel deck of the trim little stern-wheeler.

All the time, amidst the riot and panic of her heart, her cool head was asking and reiterating one question: What would Charles wish her to do? She might send a party of men to meet him, and this she suggested to Elbo.

He shook his head. "Suppose them black fellows stay for ship—they be good. They fit for fight English. Suppose I done take 'um into bush, they fight N'gombi."

"But the N'gombi people are not here." She waved her hand to the inscrutable forest. Elbo nodded his head.

"They be here for sure," he said, with conviction.

There were half-a-dozen men of the better class of native on board. Educated mission men, who acted as engineers and steersmen, and these Elbo summoned.

By their faces, the girl gathered the seriousness of the situation—she must not lose her head now, a life that was more precious to her than all the world might depend upon her courage. "What would he have wished her to do?"

She turned quickly to the chattering group. "Ask Yoga if there is steam," she said, quietly.

No, the fires were out, as was the custom when the ship lay idle. She gave an order, and instantly there was a scene of feverish activity. There was wood to be collected from the forest, a party had been engaged all the morning cutting it, and this had to be brought aboard.

Soon a lazy curl of smoke came drifting from the funnels as Yoga and his men worked at breakneck speed to feed the fires. Elbo, from the vantage place of the navigating dock, superintended the sweating gang who piled the ship's deck with fuel.

"Oh, N'kema!" he cried in the sing-song Bomongo dialect. "Oh badly wast thou named the Monkey! Better had they called thee N'dugi, the tortoise! Hast thou no shame, Nogi? Hast thou the sickness, Mongo? Haste! Haste! What is it with thee, Makala? Thou hast sickness in thy head? Ko! Ko!"

So this taciturn native laughed at them and chid them, and waxed broadly sarcastic, and stood in the blinding white heat of noontide, with the temperature at 105 in the shade, and spoke to them for his master's sake.

The last load was aboard, the steam was hissing from the escape-pipe, and the mooring ropes stood shackled for slipping, when Elbo, who had gone into the forest to reconnoitre, came leaping back, ducking and swerving.

Agatha herself stood by the telegraph, and as the Kano boy leapt the space between the bank and the deck she heard him shout warningly to the men at the mooring hawsers. Then he disappeared into her husband's cabin. He was out again in a second with a rifle in each hand and a dozen packets of ammunition folded in his arms.

Crack, crack!

She heard the firing now, and the frenzied shouting of the cannibal N'gombi.

Mechanically she stretched out her hand for one of the rifles. Charles had given her lessons, and she threw open the breech as Elbo raised his rifle and fired.

He loaded and fired again, but she could see nothing, only the shadows of great trees and the fret of sunlight on green saplings.

Again Elbo fired, and there came an answering shot close at hand.

Then she saw her husband, helmet-less, coatless, running swiftly and almost noiselessly, and she saw he was weaponless. Her mind was clear now. She judged the distance, and with her disengaged hand she threw over the handle of the telegraph to "full speed ahead," and the steersman whirled his wheel round to port.

As the big stern wheel threshed slowly round, she raised her rifle and fired at the nearest of his pursuers. The little ship swung her nose to midstream. Sir Charles gained the bank. He paused for a moment, leapt, and gained the slippery deck.

One of his pursuers followed him, but Yoga, the Christian engineer, was on the man before he rose to his feet, and in Yoga's hand was a steel spanner....

Agatha opened her eyes. She was lying in her bed. The engines were stopped, and through the open doorway she could hear her husband's voice speaking to somebody in the native dialect.

Her head was wet and the collar of hot blouse loosened. Then Charles came in.

"Hullo," he said, cheerfully, and there was a look in his eyes that she had seen once before, "feeling better?"

"Where are we?" she asked faintly, and tried to rise.

But he was down on his knees by her side, his arm about her. "You stay where you are," he whispered, and his lips brushed her cheek, "unless you are tired of this wicked world. We are on a sandbank, about a hundred yards from the place we started from, but the current is too swift for the beggars to venture out, so they are trying a little target practice, and," he added, thoughtfully, "with my rifle."

"Is there any danger?"

"None! They surprised me in the wood, and I've lost two poor chaps who were with me—"

"Snap!" Something hit the side of the cabin, splintering the wood near the roof, and he laughed joyously. "That's my rifle," he said laconically, then, "dearest, will you do something for me?"

"Anything," she murmured.

"Here's a pencil and paper. Will you scribble a note to the Commandant at Basankasu? Tell him what has happened and where we are. I'll send Elbo in a canoe down the river, and we shall be relieved by nightfall."

"In French?" she asked, and he nodded. "I'll do it, of course," she said. "But why? Don't you speak French?"

"Yes," he said quietly.

"Then why—"

He was silent for a moment. "I cannot write French," he said. "I cannot even write English."

"Charles!"

He put his head closer to hers. "I can neither read nor write," he said simply. "Neither could poor Simon. He lived in mortal terror of the fact being discovered. I, too, have since shared his fear."

"The bandaged hand!" she murmured, as a light dawned upon her.

He nodded. "That was my pitiful ruse—with an injured hand I might dictate my telegrams, and any scrawl might be accepted as my signature." She wrote the note without a word, and Elbo took it from his hand. Then he came back to her.

"Are you sure there's no danger?" she asked in so low a tone that he was forced to resume his former position. "None," he said.

"And if there was danger, would you hold me tightly as you did just now?" she murmured.

He did not trust himself to speak.

"Will you please remember," she whispered, "that in addition to being your future school mistress, I—I am your wife. And will you pretend the danger isn't really past?"

## The Derby Favourite

'Likely enough,' said P.C. Lee, 'you've heard me tell about Captain Kintock. He wasn't the sort of man you'd expect a police constable to have much to do with, because he was of the higher class of bad lot, but owin' to his livin' on my ground—a very fine house he had in Ladbroke Gardens—an' owin' to my knowin' Baine, that did most of his dirty work, I got a fair inside knowledge of what happened at Epsom.

'In a sense, this story I'm goin' to tell you is a racin' story, though I don't want you to run away with the idea that I know much about it.

'When people tell you that racin' is a game that is only followed by thieves an' blackguards, by sharps an' flats, do not believe them. Some of the worst men in England go racin', but then, again, some of the best go, too.

'The bulk lie between the two extremes, an' are sane, decent citizens, who love the sport for the sport's sake.

'But the bad men are very bad, because they are clever, an' a clever bad man is a dangerous animal.

'Kintock was one the "Heads". He'd had money enough to sink a ship, at one time or another. A gambler born an' bred, he would bet on anything from horses to windmills.

'But Kintock was a crook, it was against his nature to go straight an' when it was a question of an easy honest way of doin' a thing, an' a hard, dishonest way, he always chose the latter for the sheer devilry of it.

'Rumly enough, he never took to horses till he'd run through every other form of gamblin', but when he did, he took to it colossal scale. He bought bloodstock in every direction, bought horses at the sales, an' out of sellin' races, an' took a lease of an old trainin' establishment down in Wiltshire, an' spent half his time between there an' Kensin'ton. Everybody knew he was a crook, but nobody knew enough about him to point to any definite act he had committed, an' so, somehow, he managed to get the Jockey Club to give him a licence to train.

'He was an extraordinarily fascinatin' man. Tall, lean-limbed, with a face like one of those Greek gods you see at the British Museum, an' a head of brown, curly hair that was goin' grey.

'So far as I could find out, he'd come into a lot of money—somethin' well into six figures—when he was twenty-one. He lived for a year at the rate of £500 a day, went into bankruptcy, an' was sent abroad. He made a fortune in the Argentine an' lost it in South Africa, floated a bogus company in Egypt, got concessions from the Turkish Government in Syria, an' turned up smilin' in England a rich man for the second time.

'Then he disappeared suddenly, an' about the same time a lot of excited shareholders made the discovery that the concession in Syria wasn't worth the paper it was written on, an' the assets of the Egyptian company were just worth the market value of a roller-top desk an' an easy chair, which formed the furniture of the company's office in Mincin' Lane. I don't know how they settled it, but I rather think that some of his rich relations paid up an' liquidated the company, an' a year later Kintock was in Monte Carlo with enough banknotes to stuff a portmanteau. Soon after this it was that he came to England to work the horses.

'I don't know how he froze on to Baine, but I can guess. Baine used to call himself a commission agent, had a house in Nottin' Dale, an' was a wrong 'un through an' through. A little bullet-headed man with an enormous slit of a mouth an' bow legs that were always done up in horsey-lookin' gaiters, he was well known at small meetin's an' made his livin' by chummin' up to inexperienced young men an' "tellin' the tale". His modus operandi was to get them to invest a few sovereigns on a horse that hadn't got an earthly chance of winnin'. He would take the few sovereigns an' "invest" them by puttin' the money in his pocket. When the horse lost he'd come back to the "mug" an' spin a beautiful yarn about how the horse would have won if he hadn't been interfered with at the start.

'Just about this time there was a young chap livin' in Kensin'ton Gardens by the name of Hite. He was one of those fellows who suffer from havin' too much money, an' naturally he turned to racin' as a cure for the disease. His father was one of them scientific fellows who don't take any notice of money, but spend their lives lookin' through a microscope to see the little bugs in the blood. A professor at Oxford he was, an' so young Sanderson Hite, who wasn't scientific, except with a book of form, got into touch with Baine.

'Baine noticed him at one or two race meetin's, an' particularly noticed that he was always alone, an' so he struck up a sort of acquaintance with him, an' told him "the tale."

'It was about the winner of the Newbury Spring Cup, an' Sandy took it all in, very eagerly.

'Only when it came to the question of partin' with five pounds he hesitated an' said he'd put the money on himself.

'To Baine's annoyance he went into the ring an' backed the horse which hadn't a hundred to one chance—for £250!

'Baine absolutely gnashed his teeth when he saw all this good money goin' into the bookmaker's pocket, but he nearly died with amazement when this "dead" horse he'd recommended won the race by a short head, beatin' a hot favourite.

'Two thousand pounds young Sandy cleared, an' he handed over a hundred to Baine for his information. After that, Baine couldn't do wrong so far as Sandy Hite was concerned. Seein' that he'd got hold of the original golden egg-layin' goose, Baine clamped himself on to it, an' laid himself out to get bona fide information, an' for weeks these two reaped in a fine harvest.

'The Captain was beginnin' to win a few races just then, but was bettin' very light, for him, so that when Baine mentioned "Sandy" an' asked if he could put him "on" to a good thing that the Captain was runnin', he said he didn't mind.

'Now, the most curious feature of the whole business was this, that Kintock never met Sandy, not even when he marked the boy down for pluckin'. He preferred to do it through Baine, an' what is more, he never touched Sandy for a penny until the great Highbury Boy bet.

'Highbury Boy was a two-year-old, the property of Lord Horling. Entered for all the classic races an' tried, almost as a yearlin', to be well above the average, Kintock purchased the colt, with his engagements, for ten thousand pounds.

'If ever there was a man who knew a horse, that man was the Captain, an' when he said that Highbury Boy would win the Derby, Baine believed him.

'He ran him in a couple of his engagements an' ran a "bye". The colt could have won on both occasions, but the jockey, ridin' to orders, contrived to get himself shut in.

'Then he brought him out for the Champagne Stakes at Doncaster, an' the Captain betted. He went into the ring, an' threw the money about as though he were bettin' on the most certain of certainties, an' Highbury Boy startin' at 2 to 1 a strong favourite, won in a common canter.

'That was the last race of his two-year-old days, an' when, just before Christmas of that year, bettin' on the next year's Derby began to creep into the papers, he would have been installed a hot favourite but for the disquietin' news published in the sportin' press, that he had trained off, accordin' to the papers.

'Baine was very prosperous in those days—I think he was on the Captain's pension list—an' I don't doubt that some of the exclusive information published in the London sportin' papers came from him.

'I saw him one day—Highbury Boy bein' at 20 to 1 an' me havin' backed him at sixes I was a bit upset.

'"What about this horse of yours, Baine?" I ses.

'"Highbury Boy?" ses he, innocent, "oh, he's trained off accordin' to the papers."

'"I know all about the papers," I ses; "are you their special correspondent?"

'"Without the word of a lie," he ses, very frank, "I am."

'The Craven Stakes, the first race in which Highbury Boy was entered as a three-year-old, came, an' the "Boy" was scratched; the Two Thousand Guineas, won by Bel Mere (who also won the Craven), passed without the colt's puttin' in an appearance. He ran at Kempton for the Jubilee Handicap an' finished tenth, an' he went right out of the Derby list an' was spoken of as a doubtful starter.

'On public form it looked a thousand pounds to an orange pip on Bel Mere, an' money was laid on him, an' the first an' most enthusiastic of his supporters was Sandy.

'He was very jubilant, an' very confident, because he'd had a good season the year before, an' he'd come into somethin' like £40,000 by the death of an aunt.

'"Baine," ses he one day when we were all in the tea-room at Newbury, "if these were the old days when one could bet in ten thousands, I could double my fortune on Bel Mere."

'"What do you mean by old days, Mr. Hite?" ses Baine. "It is just as easy to get a bet on for ten thousand, or one of even twenty thousand for the matter of that, as it ever was."

'Then he went on to tell him of Captain Kintock, of what a fine, generous "better" he was, an' how, even though Highbury Boy was a physical wreck, he was so cocksure that it would beat Bel Mere that he'd stake his life on it.

'Sandy bit at the bait quicker than Baine thought possible.

'"Would he?" he said eagerly. "What! After the Jubilee runnin'? I wish to goodness he would!"

'If you wonder why this young man was prepared to make such a huge bet, you have got to remember that Bel Mere was extraordinarily superior to any other horse in that race except Highbury Boy, an' that Highbury Boy was popularly supposed to be a cripple on crutches. Well, the long an' the short of the discussion was that Baine promised to see the Captain an' ask him if he was prepared to back Highbury Boy against Bel Mere, an' after a lot of palaver an' an exchange of polite letters, the Captain expressed himself as willin' to lay one bet of £15,000 against Bel Mere beatin' Highbury Boy.

'I heard all this afterwards.

'Derby Day came nearer, an' then I believe there was some more correspondence, an' the £15,000 bet was increased to £25,000, an' then the Captain had a bit of bad luck, for the story of this wager got into the papers, an' the first thing that happened was old Mr. Sanderson Hite got to hear of the foolish tricks that his son was playin', an' puttin' aside his microscope an' his test-tubes an' his electric batteries, he came down to see Kintock, one simple old man with no worldly knowledge worth speakin' about—an' Kintock so wise an' cunnin' an' glib.

'It was a gorgeous spring mornin' when he arrived at Epsom. Kintock had rented a house just outside the town, an' Highbury Boy was in the stable, guarded day an' night by a couple of men.

'They were sittin' out on the lawn takin' eleven o'clock tea—he was a very abstemious man was the Captain—when old Mr. Hite was announced.

'He came up the garden path, by Baine's account, a neat old figure dressed with scrupulous care. Spotless linen, perfectly fittin' frock coat, an' a big old-fashioned satin bow to his wing collar. His fashion was the fashion of forty years ago, he might have stepped out of an 1874 fashion plate.

'He got straight to business with Kintock with an old-fashioned quietness of speech an' courtesy that was very puzzlin' to Baine. Without any preliminary he started in about Highbury Boy.

'"I have taken the trouble," he ses, "to study the form—is that the word?—of Highbury Boy, an' to my surprise I find that it is quite possible to anticipate winners from the study of a horse's performances. If Highbury Boy were in good health, would he win the Derby, Mr. Kintock?"

'The Captain hesitated.

"Yes," he admitted after a pause.

'"Is he well?"

'The old man sat bolt upright in his chair, his thin white hands crossed upon his stick, an' the question was hurled at Kintock with a sudden ferocity that was surprisin'.

'Baine saw the Captain shift uneasily at the directness of the attack.

'Then the old man went on.

'"You have told me all I want to know," he ses. "I have made diligent search for the origin of the stories of your horse's illness, an' I have traced the rumours an' head shakin's an' whispered reports. Now, I ask you, sir," he went on, "to do me a favour."

'"I shall be happy to do anythin' in reason," said Kintock.

'"I ask you to take your bettin' book an' run your pen through the bets my son has made with you concernin' your horse."

'Kintock laughed.

'"That I shall not do," he said calmly.

'The old man rose with a little inclination of his head.

'"Then your horse will not win," he said with such an air of confidence that the Captain was startled. "I have given you a chance, an' you have refused to take it. I do not care a straw how much money you may make from your other dupes, I am satisfied that the foolish young man who is my son shall be saved from his folly." 'Then Kintock got wild at the old man's confidence, an' did a foolish thing, for he lost his temper an' spoke frankly.

'"My horse will win," he said angrily, "that's the truth, an' you might as well know it. Win! Why, Bel Mere will not see the way the Boy will go! An' as for your son, I hold him to his bargain. If he doesn't pay I'll post him, yes, by—"

'The old man turned to go; then he hesitated an' came back.

'"Would it be askin' too much if I asked your permission to see this wonderful horse of yours?" Then, as a suspicious frown gathered on Kintock's face, he went on, with a wry smile, "My interest is not an unnatural one, is it?"

'But Kintock's suspicions were aroused.

'"You may see the horse," he said, "but at a distance."

'He called Baine aside, an' told him to watch the old man closely, an' if he made any movement that threatened the horse's safety to grip him.

'He went to the stables himself, an' by-an'-by came back to invite the professor into the little meadow that adjoined the house, an' after a while the two grooms come in leadin' Highbury Boy.

'The old man stood with his 'ands behind him watchin' the beautiful bay as they led him up an' down.

'There never was a more perfect-lookin' colt than the Boy, an' somethin' like pride came into Kintock's face as he watched the horse movin'.

'Then the old man spoke.

'"Once more, Mr. Kintock, will you cancel my son's bet?"

'"No," said Mr. Kintock briefly, an' the old man nodded.

'Baine was watchin' him as a cat watches a mouse, but he made no sign. Still, with his hands clasped behind him, he stood like one lost in thought. Then he roused himself.

'"Very well," was all he said, an' with bent head an' knitted brows he accompanied us back to the garden.

'"I have one thing to say to you," he said to Kintock, "have you ever heard of a sayin', falsely ascribed to the Jesuits, that a man may do harm that good may come?"

'"I have heard that very frequently," said Kintock. "Moreover, that has been my creed."

'"Suppose," the old man said slowly, "suppose somebody got into the stable of this fine horse of yours, an'—"

'"Nobbled it?" smiled Kintock.

'"I think that is the word I have read in connection with similar occurrences," said Mr. Hite; "suppose this happened—suppose I sent my friends—"

'"Try," said Kintock with an ugly smile; "if you or they succeed in gettin' at Highbury Boy they're welcome. I shall not complain. If that is your hope of preventin' him winnin', you are buildin' upon sand. Good-morning."

'"We shall see," said old Mr. Sanderson Hite, an' he walked down the path to the gate.

'Baine went round to see the Boy boxed for the day, an' after Kintock had issued his orders to the grooms, who were devoted to him body an' soul, he walked back across the meadow.

'The Captain had already shaken off his annoyance, an' was laughin' quietly at the old man an' his threat.

'"He is certainly an original, an' if young Sandy had half his brains—hullo!"

'He stopped suddenly an' picked up a matchbox—he was the tidiest man I ever knew.

'"Who dropped this?" he said. Then he looked at the box an' whistled. On the outside was printed in red letters—Tompkins, Tobacconist, Cambridge. "The old man dropped that," he said with a frown, "he was standin' close to this spot. He is not the sort of man to carry an empty matchbox about for fun, he didn't look like a smoker; now, what is the meanin' of this?"

'Somehow old Mr. Hite's threat had a depressin' effect upon Kintock, an' he must have taken him more seriously than did Baine, for he ordered his bed to be taken to the room above the stables, an' had a square hole cut in the floor immediately over Highbury Boy's box, an' a pane of glass fitted. He was thus able to see all that was happenin' in the stable from the room above. He went farther than this, for he went to the police an' got a couple of officers specially detailed to watch the outside of the stable for the two nights that intervened between Mr. Hite's visit an' Derby Day. I was one of 'em, an' that's how I come to know all about this story.

'The Epsom summer meetin' begins on the Tuesday, an' it was on the Tuesday that Kintock started to bet. Highbury Boy stood at 50 to 1 in the list when Kintock started operations. He was a clever gambler, for he never showed his hand thoroughly. He had an agent in Holland backin' the horse, whilst he was simultaneously gettin' the odds from the biggest bookmakers on the course, an' by night Highbury Boy had been "backed down" to 4 to 1 an' was co-favourite with Bel Mere.

'Kintock's great fear had been that his foolish outburst might have been taken advantage of by old Hite; that he would spoil his market, an' he put a man on to watch the old fellow.

'The Captain came home to dinner the night before the Derby jubilant.

'"He's gone back to Cambridge," he said, with a triumphant laugh, "an' to think I was worryin' about him!"

'"He's thrown up the sponge," said Baine.

'"Capitulated without firin' a shot," smiled Kintock, "but it may be a ruse to throw us off our guard. The Boy must not be left out of our sight."

'Nothin' happened that night so far as I know, an' Derby Day dawned with me sittin' on a chair outside the favourite's stable smokin' a pipe.

'It was a glorious May day, with bright sunshine, an' a fleck or two of white cloud in the sky, an' the Downs were crowded. The people stood in a solid black mass up the hill, an' ten deep from the startin' gate, round Tattenham Corner, to the winnin' post. In the paddock, big as it is, there was scarcely room to walk about, but we found a corner where the crowd was thin, an' there we saddled Highbury Boy an' gave him his final preparation.

'Kerslake was the jockey, a lad who had won two Derbies, an' knew exactly every inch of the course.

'The bell rang, an' Kerslake mounted.

'Kintock had a few words with him, an' what the jockey said, I think, restored some of the Captain's assurance.

'"I stand to win £60,000," he said to me, as he an' Baine walked back to the rings, me an' Baine to Tattersalls, an' he to the Members' enclosure, "an' that old man got on my nerves."

'"Is he still at Cambridge?" says Baine, an' Kintock nodded.

'"I've had a man watchin' him there, an' I received a wire from him only half an hour ago, sayin' that Hite was lecturin' this mornin' at eleven, an' he had seen him a few minutes before he sent the wire."

'There was the usual parade an' canter, the usual string of horses pickin' a slow way across the Downs to the startin' gate, the usual delay, an' then—

'"They're off!"

'A roar from the stands an' an answerin' roar from the packed course as the bell rang, an' away went the field in a perfect line.

'Baine was on the rails just behind me, an' was readin' the race through his glasses.

'"Bel Mere is makin' the runnin' from Handy Lad, Mosempions, Highbury Boy, an' Cattino," he said.

'They breasted the hill in a bunch, an' came sweepin' to the left to the famous corner.

'They were all together when they turned into the straight, an' then without any glasses I saw Kerslake prepare to take his position.

'Bel Mere was leadin' an' already stands an' course resounded with the yell: "Bel Mere wins!"

'Then Kerslake went after the leader, caught him an' passed him in with one run an' down below in the ring a bookmaker shouted: "I'll back Highbury Boy!"

'Up went the whip of Bel Mere's rider, but he could get no nearer, an' Highbury Boy came with his devastatin' strides nearer an' nearer the post.

'Then he stopped . . .

'There is no other word to describe what happened.

'Stopped as dead as that horse did that was shot by the anti-gamblin' fanatic; then swerved right across the course, stopped again an' went down all of a heap as Bel Mere flashed past the post an easy winner.

'I saw Kintock's white face on the Members' stand as I ran across to the horse.

'Baine was at the horse's side first, an' with another policeman helped to lift the unconscious jockey. He was badly shaken by his fall, but was not seriously injured.

'But Highbury Boy was finished, you could see that, long before the vet came with the horse ambulance.

'Kintock, very quiet and self-possessed, directed operations.

'As it happened there were two famous veterinary surgeons on the course an' they accompanied us back to the house—the Captain, Baine, Inspector Carbury an' me.

'Highbury Boy was taken from the ambulance an' collapsed on the grass as we gathered round him.

'Very carefully one of the surgeons made his examination.

'"Has he been shot?" asked Kintock, but the doctor shook his head.

'He continued his examination; then asked if we had a microscope.

'Baine went into the town to borrow one, whilst the vet applied one or two rough an' ready remedies to the horse. By-an'-by he rose an' stood by the horse, eyein' him thoughtfully.

'"Remarkable, very remarkable," he ses; then he asked if he might see the stable.

'He went in by himself an' was there ten minutes, an' when he came out he held in his hand—a matchbox!

'Kintock started back with an oath.

'"Where did you get that?" he demanded.

'The surgeon looked surprised.

'"Out of my pocket," he said, an' just then Baine came back with the microscope.

'The veterinary surgeon took a little blood from the horse with the point of a needle an' adjourned to the house.

'He was back in five minutes.

'"Have you had any person here interested in tropical diseases?" he asked.

'A slow light dawned on Kintock's face an' he nodded.

'"Because," said the vet, "whoever it was must have inadvertently left behind him, these."

'He opened the matchbox he still held in his hand an' produced two dead flies.

They were a little larger than the house-fly, of a dark-brown colour, an' their wings were folded over their backs in the shape of scissors.

'"This," said the vet, "is the fly which is known to science as the Glossina morsitans, or as it is commonly called the 'tsetse fly'. Its bite is almost certain death to a horse, though, curiously enough, the usual symptoms peculiar to the disease are absent in your horse. Do you know who brought the flies here?"

'"I can guess," ses the Captain with a grim smile.'

Bailman made things snug for the night in his own characteristic fashion: walked round the tent; saw to the guide ropes; put his lantern over the strands of barbed-wire pegged firmly into the ground; carefully inspected his mosquito-net for signs of a stray musca; then turned his attention to the boys. They were squatting round their fire—a voluble, light-hearted assembly.

"Hast night your noise disturbed me," he said, as he passed them. "To-night, when the lo-koli sounds, you will sleep, and, if I be awakened, I will come with my whip, and you will feel great shame."

He spoke in the sonorous tongue of the Bo-mongo people, and, despite the awfulness of his threat, a titter of amusement ran round the circle. Bailman himself grinned into the darkness as he made his way down to the river, not that he would hesitate to use his chicotte upon a disobedient servant. He had too full an acquaintance with the Congo folk to be overmuch exercised at the necessity for employing the stick; but he grinned because twelve months in the wilds had made him half a savage, and he appreciated the humours of pain.

By the river side the little steamer was moored. There was a tiny bay here, and the swift currents of the river were broken to a gentle flow; none the less, he inspected the shore-ends of the wire hawsers before he crossed the narrow plank that led to the deck of the Zaire. The wood was stacked on the deck, ready for tomorrow's run. The new water-gauge had been put in by N'kema, the engineer, as he had ordered; the engines had been cleaned, and Bailman nodded approvingly. He stepped lightly over two or three sleeping forms curled up on the deck, and gained the shore. "Now I think I'll turn in," he muttered, and looked at his watch. It was nine o'clock. He stood for a moment on the crest of the steep bank, and stared back across the river. The night was black; but he saw the outlines of the forest on the other side. He saw the jewelled sky, and the pale reflection of stars in the water. Then he went to his tent, and leisurely got into his pyjamas. He jerked two tabloids from a tiny bottle, swallowed them, drank a glass of water, and thrust his head through the tent opening. "Ho, Sokani!" he called, speaking in the vernacular, "let the lo-koli sound!"

He went to bed.

He heard the rustle of men moving, the gurgles of laughter as his threat was repeated, and then the penetrating rattle of sticks on the native drum—a hollow tree trunk. Fiercely it beat—furiously, breathlessly, with now and then a deeper note as the drummer, using all his art, sent the message of sleep to the camp.

In one wild crescendo the lo-koli ceased, and Bailman turned with a sigh of content and closed his eyes... he sat up suddenly. He must have dozed; but he was wide awake now.

He listened, then slipped out of bed, pulling on his mosquito boots. Into the darkness of the night he stepped, and found N'kema, the engineer, waiting.

"You heard, master?" said the native.

"I heard," said Bailman with a puzzled face, "yet we are nowhere near a village."

He listened.

From the night came a hundred whispering noises, but above all these, unmistakable, the faint clatter of an answering drum. The white man frowned in his perplexity. "No village is nearer than the Bongindanga," he muttered, "not even a fishing village; the woods are deserted—"

The native held up a warning finger, and bent his head, listening. He was reading the message that the drum sent. Bailman waited; he knew the wonderful fact of this native telegraph, how it sent news through the trackless wilds. He could not understand it, no European could, but he had respect for its mystery.

"A white man is here," read the native; "he has the sickness."

"A white man!"

In the darkness Bailman's eyebrows rose incredulously.

"He is a foolish one," N'kema read; "he sits in the Forest of Happy Thoughts and will not move."

Bailman clicked his lips impatiently. "No white man would sit in the Forest of Happy Thoughts," he said, half to himself, "unless he were mad."

But the distant drum monotonously repeated the outrageous news. Here, indeed, in the heart of that loveliest glade in all Africa, encamped in the very centre of the Green Path of Death, was a white man, a sick white man... in the Forest of Happy Thoughts... a sick white man....

So the drum went on and on, till Bailman, rousing his own lo-koli man, sent an answer crashing along the river, and began to dress hurriedly.

In the forest lay a very sick man. He had chosen the site for the camp himself. It was in a clearing, near a little creek that wound between high elephant-grass to the river. Mainward chose it, just before the sickness came, because it was pretty. This was altogether an inadequate reason, but Mainward was a sentimentalist, and his life was a long record of choosing pretty camping places, irrespective of danger. "He was," said a newspaper, commenting on the crowning disaster which sent him a fugitive from justice to the wild lands of Africa, "overburdened with imagination." Mainward was cursed with ill-timed confidence; this was one of the reasons he chose to linger in that deadly strip of the Ituri which is clumsily named by the natives "The Lands-where-all-bad-thoughts-become-good-thoughts," and poetically adapted by explorers, and daring traders, as "The Forest of Happy Dreams." Over-confidence had generally been Mainward's undoing—over-confidence in the ability of his horses to win races; over-confidence in his own ability to secure money to hide his defalcations—he was a director of the Welshire County Bank once—over confidence in securing the love of a woman who, when the crash came, looked at him blankly and said she was sorry, but she had had no idea that he felt towards her like that....

Now Mainward lifted his aching head from the pillow and cursed aloud at the din. He was endowed with the smattering of pigeon-English which a man may acquire from a three months' sojourn, divided between Sierra Leone and Grand Bassam.

"Why for they make 'em cursed noise, eh?" he fretted. "You plenty fool-man, Abiboo."

"Si, senor," agreed the Kano boy calmly.

"Stop it, d'ye hear; stop it!" raved the man on the tumbled bed; "this noise is driving me mad—tell them to stop the drum."

The lo-koli stopped of its own accord, for the listeners in the sick man's camp had heard the faint answer from Bailman's.

"Come here, Abiboo—I want some milk: open a fresh tin; and tell the cook I want some soup, too."

The servant left him muttering and tossing from side to side on the creaking camp bedstead. Mainward had many things to think about. It was strange how they all clamoured for immediate attention; strange how they elbowed and fought one another in their noisy claims to his notice. Of course there was the bankruptcy and the discovery at the bank—it was very decent of that inspector fellow to give him the tip to clear out—and Ethel, and the horses, and—and...

The Valley of Happy Dreams! That would make a good story if Mainward could write, only, unfortunately, he could not write. He could sign things, sign his name "Three months after date pay to the order of—" he could sign other people's names... he groaned and winced at the thought.

But here was a forest where bad thoughts became good, and, God knows, his mind was ill-furnished. He wanted peace and sleep and happiness—he greatly desired happiness. Now suppose "Fairy Lane" had won the Wokingham Stakes? It did not, of course (he winced again at the bad memory), but suppose it had? Suppose he could have found a friend who would have lent him £16,000, or even if Ethel....

"Master," said Abiboo's voice "dem puck-a-puck, him lib for come."

"Eh, what's that?"

Mainward turned almost savagely on the man.

"Puck-a-puck—you hear 'um?"

But the sick man could not hear the smack of the Zaire's stern wheel, as the little boat breasted the downward rush of the river; he was surprised to see that it was dawn, and grudgingly admitted to himself that he had slept. He closed his eyes again and had a strange dream. The principal figure was a tall, tanned, clean-shaven man in a white helmet, who wore a dingy yellow overcoat over his pyjamas.

"How are you feeling?" said the stranger.

"Rotten bad," growled Mainward, "especially about Ethel; don't you think it was pretty low down of her to lead me on to believe that she was awfully fond of me, and then at the last minute to chuck me?"

"Shocking," said the strange white man gravely; "but put her out of your mind just now: she isn't worth troubling about What do you say to this?"

He held up a small greenish pellet between his forefinger and thumb, and Mainward laughed weakly.

"Oh, rot!" he chuckled faintly, "you're one of those Forest of the Happy Dreams johnnies; what's that? a love philter?" He was hysterically amused at the witticism.

Bailman nodded.

"Love or life, it's all one," he said, but apparently unamused, "swallow it."

Mainward giggled and obeyed.

"And now," said the stranger—this was six hours later—"the best thing you can do is to let my boys put you on my steamer and take you down river."

Mainward shook his head. He had awakened irritable and lamentably weak. "My dear chap, it's awfully kind of you to have come—by the way, I suppose you are a doctor?"

Bailman shook his head.

"On the contrary, I am a journalist," he said flippantly, "I'm Bailman, the special correspondent, of The Megaphone. I've been doing atrocities for a year—you know the stuff that is associated with the Congo—but you were saying?"

"I want to stay here—it's devilish pretty."

"Devilish is the very adjective I should have used—my dear man, this is the plague spot of the Congo; it's the home of every death-dealing fly and bug in Congo Land."

He waved his hand to the glorious vista of fresh green glades, of gorgeous creepers that hung their garlands from tree to tree.

"Look at the grass," he said; "it's homeland grass—that's the seductive part of it; I nearly camped here myself—come my friend, let me take you to my camp."

Mainward shook his head obstinately.

"I'm obliged, but I'll stay here for a day or so. I want to try the supernatural effects of this pleasant place," he said with a little smile. "I've got so many thoughts that need treatment."

"Look here," said Bailman roughly, "you know jolly well how this forest got its name; it is called Happy Dreams because it's impregnated with fever, and with every disease from beri-beri to sleeping sickness. You don't wake from the dreams that you dream here. Man, I know this country, and you're a new comer; you've trekked here because you wanted to get away from life and start all over again."

"I beg your pardon." Mainward's face flushed and he spoke a little stiffly.

"Oh, I know all about you—didn't I tell you I was a journalist? I was in England when things were going rocky with you, and I've read the rest in the papers I get from time to time. But all that is nothing to do with me. I'm here to help you to start fair. If you had wanted to commit suicide, why come to Africa to do it? Be sensible and shift your camp; I'll send my steamer back for your men—will you come?"

"No," said Mainward sulkily. "I don't want to, I'm not keen; besides, I'm not fit to travel."

Here was an argument which Bailman could not answer. He was none too sure upon that point himself, and he hesitated before he spoke again.

"Very well," he said at length, "suppose you stay another day to give you a chance to pull yourself together. I'll come along to-morrow with a tip top invalid chair for you—is it a bet?"

Mainward held out his shaking hand, and the ghost of a smile puckered the corners of his eyes. "It's a bet," he said.

He watched the journalist walk through the camp, speaking to one man after another in a strange tongue. A singular, masterful man this, thought Mainward. Would he have mastered Ethel? He watched the stranger with curious eyes, and noted how his own lazy devils of carriers jumped at his word....

"Good-night," said Bailman's voice, and Mainward looked up. "You must take another of these pellets, and tomorrow you'll be as fit as a donkey-engine. I've got to get back to my camp tonight, or I shall find half my stores stolen in the morning; but if you'd rather I stopped?"

"No, no," replied the other hastily. He wanted to be alone. He had lots of matters to settle with himself. There was the question of Ethel, for instance.

"You won't forget to take the tabloid?"

"No. I say, I'm awfully obliged to you for coming. You've been a good white citizen."

Bailman smiled. "Don't talk nonsense," he said, good-humouredly. "This is all brotherly love. White to white, and kin to kin, don't you know? We're all alone here, and there isn't a man of our colour within five hundred miles. Goodnight, and please take the tabloid—"

Mainward lay listening to the noise of the departure. He thought he heard a little bell tingle. That must be for the engines. Then he heard the puck-a-puck of the wheel—so that was how the steamer got its name.

Abiboo came with some milk. "You take um medicine, master?" he inquired.

"I take um," murmured Mainward; but the green tabloid was underneath his pillow.

Then there began to steal over him a curious sensation of content. He did not analyse it down to its first cause. He had had sufficient introspective exercise for one day. It came to him as a pleasing shock to realise that he was happy.

He opened his eyes and looked round. His bed was laid in the open, and he drew aside the curtains of his net to get a better view.

A little man was walking briskly toward him along the velvet stretch of grass that sloped down from the glade, and Mainward whistled.

"Atty," he gasped. "By all that's wonderful."

Atty, indeed, it was: the same wizened Atty as of yore; but no longer pulling the long face to which Mainward had been accustomed. The little man was in his white riding-breeches, his diminutive top-boots were splashed with mud, and on the crimson of his silk jacket there was evidence of a hard race. He touched his cap jerkily with his whip, and shifted the burden of the racing saddle he carried to his other arm,

"Why, Atty," said Main ward, with a smile, "what on earth are you doing here?"

"It's a short way to the jockeys' room, sir," said the little man. "I've just weighed in. I thought the Fairy would do it, sir, and she did."

Mainward nodded wisely. "I knew she would too," he said. "Did she give you a smooth ride?"

The jockey grinned again. "She never does that," he said, "but she ran gamely enough. Coming up out of the Dip, she hung a little, but I showed her the whip, and she came on as straight as a die. I thought once The Stalk would beat us—I got shut in, but I pulled her round, and we were never in difficulties. I could have won by ten lengths," said Atty.

"You could have won by ten lengths," repeated Mainward in wonder. "Well, you've done me a good turn, Atty. This win will get me out of one of the biggest holes that ever a reckless man tumbled into—I shall not forget you, Atty."

"I'm sure you won't, sir," said the little jockey gratefully; "if you'll excuse me now, sir?"

Mainward nodded and watched him as he moved quickly through the trees.

There were several figures in the glade now, and Mainward looked down ruefully at his soiled duck suit. "What an ass I was to come like this," he muttered in his annoyance. "I might have known that I should have met all these people."

There was one he did not wish to see; and as soon as he sighted Venn, with his shy eyes and his big nose, Mainward endeavoured to slip back out of observation. But Venn saw him, and came tumbling through the trees, with his big flabby hand extended and his dull eyes aglow,

"Hullo, hullo!" he grinned, "been looking for you."

Mainward muttered some inconsequent reply. "Rum place to find you, eh?" Venn removed his shining silk hat and mopped his brow with an awesome silk handkerchief.

"But look here, old feller--about that money."

"Don't worry, my dear man," Mainward interposed easily. "I can pay you now."

"That ain't what I mean," said the other impetuously; "a few hundred more or less docs not count. But you wanted a big sum—

"And you told me you'd see me—"

"I know, I know," Venn put in hastily; but that was before Kaffirs started jumpin'. Old feller, you can have it!"

He said this with grotesque emphasis, standing with his legs wide apart, his hat perched on the back of his head, his plump hands dramatically outstretched, and Mainward laughed outright.

"Sixteen thousand?" he asked.

"Or twenty," said the other impressively. "I want to show you—"

Somebody called him, and with a hurried apology he went blundering up the green slope, stopping and turning back to indulge in a little dumb show illustrative of his confidence in Mainward and his willingness to oblige.

Mainward was laughing, a low, gurgling laugh of pure enjoyment. Venn of all people! Venn, with his cursed questions and talk of securities. Well! well! Then his merriment ceased, and he winced again, and his heart beat faster and faster, and a curious weakness came over him.

How splendidly cool she looked.

She walked in the clearing, a white, slim figure: he heard the swish of her skirt as she came through the long grass... white, with a green belt all encrusted with dull gold embroidery. He took in every detail hungrily—the dangling gold ornaments that hung from her belt, the lace collar at her throat, the....

She did not hurry to him: that was not her way.

But her eyes dawned a gradual tenderness—those dear eyes that dropped before his shyly.

"Ethel!" he whispered, and dared to take her hand.

"Aren't you wonderfully surprised?" she said.

"Ethel! here!"

"I—I had to come."

She would not look at him, but he saw the pink in her cheek and heard the faltering voice with a wild hope. "I behaved so badly dear—so very badly."

She hung her head.

"Dear! dear!" he muttered, and groped toward her like a blind man.

She was in his arms, crushed against his breast, the perfume of her presence in his brain.

"I had to come to you—" Her hot cheek was against his. "I love you so."

"Me—love me? Do you mean it?" He was tremulous with happiness, and his voice broke—"dearest."

Her face was upturned to his, her lips so near; he felt her heart beating as furiously as his own. He kissed her—her lips, her eyes, her dear hair....

"O God, I'm happy," he sobbed, "so—so happy...."

Bail man sprang ashore just as the sun was rising, and came thoughtfully through the undergrowth to the camp. Abiboo, squatting by the curtained bed, did not rise. Bailman walked to the bed, pulled aside the mosquito netting and bent over the man who lay there.

Then he drew the curtains again, lit his pipe slowly, and looked down at Abiboo.

"When did he die?" he asked.

"In the dark of the morning, master," said the native.

Bailman nodded slowly. "Why did you not send for me?"

For a moment the squatting figure made no reply, then he rose and stretched himself.

"Master," he said, speaking in Swaheli—that is a language which allows of nice distinctions—"this white man was happy; he walked in the Forest of Happy Thoughts: why should I call him back to a land where there was neither sunshine nor happiness, but only night and the pain of sickness?"

"You're a philosopher," said Bailman irritably.

"I am a follower of the Prophet," said Abiboo, the Kano boy; "and all things are according to God's wisdom."


The Education of King Peter

In the land that curves along the borders of Togoland, the people understand punishment to mean pain and death, and nothing else counts. There was a foolish commissioner who was a great humanitarian, and he went up to Akasava—which is the name of this land—and tried moral suasion.

It was a raiding palaver. Some of the people of Akasava had crossed the river to Ochori and stolen women and goats, and I believe there was a man or two killed, but that is unimportant. The goats and the women were alive, and cried aloud for vengeance. They cried so loud that they were heard down at Headquarters; and Mr. Commissioner Niceman—that was not his name, but it will serve—went up to see what all the noise was about. He found the Ochori people very angry and more frightened.

"If," said their spokesman, "they will return our goats, they may keep the women, because the goats are very valuable."

So Mr. Commissioner Niceman had a long, long palaver, that lasted days and days, with the Chief of the Akasava people and his councilors; and in the end moral suasion triumphed, and the people promised on a certain day, at a certain hour, when the moon was in such a quarter and the tide at such a height, the women should be returned, and the goats also.

So Mr. Niceman returned to Headquarters swelling with admiration for himself, and wrote a long report about his genius and his administrative abilities, and his knowledge of the native, which was afterward published in Blue Book (Africa) 7,943-09.

It happened that immediately afterward Mr. Niceman went home to England on furlough, so that he did not hear the laments and woeful waitings of the Ochori folk when they did not get their women or their goats.

Bailman, working round the Isisi River with ten houssas and an attack of malaria, received a helio message:

"Go Akasava and settle that infernal woman palaver. Administration."

So Bailman girded up his loins, took twenty-five grains of quinine, and, leaving his good work, he was searching for M'Beli, the witchdoctor, who had poisoned a friend,—trekked across country for the Akasava.

In the course of time he came to the city, and was met by the Chief.

"What about these women?" he asked.

"We will have a palaver," said the Chief. "I will summon my headmen and my councilors "

"Summon nothing," Bailman said shortly. "Send back the women and the goats you stole from the Ochori."

"Master," promised the Chief, "at full moon, which is our custom, when the tide is so, and all signs of gods and devils are propitious, I will do as you bid."

"Chief," said Bailman, tapping the ebony chest of the other with the handle of his walking-stick, "moon and river, gods or devils, those women and the goats go back to the Ochori folk by sunset, or I tie you to a tree and flog you till you bleed."

"Master," said the Chief, "the women shall be returned."

"And the goats," added Bailman.

"As to the goats," said the Chief airily, " they are dead—having been killed for a feast."

" You will bring them back to life," said Bailman.

"Master, do you think I am a magician?" asked the Chief of the Akasava.

"I think you are a liar," said Bailman impartially, and there the palaver ended.

That night, goats and women returned to the Ochori, and Bailman prepared to depart.

He took the Chief aside, not desiring to put shame upon him, or to weaken his authority.

"Chief," he remarked, "it is a long journey to Akasava, and I am a man fulfilling many tasks. I desire that you do not cause me any further journey to this territory."

"Master," said the Chief truthfully, "I never wish to see you again."

Bailman smiled inwardly, collected his ten houssas, and went back to the Isisi River to continue his search for M'Beli.

It was not a nice search, for many reasons; and there was every excuse for believing that the King of the Isisi himself was the murderer's protector. Confirmation of this view came, one morning, when Bailman, encamped by the big river, was taking a breakfast of tinned milk and toast. There arrived hurriedly Sato-Koto, the brother of the King, in great distress of mind, for he was a fugitive from the King's wrath. He babbled forth all manner of news, in much of which Bailman took no interest whatever. But what he said of the witch, doctor who lived in the King's shadow was very interesting indeed, and Bailman sent a messenger to Headquarters, and, as it transpired, Headquarters despatched, in the course of time, Mr. Niceman—who by this time had returned from furlough—to use moral suasion on the King of the Isisi.

From such evidence as we have been able to collect, it is clear that the King was not in a melting mood: it is an indisputable fact that poor Niceman's head, stuck on a pole before the King's hut, proclaimed the King's high spirits.

His Majesty's ships St. George, Thrush, Philome, and Phoebe sailed from Simons Town, and H.M.S. Dwarf came down from Sierra Leone, and in less than a month after the King had killed his guest he wished he had not.

Headquarters sent Bailman to clear up the political side of the trouble.

He was shown round what was left of the King's city, by the flag lieutenant of the St. George.

"I'm afraid," remarked that gentleman apologetically,—"I am afraid that you will have to dig out a new king. We've rather killed the old one."

Bailman nodded.

"I shall not go into mourning," he said.

There was no difficulty in finding candidates for the vacant post. Sato- Koto, the dead King's brother, expressed with commendable promptitude his willingness to assume the cares of office.

"What do you say?" asked the admiral commanding the expedition.

"I say 'no,' sir," said Bailman, without hesitation. "The King has a son, a boy of nine; the kingship must be his. As for Sato-Koto, he shall be Regent at pleasure."

And so it was arranged, Sato-Koto sulkily assenting.

They found the new King hidden in the woods with the women folk, and he tried to bolt; but Bailman caught him and led him back to the city by his ear.

"My boy," he asked kindly, "how do people call you?"

"Peter, master," whimpered the wriggling lad, "in the fashion of the white people."

"Very well," said Bailman. "You shall be King Peter, and rule this country wisely and justly, according to custom and the law. And you shall do hurt to none, and put shame on none; nor shall you kill, or raid, or do any of those things that make life worth living; and if you break loose, may the Lord help you!"

Thus was King Peter anointed monarch of the Isisi people, and Bailman, with the little army of blue-jackets and houssas, went back to Headquarters; for M'Beli, the witch-doctor, had been slain at the taking of the city, and Bailman's work was finished.

The story of the taking of Isisi and the crowning of the young King was told in the London newspapers, and lost nothing in the telling. It was so described by the special correspondents who accompanied the expedition that many dear old ladies wept, and many dear young ladies of Mayfair said, "How sweet!" And the outcome of the many emotions that the descriptions evoked was the sending out from England of Miss Clinton Calbraith, who was an M.A. and unaccountably pretty.

She came out to "mother" the orphan King, to be a mentor and a friend. She paid her own passage, but the books that she brought and the school- paraphernalia that filled two large packing-cases were subscribed for by the tender readers of Tiny Toddlers, a magazine for infants. Bailman met her on the landing-stage, being curious to see what a white woman looked like.

He put a hut at her disposal, and sent the wife of his coast clerk to look after her.

"And now, Miss Calbraith," he asked, at dinner that evening, "what do you expect to do with Peter?"

She tilted her pretty chin in the air reflectively.

"We shall start with the most elementary of lessons—the merest kindergarten—and gradually work up; I shall teach him calisthenics, a little botany—Mr. Bailman, you're laughing!"

"No, I wasn't," he hastened to assure her; "I always make a face like that— er—in the evening. But tell me this; do you speak the language—Swaheli, Bomongo, Fingi--"

"That will be a difficulty," she said thoughtfully.

"Will you take my advice?" he asked.

"Why, yes."

"Well, learn the language." She nodded. "Go home and learn it." She frowned. "It will take you about twenty-five years."

"Mr. Bailman," she said, not without dignity, "you are making fun of me."

" Heaven forbid," said Bailman piously, " that I should do anything so wicked."

The end of the story, so far as Miss Clinton Calbraith was concerned, was that she went to Isisi, stayed three days, and came back incoherent.

" He is not a child," she cried wildly. " He is—a—a little devil!"

"So I should say," agreed Bailman philosophically.

"A king! It is disgraceful! He lives in a mud hut, and wears no clothes! If I'd known--"

"A child of nature," said Bailman blandly. "You didn't expect a sort of Louis Quinze, did you?"

"I don't know what I expected," she said desperately; "but it was impossible to stay—quite impossible."

"Obviously," murmured Bailman.

"Of course, I knew he would be black," she went on; "and I knew that—oh, it was too horrid!"

"The fact of it is, my dear young lady," said Bailman, "Peter wasn't as picturesque as you imagined him; he wasn't the gentle child with pleading eyes; and he lives messy. Is that it?"

This was not the only attempt to educate Peter. Months afterward, when Miss Calbraith had gone home and was busily writing her famous book, "Alone in Africa—By an English

Gentlewoman," Bailman heard of another educative raid. Two members of the Ethiopian Mission came into Isisi by the back way. The Ethiopian Mission is made up of Christian black men, who very properly, basing their creed upon holy writ, preach the gospel of equality. A black man is as good as a white man any day of the week, and infinitely better on Sundays, if he happens to be a member of the Reformed Ethiopian Church.

They came to Isisi, and achieved instant popularity, for the kind of talk they provided was very much to the liking of Sato-Koto and the King's councilors.

Bailman sent for the missioners. The first summons they refused to obey; but they came on the second occasion, for the message Bailman sent was both peremptory and ominous.

They came to Headquarters—two cultured American negroes of good address and refined conversation. They spoke English faultlessly, and were in every sense perfect gentlemen.

"We cannot understand the character of your command," said one, "which savors somewhat of an interference with the liberty of the subject."

"You'll understand me better," remarked Bailman, who knew his men, "when I tell you that I cannot allow you to preach sedition to my people."

"Sedition, Mr. Bailman!" said the negro, in shocked tones. "That is a grave charge." Bailman took a paper from a pigeonhole in his desk—the interview was taking place in his office.

"On such a date," he said, "you said this, and this, and that."

In other words, he accused them of overstepping the creed of equality and encroaching upon the borderland of political agitation.

"Lies," said the elder of the two, without hesitation.

"Truth or lie," answered Bailman, "you go no more to Isisi."

"Would you have the heathen remain in darkness?" asked the man reproachfully. "Is the light we kindle too bright, friend?"

"No," said Bailman, "but a thought too warm."

So he committed the outrage of removing the Ethiopians from the scene of their earnest labors, in consequence of which questions were asked in the English Parliament.

Then the Chief of the Akasava people—an old friend—took a hand in the education of King Peter.

Akasava adjoins that King's territory, and the Chief came to give hints in military affairs.

He came with drums a-beating, with presents of fish and bananas and salt.

"You are a great King," he said to the sleepy-eyed boy, who sat on the stool of state, regarding him with open-mouthed interest. "When you walk, the world shakes at your tread; the mighty river that goes flowing down to the big water parts asunder at your word; the trees of the forest shiver; and the beasts go slinking to cover when your mightiness goes abroad."

"Oh ko ko!" giggled the King, pleasantly tickled.

"The white men fear you," continued the Chief of the Akasava; "they tremble and hide at your roar."

Sato-Koto, standing at the King's elbow, was a practical man.

"What seek ye. Chief?" he asked, cutting short the compliments.

So the Chief told him of a land peopled by cowards, rich with the treasures of the earth, goats and women.

"Why do you not take them yourself?" demanded the Regent.

"Because I am a slave," said the Chief, "the slave of Baili, who would beat me. But you, lord, are of the great. Being King's headman, Baili would not beat you, because of your greatness."

There followed a palaver that lasted two days.

"I shall have to get busy with Peter," wrote Bailman despairingly to the Administrator. "The little beggar has gone on the war-path against those unfortunate Ochori. I should be glad if you would send me a hundred men, a Maxim gun, and a bundle of rattan canes, I'm afraid I must attend to Peter's education myself."

"Lord, did I not speak the truth?" said the Akasava Chief, in triumph. " Baili has done nothing! Behold, we have wasted the city of the Ochori, and taken their treasure, and the white man is dumb because of your greatness! Let us wait till the moon comes again, and 1 will show you another city."

"You are a great man," bleated the King, "and some day you shall build your hut in the shadow of my palace."

"On that day," said the Chief, with splendid resignation, " I shall die of joy."

When the moon had waxed and waned, and come again, a penciled silver hoop of light in the eastern sky, the Isisi warriors gathered, with spear and broad- bladed sword, with ingola on their bodies and clay in their hair.

They danced a great dance by the light of a huge fire, and all the women stood around, clapping their hands rhythmically.

In the midst of this there arrived a messenger in a canoe, who prostrated himself before the King, saying:

"Master, one day's march from here is Baili. He has with him five score of soldiers and the brass gun which says ha-ha-ha-ha-ha!"

A silence reigned in court circles, which was broken by the voice of the Akasava Chief.

"I think I will go home," he said. "I have a feeling of sickness. Also, it is the season when my goats have their young."

"Do not be afraid," said Sato-Koto brutally. "The King's shadow is over you, and he is so mighty that the earth shakes at his tread, and the waters of the big river part at his footfall; also, the white men fear him."

"Nevertheless," said the Chief, with some agitation, "I must go, for my youngest son is sickening with fever and calls all the time for me."

"Stay," said the Regent, and there was no mistaking his tone.

Bailman did not come the next day, nor the next. He was moving leisurely, traversing a country where many misunderstandings existed that needed clearing up. When he arrived, having sent a messenger ahead to carry the news of his arrival, he found the city peaceably engaged.

The women were crushing corn, the men smoking, the little children playing and sprawling about the streets.

He halted on the outskirts of the city, on a hillock that commanded the main street, and sent for the Regent.

"Why must I send for you?" he asked. "Why does the King remain in his city when I come? This is shame."

"Master," said Sato-Koto boldly, "it is not fitting that a great king should so humble himself."

Bailman was neither amused nor angry. He was dealing with a rebellious people, and his own fine feelings were as nothing to the peace of the land.

"It would seem that the King has had bad advisers," he reflected aloud, and Sato-Koto shuffled uneasily.

"Go now and tell the King to come—for I am his friend."

The Regent departed, but returned again alone.

"Lord, he will not come," he said sullenly.

"Then I will go to him," said Bailman.

King Peter, sitting before his hut, greeted Mr. Commissioner with downcast eyes.

Bailman's soldiers, spread in a semi-circle before the hut, kept the rabble at bay.

"King," said Bailman,—he carried in his hand a rattan cane of familiar shape, and as he spoke he whiffled it in the air, making a little humming noise,—"stand up."

"Wherefore?" said Sato-Koto.

"That you shall see," said Bailman.

The King rose reluctantly, and Bailman grabbed him by the scruff of his neck.

Swish!

The cane caught him most undesirably, and he sprang into the air with a yell.

Swish, swish, swish!

Yelling and dancing, throwing out wild hands to ward off the punishment, King Peter blubbered for mercy.

"Master!" Sato-Koto, his face distorted with rage, reached for his spear.

"Shoot that man if he interferes," ordered Bailman, without releasing the King.

The Regent saw the leveled rifles, and hastily stepped back.

"Now," said Bailman, throwing down the cane, "now we will play a little game."

"Wow, wow—oh ko!" sobbed His Majesty.

"I go back to the forest," said Bailman. "By and by a messenger shall come to you saying that the Commissioner is on his way—do you understand?"

"Yi-hi," sobbed the King.

"Then will you go out with your councilors and your old men, and await my coming according to custom. Is that clear?"

"Ye-es, Master," whimpered the boy.

"Very good," said Bailman, and withdrew his troops.

In half an hour came a grave messenger to the King, and the court went out to the little hill to welcome the white man.

This was the beginning of King Peter's education, for thus was he taught obedience.

Bailman went into residence in the town of Isisi, and there he held court.

"Sato-Koto," he said on the second day, "do you know the village of Ikau?"

"Yes, master; it is two days' journey into the bush."

Bailman nodded.

"You will take your wives, your children, your servants, and your possessions to the village of Ikau, there to stay until I give you leave to return. The palaver is finished."

Next came the Chief of the Akasava, very ill at ease.

"Lord, if any man says I did you wrong, he lies," said the Chief.

"Then I am a liar," answered Bailman; "for I say that you are an evil man, full of cunning."

"If it should be," said the Chief, "that you order me to go to my village, as you have ordered Sato-Koto, I will go, since he who is my father is not pleased with me."

"That I order," said Bailman; "also, twenty strokes with a stick, for the good of your soul. Furthermore, I would have you remember that down by Tembeli, on the great river, there is a village where men labor in chains because they have been unfaithful to the Government and have practised abominations."

So the Chief of the Akasava people went out to punishment.

There were other matters, of a minor character, requiring adjustment; but when these were all settled to the satisfaction of Bailman, but by no means to the satisfaction of the subjects, the Commissioner turned his attention to the further education of the King.

"Peter," he said, "to-morrow, when the sun comes up, I go back to my own village, leaving you without councilors."

"Master, how may I do without councilors, since I am a young boy?" asked the King, crestfallen and chastened.

"By saying to yourself, when a man calls for justice, 'If I were this man, how should I desire the King's justice?'"

The boy looked unhappy. "I am very young," he repeated, "and to-day there come many from outlying villages, seeking redress against their enemies."

"Very good," said Bailman; "to-day I will sit at the King's right hand and learn of his wisdom."

The boy stood on one leg in his embarrassment, and eyed Bailman askance.

There was a hillock behind the town. A worn path led up to it, and atop it was a thatched hut without sides. From this hillock could be seen the broad river with its sandy shoals, where the crocodiles slept with open mouth, and the rising ground toward Akasava, hills that rose one on top of another, covered with a tangle of vivid green. In this house sat the King in judgment, beckoning the litigants forward. Sato-Koto was wont to stand beside the King, bartering justice.

To-day Sato-Koto was preparing to depart, and Bailman sat at the King's side.

There were indeed many litigants.

There was a man who had bought a wife, giving no less than a thousand rods and two bags of salt for her. He had lived for three months with her, when she departed from his house.

"Because," said the man philosophically, "she had a lover. Therefore, Mighty Sun of Wisdom, I desire the return of my rods and my salt."

"What say you?" asked Bailman.

The King wriggled uncomfortably.

"What says the father?" he said hesitatingly, and Bailman nodded.

"That is a wise question," he approved, and called the father—a voluble and eager old man.

"Lord King," he said hurriedly, "I sold this woman, my daughter. How might I know her mind? Surely I fulfil my contract when the woman goes to the man—how shall a father control when a husband fails?"

Bailman looked at the King again, and the boy drew a long breath.

"It would seem, M'bleni, that the woman, your daughter, lived many years in your hut, and if you do not know her mind either you are a great fool or she is a cunning one. Therefore, I judge that you sold this woman knowing her faults. Yet, the husband might accept some risk also. You shall take back your daughter and return five hundred rods and a bag of salt; and if it should be that your daughter marries again, you shall pay one half of her dowry to this man."

Very, very slowly he gave judgment, hesitatingly, anxiously, glancing now and again to the white man for approval.

"That was good," said Bailman, and called forward another pleader.

"Lord King," said the new plaintiff, "a man has put an evil curse on me and my family, so that they sicken."

Here was a poser for the little judge, and he puzzled the matter out in silence, Bailman offering no help.

"How does he curse you?" at last asked the King.

"With the curse of death," said the complainant in a hushed voice.

"Then you shall curse him also," said the King, "and it shall be a question of whose curse is the stronger."

Bailman grinned behind his hand, and the King, seeing the smile, smiled also.

From that time on, Peter's progress was rapid, and there came to Headquarters from time to time, in the course of years, stories of a young king who was a Solomon in judgment.

So wise he was (who knew of the formula he applied to each case?), so beneficent, so peaceable, that the Chief of the Akasava, from whom tribute was periodically due, took advantage of the gentle administration, and sent neither corn nor fish nor grain. He did this after a journey to far-away Ikau, where he met the King's uncle, Sato-Koto, and they agreed upon common action. Since the crops were good, the King overlooked the first fault; but the second tribute came due, and neither Akasava nor Ikau sent; and the people of Isisi, angry at the insolence, murmured, and the King sat down in the loneliness of his hut to think upon a course that would be both just and effective.

"I really am sorry to bother you," wrote Bailman to the Administrator, again, "but I shall have to borrow your houssas for the Isisi country. There has been a tribute palaver, and Peter went down to Ikau and wiped up his uncle; he filled in his spare time by giving the Akasava the worst licking they ever have had. I thoroughly approve of all that Peter has done, because I feel that he is actuated only by the keenest sense of justice and a desire to do the right thing at the right time—and it was time Sato-Koto was killed; but I shall have to reprimand Peter, for the sake of appearances. The Akasava Chief is in the bush, hiding."

Peter came back to his capital after his brief but strenuous campaign, leaving behind him two territories that were all the better for his visit, though somewhat sore.

The young King brought together his old men, his witch-doctors, and other notabilities.

"By all the laws of white men," he said, "I have done wrong to Baili; because he has told me I must not fight, and, behold, I have destroyed my uncle, who was a dog, and I have driven the Chief of the Akasava into the forest. But Baili told me, also, that I must do what was just, and that I have done, according to my lights, for I have destroyed a man who put my people to shame. Now, it seems to me that there is only one thing to do, and that is to go to Baili, telling the truth and asking him to judge."

"Lord King," said the oldest of his councilors, "what if Baili puts you to the chain- gang?"

"That is with to-morrow," quoth the King, and gave orders for preparations to be made for departure.

Half way to Headquarters, the two met, King Peter going down and Bailman coming up. And here befell the great incident.

No word was spoken of Peter's fault before sunset.

When blue smoke arose from the fires of houssa and warrior, and the little camp in the forest clearing was all a-chatter, Bailman took the King's arm and led him along the forest path.

Peter told his tale, and Bailman listened.

"And what of the Chief of the Akasava?" he asked.

"Master," said the King, "he fled to the forest, cursing me, and with him went many bad men."

Bailman nodded again gravely.

They talked of things till the sun threw long shadows, and then they turned to retrace their footsteps. They were within half a mile of the camp, and the faint noise of men laughing and the faint scent of fires burning came to them, when the Chief of the Akasava stepped out from behind a tree and stood directly in their path. With him were some eight fighting-men, fully armed.

"Lord King," said the Chief of the Akasava, "I have been waiting for you."

The King made neither movement nor reply, but Bailman quickly reached for his revolver.

His hand had closed on the butt, when something struck him, and he went down like a log.

"Now we will kill the King of the Isisi, and the white man also."

The voice was the Chief's; but Bailman was not taking any particular interest in the conversation, because there was a hive of wild bees buzzing in his head, and a mazy pain; he felt sick.

"If you kill me, it is little matter," said the King's voice, "because there are many men who could take my place. But if you slay Baili, you slay the father of the people, and none can replace him."

"He whipped you, little King," said the Chief of the Akasava mockingly.

"That also is true," said the King's voice calmly; "yet many little boys have been whipped without shame."

After a long interval:

"I would throw him into the river," said a strange voice; "thus shall no trace be found of him, and no man will lay his death to our door."

"What of the King?" said another. Then came a crackling of twigs and the voices of men.

"They are searching," came a voice, in a whisper. "King, if you speak, I will kill you now."

"Kill," said the young King's even voice; and he shouted, "Oh, M'sabo! Beteli! Baili is here!"

That was all that Bailman heard.

Two days later he sat up in bed and demanded information. There was a young doctor with him, when he woke, who had providentially arrived from Headquarters.

"The King?" He hesitated. "Well—they finished the King. But he saved your life—I suppose you know that?"

Bailman said "yes" without emotion.

"A plucky little beggar," suggested the doctor.

"Very," said Bailman; then, "Did they catch the Chief of the Akasava?"

"Yes. He was so keen on finishing you that he delayed his bolting; the King threw himself on you and covered your body--"

"That will do."

Bailman's voice was harsh and his manner brusque at the best of times, but now his rudeness was brutal.

"Just go out of the hut, doctor—I want to sleep."

He heard the doctor move, heard the rattle of the "click" at the hut door; then he turned his face to the wall and wept.


## A Case for Angel, Esquire

There was a Minister of France—was it Necker?—who suggested on a memorable occasion that the people should eat grass. He was no vegetarian, he was just being rude; and when, on a subsequent occasion, an indignant populace slew him, in some grim way they decorated the body significantly.

If it should happen that the lawless folk of Notting Dale should ever fall upon Police Constable Lee, I doubt not that the jibe with which they will assail him will have some reference to 'sparrows,' for to the mysterious agency of the 'little sparrow' is due a great deal of the worthy officer's unpopularity amongst a certain class of people in his salubrious district.

PC Lee, in mufti, stepped round to the marine store of Cokey Salem, and asked to see the proprietor.

Cokey, so-called because of the commodity he runs as a side line to the rag-and-bone business, was not at home.

He shouted down the stairs to his frowsy wife to that effect and PC Lee was not convinced.

After a while, Cokey was induced to come down into the evil-smelling shop, and he did this with an ill grace.

'Hullo,' he said, gruffly, 'what's this—water rates?'

'To be exact,' said PC Lee, gently, 'it's a question of lead pipin', feloniously removed from unoccupied premises, to wit, 914, Kensington Park Road.'

'Ho!' said the defiant Cokey, 'an' what's that gotter do with me?'

'If you'll kindly step round to the station,' said the police-constable, 'I daresay you can explain the whole matter to our inspector in a few words.'

'Suppose I don't?'

'In that case,' said the thoughtful constable, 'I shall be under the painful necessity of takin' you.'

Cokey choked back a wicked word, put on his coat and hat, and accompanied the constable.

'Where did you nose this job?' he asked, vulgarly.

'A little sparrer,' said the reflective PC, 'happened—'

'I'd like to get hold of that sparrer of yours,' said Cokey, between his teeth, I'd wring his blanky neck.'

On the occasion under review, Cokey did not convince a sceptical inspector of his innocence. Nor had he any better luck with a frozen-faced magistrate, who listened dispassionately to Cokey's somewhat involved story. According to Cokey the lead piping found on his premises had

'Fallen like the gentle rain from heaven, upon the place beneath.'

This magistrate, who had never been known to smile, relaxed when Cokey adduced his crowning argument that the piping had been placed in his yard by the police, and committed Cokey to the Middlesex Sessions.

The Chairman of that Court, aided by a bored jury, found Cokey guilty of receiving, and the Chairman having, figuratively speaking, said it would be as much as his place was worth to give him less, sent Cokey to prison with hard labour for nine calendar months.

Whereupon the prisoner, affectionately addressing PC Lee, said that on some future occasion he would have the heart, lungs, and important blood vessels of the impassive officer—though exactly what he would do with them he did not say.

I saw PC Lee some nine months later, and knowing that Cokey was at liberty, I expressed my surprise at finding him still alive.

PC Lee smiled.

'If the Government would give prisoners leave of absence on the day they are sentenced,' he said, 'I daresay he might have caused me inconvenience; but barrin' that, I shall die a natural death. If a chap who had been sentenced heavily suddenly found himself pardoned, he'd be so overjoyed that he wouldn't have any time to hate me or any other constable, an' even a man who goes to a long term soon loses all the bad feelin' he ever had, an' comes out of "stir" full of a peace-on-earth-an'-good-will feelin'.

'In prison you've got a lot of time to think, an' if a man isn't a lunatic, he works out the situation reasonably an' comes to the conclusion that the constable has only done his duty, an' by the time the sentence is worked out, he's lost all his dislike for the man who lagged him.

'The only time I ever knew a man to bear animosity was in the case of the Newton Lane Robbery.

'If you don't remember the case. I'll give it to you in a few words. A cashier from one of the Ladbroke Grove shops was goin' back to his premises from the bank at Notting Hill Gate, when he was set upon by half-a-dozen roughs, knocked down an' robbed. All this happened in broad daylight, but in an unfrequented little turning, an' the assailants got away.

'It so happened that I was off duty (I was in X Division at the time), but I got to hear of the case when I reported for duty that night.

'The young fellow who was robbed had been taken to the hospital, but as he wasn't so badly hurt, he was allowed to go home. Accordin' to him, he wouldn't be able to recognise any of the party.

'Now, the detection of crime, as I see it, is a simple matter. The criminal is the obvious person. Don't you believe these detective stories that tell you that the feller found with the diamonds in his pocket is the innocent hero—he's only the innocent hero in story books. In real life he's the feller that did the robbery.

'When the police find a little sub-post-office has been robbed, an' the postmaster lyin' bound an' gagged, or when they see a bank clerk lyin' on the floor with the smell of chloroform hangin' round an' the safe open, they know it's 33 to 1 that they've got the robber first pop, an' that the enterprisin' burglar, as the song says, is the young feller found in such a romantic attitude.

'Unprofessional criminals spend too much of their time in preparin' picturesque scenes, an' professional criminals spend too much time in gettin' ready alibis, an' between one an' the other the police have a fairly easy time.

'So that it was only natural that our first suspicions fastened on the feller that had been robbed, an' there were certain features of it that made this view likely. Nobody had seen him attacked, nobody had seen men comin' away from the scene of the crime, an' if he hadn't been so badly injured there would have been no doubt whatever that he was the robber himself, an' the whole 'outrage' a fake.

'This might have been the case with the young cashier, only there was a remarkable flaw in the theory. He'd left the bank with five notes for a hundred pounds (which had been drawn for the purpose of sendin' to Russia to settle an account), an' this he placed in a big handbag which he carried, an' which was found open an' empty.

'He was carefully searched, but no money was on him when he was found. He had been seen enterin' the little street. One of the bank clerks, who happened to leave the bank at the same time, had walked with him to the entrance of the street, an' nobody had been seen to leave at either end before he was discovered. If he'd stolen 'em himself—what had happened to the banknotes? He couldn't bury 'em. There was no place in the street itself where they could have been hidden—you may be sure that we searched every possible hidin' place—an' the police were forced to believe that his story was true.

'The only thing against the man was that his firm had lost money before from their office. Ten, twenty, an' fifty pound notes had vanished, but the cashier was so above suspicion, an' had always insisted upon bein' the first to be searched, that they had never dreamt of connectin' him with any theft, an' had discharged clerk after clerk in consequence.

'It was such an interestin' case that the Yard sent down Mr Angel—you wrote about him didn't you?—a rare nice gentleman, who's always pullin' your leg, but very pleasant with it.

'Our inspector was asked to tell off a man to accompany Mr Angel, an' to my surprise I was chosen instead of some of our smart fellers.

'"Lee," says the inspector, "you go round with Mr Angel, an' introduce him to some of the 'heads' in your neighbourhood." So, in a manner of speakin', I was put in charge of Angel.

'But, bless you, he didn't want any introducin'! He knew all the toughs: knew Nick Moss, an' Percy Steel, an' Jim the Fence; knew 'em as if he'd been brought up with 'em—an' they knew him.

'We might have saved ourselves the trouble, because we learnt very little from these chaps, except from Nick Moss.

'"Hullo. Nick," says Angel, Esquire, most cheerfully, "how is the ladder larceny business?"

'Nick grinned a bit sheepish.

'"I'm straight now, Mr Angel," he says; "the other game's a mug's game."

'"Cutting out all your blessed platitudes," says Angel, "which of your college companions did this last little job?"

'"If I never move from here," says Nick, most solemn, "if I die this very minute, if—"

'"Havin' been duly sworn," says Mr Angel, "it is unnecessary to go any further—I gather from your interestin', but altogether unnecessary, protestation that you don't know."

'"That's right, sir," says Nick.

'Mr Angel told me later that he quite believed Nick didn't know for sure, but he thought that he had a suspicion.

'We examined the street where the robbery was committed. It is a street with stables on one side an' little houses on the other, an' connects Portobello Road with Pembridge Road.

'Nobody could give us any information about the robbery; in the majority of cases the first they knew about it was when the cashier had been found lyin' on the side-walk. Next we made a few inquiries about the cashier an' found that he was a most respectable man, with money of his own in the bank, a churchwarden, an' a member of the Young Men's Christian Association. What was most important was, he'd got money of his own in the bank.

"I'm afraid, Lee," says Mr Angel, "that this case must go down to history as 'The Notting Hill Mystery,'" and so it might have done but for the fact that one of the most curious coincidences happened that you could ever imagine.

'You've heard me talk about my "little sparrow?" It's a wheeze I work on the lads who want to know where I get all my valuable information from. This "cod" of mine got round to Mr Angel's ears, an' he remarked to me, in that jokin' way of his:

'"What a pity, Lee, your feathered friend can't supply us with a brilliant word picture of what happened—"

'He stopped short sudden, an' frowned thoughtfully.

'"By George!" says he, "I wonder if that is possible?"

'I couldn't see what he was gettin' at, so I waited.

'"We'll go round an' see our cashier friend," says Angel, so off we went to a neat little house near Wormwood Scrubbs.

'He was a bachelor, but rented a house, an' he opened the door to us himself, an' invited us in.

'It was a comfortably furnished sittin'-room, an' I saw Angel give a quick glance round as though sizing up the place. The only thing I noticed was that Mr Killun—that was his name—made a hasty attempt to fold up a newspaper that he'd been readin'.

'Killun was a pale-faced youth with uneven features an' a shifty eye, an' I disliked him from the first.

'"Readin', Mr Killun?" says Angel.

'"Yes," says Killun, quickly, "I'm naturally interested in learnin' if the police have any clue as to the people who robbed me."

'Angel, Esquire nodded, but said nothin'.

'By-an'-bye, he asked carelessly: "By the way, what are Southern Pacific Preferred?"

'"Sixty-four," said Killun, quick—then checked himself—"at least, I believe so—I don't take much interest in Stock Exchange transactions."

'"I suppose not," says Angel, an' went on talkin' about the robbery an' about things in general. He touched on the Lincoln Handicap, but Mr Killun said he knew nothin' about racin', an' that was probably so, because Angel referred to the Lincoln as a two mile race, an' no racin' man could have resisted the temptation to correct him.

'We left, an' Angel went away to London to make a few inquiries. He came back that night, an' together we went to Killun's house.

'"I want to see the bag you carried the notes in," says Angel.

'To my surprise the man produced it. I was surprised, because the bag ought to have been in the possession of the police, an' it only shows you how we are sometimes caught nappin', for without that bag the robber might never have been caught.

'Angel took the bag and examined it.

'"This is an enormous bag to carry five hundred pound notes in?"

'"It's the only one I've got," said the man, a little sullenly.

'Angel took it under the light an' inspected the inside. Then he laid a sheet of paper on the table an' shook out the contents. There was nothin' in it, except a few crumbs of tobacco, a little dust, an' somethin' that Angel, Esquire picked up an' examined carefully.

'It was a tiny grey feather, an' he nodded slowly.

'Then he turned to Killun.

'"I shall take you into custody," he said, "on a charge of stealin' five hundred pounds, the property of your employer."

'"It's a lie!" said Killun, hoarsely, an' tried to bolt. But I caught him, an' as he was inclined to be a little bit fresh, I put the handcuffs on him.

'We took him down to the station, an' then went back an' searched the house. On the roof, in a cage, we found a pigeon.

'"There's your little bird, Lee," says Angel, with a chuckle. "That's one of the little birds that was in Mr Killun's big bag. Not this chap, but others like him. A hundred-pound note fastened with an elastic band round each leg—an' whiff!—goes five hundred. He must have sent three birds."

'Angel spent some time that night concoctin' a message. He wrote it on a slip of thin paper an' fitted it to the pigeon's leg. Then he flew the pigeon.

'Next mornin', at eleven o'clock, we arrested an eminent bucket-shop* keeper, who turned up outside the Mansion House by appointment—Angel made the appointment.

*[Bucket-shop: A fraudulent brokerage operation in which orders to buy and sell are accepted but no executions take place. Instead, the operators expect to profit when customers close out their positions at a loss.]*

'This,' said PC Lee, impressively, 'proves my words, that the real criminal is the obvious criminal. Killun had been speculatin' an' had got into difficulties with the bucket-shop. The man that ran the shop wanted the money, an' bein' a bit of a pigeon fancier, had suggested a way of gettin' Killun out of his difficulties.

'Killun would take the birds in his bag to the office, an' whenever he could lay his hands on paper money, would nip out into the cloakroom, fix the note, an' fly the bird through a window, an' be back at his desk before anybody noticed his absence.'


The Barford "Snake"

Every railway man knows the Barford "Snake." There isn't one of us on the road that can hear the very words without shuddering. It has brought bad luck enough to a hundred poor souls, as I well know, and might have added me to its list of dead and crippled and mad victims, but for the strange fact that down in Bymouth, where I went to school, the teacher knocked a whole chapter of Shakespeare's play, Julius Caesar, into my thick head. How I used to curse Wednesdays!—that was poetry day at our board school—when I had to stand up before the class and stammer and stutter those words, to me without sense or meaning.

When the time came for me to go into the engine shed at Trentbury and change my books for a bundle of cotton waste, and my atlas for the Manual for Firemen, I felt a great load drop from my mind, and, in my fancy, I kicked Julius Caesar from one end of the fitters' shop to the other.

I didn't know much about Barford in those days. I'd heard drivers and firemen grumble and grouse about it, but it had not earned its reputation then. What was wrong about Barford, was the road in and out! If you want to get a rough idea of what it was like, you've got to put three "s's" end to end like this and remember that the whole distance they represent is about three-quarters of a mile, to realise what it meant to drivers. It was dead slow driving from end to end, and it spoilt the finest non-stop run in England, for it was a company order that no train should run through Barford junction.

The Barford Snake—as we called it—had a curious history. The Great Radial was one of the first roads to be built, and, at the time, there was a lot of opposition. It seems strange to us up-to-date folks that olden people should try to stop railway building, but so it was, and the bitterest enemy the rail had in the country round Barford was a chap named Germott: a regular savage fellow he was; said that railroads would ruin the country, and when the company came to him and offered to buy his land, he not only flatly refused, but induced other landowners to do the same. They tried (the company) all sorts of legal methods of making him quit, but he was protected with freeholds and every kind of ancient rights, and they couldn't get round him. He was only a young chap at that time, full of energy, and he worked his hardest to keep the railway out of Barford. He might have succeeded, too, only one or two of the men who had promised to support him turned traitor and sold their lands, and the consequence was that the company was just able to get a road into Barford and out again; but it was a devilish road to make, for it had to twist and turn and dodge in and out to avoid Farmer Germott's lands.

He never forgave the Great Radial for outwitting him. For years and years he fought the company in the courts and out of the courts for damage to crops by fire, trespass by employees, damage to stock by fright: there wasn't a single sin that the railway company didn't commit. Sometimes he would succeed, for juries were very prejudiced against railways in those days, and it wasn't a very difficult matter to get a verdict—at least, so I've heard Mr. Dash, the Company solicitor, say.

But as often as he won, he lost, and even when he got damages against the railway, they were all swallowed up in legal expenses.

It became a perfect mania with him, fighting the company, and it was the talk of the country that he was ruining himself in his desire for revenge. He got as near ruin as he could, and that made him the more bitter. Then he took up with a girl from Ouseleigh named Lune—an elf of a wench all eyes and hair. Lune her name was, and she was well named, for there wasn't one of the Lunes that hadn't a touch of madness somewhere in them, from Cabel Lune, who became a celebrated fiddle-player in London, to Jim Lune, who did ten years' for shooting a gamekeeper. It was the worst kind of wife he could have had by all accounts, but he took her, and in course of time had three children, two of which died young; the third lived long enough to get married, then he died—killed on the railway by ill-luck, and there was an action at law, which was decided in favour of the company. Gwen Germott was born after her father's death, and lived with her mother and grandfather on the farm, this side Barford.

In course of time the mother died—old Dame Germott went to glory twenty years ago—and this old man and his grand-daughter lived together in solitude, the man teaching the child his creed, the young one feeding the fires of hatred in her very ignorance.

I mind the first time I ever saw them. It was the day I took my own engine out of the shed, and a proud day it was for me.... "97 Up" was the train, minerals and empties to Barford, but for me it was the "Flying Londoner," and I trod on air.

We pulled into Barford thirty seconds ahead of time, or rather we pulled up at the distance signal that stood at "danger," when my mate said:

"Dan, do you want to see the man who made the Barford Snake?" and pointed.

They stood by a gate of a level crossing. The old man must have been nigh on seventy then, and the girl was a lanky, thin-legged girl with the same eyes as, from what I've heard, her grandmother had, big and black and solemn. They stood hand in hand—a strange picture: for the old man had a long white beard that reached below his waistcoat, and a shaggy mane of white hair hanging over his collar. His face was pinched and scarred as though his fight with the railway had been a physical fight, and his thin hooked nose was more like the beak of a bird than a human feature. He saw us looking at him, and raised his fist passionately, and the girl followed suit, her thin little hands clenched and her small face all twisted with anger.

"Curse you!" I heard him roar above the hissing of the exhaust, and just then the signal fell with a "clack" and I took "97" into the junction.

A driver who has got his heart in his job as I had, and was as anxious to get on as I was, hadn't got much time to worry his head about the feuds of a mad old farmer and his impish grandchild, but from time to time I heard of them, though I never saw either again for five years—an eventful five years for me. I rose rapidly, passing to slow passenger work and fast mail work, till I was chosen to run the "17 Up" one of the most important passenger services of the day. "17 Up" and "112 Down" on alternate days: this was the service I was chosen for, over the heads of older, and I dare say better, men. There was only one higher step I could take and that was to run the "Flying Londoner," but it was not a step I expected for many years, for three of the best drivers in England were engaged in that run. They were all men at the top of their class, men who knew their engines as a mother knows her baby, who could hear above the roar and the thunder of their pounding machines every single part at its work, and knew instinctively the cause of every tiny ailment that affected her.

The first definite news I got of the Germotts was that they had taken a house in Trentbury—they'd driven forty miles by trap sooner than come by railway. It was Bill Sanders, a fireman on one of the locals, who told me. "They've got religion," he said, "at least the girl has."

"Starting a mission to railway men, I'll he bound," said old Carter jokingly—old Carter was one of the drivers of the "Londoner."

There's many a true word spoken in jest, and it turned out to be just as old Carter said.

She held little meetings in a disused workshop in the town and sent round handbills to the fitters and the cleaners asking them to come. A good many went out of curiosity, although the district superintendent passed the word privately that no good could come of having anything to do with the Germotts.

I did not go myself: from all accounts it wasn't so much religion the Germotts had got, as spiritualism, and there's no doubt at all about it, that, wherever she picked the jargon up, she had got it all at her fingers' ends, and folk who went to scoff at her came away half-converted. They told me she had grown into a beautiful woman, and that may have been one of the reasons our young sparks found spiritualism so attractive. But it wasn't only the young ones—the old fellows, staid sober men like Carter, were influenced.

They say she spent hours struggling with old Carter, wrestling for his astral soul, or whatever you call it, only she and him and her arguments must have been mighty powerful, for when the old man left her house, he was as white as a sheet. I could name a dozen other men, Nick Fremlin, George Willowby, Dick Selby, who took up most powerfully with this new-fangled business.

I had half made up my mind to go to the little hall one evening and see and hear for myself, when something occurred to stop me.

I pulled out of Barford one night on the down trip, went dead slow round the curves of the Snake, got "All right" from the guard, and opened up for the last spin of forty miles. It was a beautiful night. There was a young moon, and the hoar frost glittered on hedge and field, as if some mighty hand had sprinkled the world with the dust of diamonds.

We ran shrieking through Marborne and Mutwell, and struck the straight level road between the last station and Trentbury. Halfway home we saw the lights of the "Flying Londoner" ahead, and I never realised so vividly why she got her name as I did that night—for,she came past us like a flash, and with a buffet of wind that nearly made me lose my balance.

I looked hack over the side of the cab and saw her red tail lights vanish, then looked at my mate. "What's wrong with old Carter—is he late?" he asked.

I looked at my watch. I was running to time, and was due to cross the "Londoner" at a point ten miles north of Trentbury.

"He's not late," I said; "we don't usually cross him so soon." And it was not till ninety seconds later that we reached the little bridge where, day by day, year in and year otit, as regular as clockwork, the "112" and the "Flying 6" passed each other.

Nothing upsets a railway man so much as to meet a train unexpectedly, and a train that is ahead of time is always unexpected. My mate did not speak till Trentbury was in sight, then he turned his troubled face to me.

"Was there a director on board?" he asked; but I shook my head, for I knew on our line that if the greatest man in the land were on board, it would make no difference in running time.

We drew into the station, were uncoupled, and instantly got a clear road to the shed.

I had my hand on the regulator when the shed signal swung to danger and the "three siding" lamps went green, then I heard my name shouted.

I looked out of the cab.

Somebody was running along the platform toward me.

It was the district superintendent, and his face was the colour of ashes.

He sprang on to the footplate.

"Pull out!" he gasped. "Couple the breakdown. The 'Flying 6'..."

"What?" I whispered, and my heart almost stopped beating.

"She's a wreck at Barford," he said, with almost a sob.

"She took the Snake at eighty miles an hour," he groaned. "Oh, my God!"

Ten minutes later I was flying back to Barford with the breakdown train and a gang of about a hundred men. On the way I had time to mention the incident of passing the "Londoner" ninety seconds ahead of time.

"That means he'd gained three minutes in twelve miles—it's incredible, it's unthinkable!" said the superintendent. "Why, Carter is the steadiest man on the road." I was silent. The watch could not lie, and the superintendent knew it. Incredible or not, it was true.

He gave me some information about the wreck—just as much as he had been able to get through. The "Flying 6" had run past the danger signals, both the "distant off" and the "home."

"What was the engine?" I asked.

"794—she wouldn't go wrong," he said; and, indeed, I knew there wasn't an engine on the road less likely to play tricks than No. 794.

I won't describe to you the ghastly sight that met our eyes at Barford; the engine crumpled like a piece of paper, the carriages splintered as if they were so many match-boxes, the horrible, silent rows of dead that were laid on the station platform.

I was sick at heart and weary when I drew into Trentbury next morning. I had helped to draw poor old Carter from underneath his engine....

It was the sensation of the day. The newspapers were filled with speculations. Why did the accident occur? How it happened was obvious. No engine that was ever built could negotiate those damnable curves at eighty miles an hour. Even at forty it would have meant disaster. Was Carter drunk? They hinted as much, but we knew him for a staunch teetotaller. Had he gone mad? There wasn't a saner man living. Had he had a fit? Against this theory there was his mate, the fireman—it was not possible that both men should succumb at the identical moment.

If it was a mystery to the newspapers, it was doubly a mystery to us who knew the inside working of a railway. But it was a mystery which seemed as though it would never be solved.

There were inquests and Board of Trade inquiries, and a private inquiry by the company, and then we buried our dead, and the story of the Barford disaster passed into history. Dick Selby was given poor old Carter's job, and Barford became a bad memory.

Two months afterwards I steamed out of Barford at the usual hour for the home run, as I had done for a year.

It was not curious that I should have been reminded of that dreadful night when we met the "Flying 6" thundering to her doom. I never passed the little bridge to meet the oncoming rush of the "Londoner" without breathing a silent prayer of thanks. But to-night something loosened my tongue, and I turned to Dixon as we cleared Mutwell and said: "This is the worst part of the run, Ned."

He understood me and nodded.

"I've never got her out of mind. Good God!" He stared ahead, and I looked.

Right ahead of us, tearing along the up road, swaying from side to side, came the "Londoner."

"Whar-r-r-!" she roared, and was past.

We stared at each other: mechanically my hand went to my watch.

"She's two minutes ahead!" I whispered hoarsely, and there came to me a horrible premonition of disaster.

How well justified that foreboding was, all the world knows; for the tragedy of two months previous had been re-enacted. The "Flying 6" was a blazing wreck in exactly the same place where poor Carter had gone to his death.

Dick Selhy, the driver, was alive when they got him out, and they did all that they could for him, not only for humanity's sake, but because they knew that their only hope of clearing up the mystery lay in him.

Crushed and mangled and burnt, with scarcely a sound bone or organ in his body, they carried him into Barford Cottage hospital, and officials watched him through the night, trying to piece together from his mutterings some story of the disaster as he had seen it. "Straight!" he muttered all night long, "straight as an arrow—straight as an arrow!" and no other word passed his lips till he died in the early hours of the morning.

If the first wreck had caused a sensation, the second seemed to electrify all England. It was the horrible coincidence that startled everybody. On the same spot two trains had been wrecked. Both were driven by sober, competent drivers; both met their fate through a glaring breach of regulations; both drivers had ignored the company orders which prohibit a greater speed than seven miles an hour when passing the Snake, and both had been wilfully blind to signals.

One morning after the inquest I was sent for from the loco-superintendents office.

When I got there I found the general manager and the secretary of the company. They looked very grave, and the manager, a courteous, elderly gentleman whom I knew by sight, motioned me to a seat.

"We have sent for you, Willis," he said, "because we have decided to appoint you to the 'Flying 6' in place of the unfortunate man who has just met with so terrible a death."

I murmured my thanks. A year ago the appointment would have fulfilled my most ambitious hopes, but now there seemed a bitter taste to the sweet I had craved.

"I want to tell you," said the manager, "that I have made most careful inquiries into your life, and I am satisfied that you have all the advantages of the men who preceded you—and one more."

He paused, and I wondered what particular gift I had that poor Dick Selby had not. He soon enlightened me.

"You have not meddled with the Germotts," he said quietly, "and I trust you will give them a wide berth."

I gasped: I hadn't connected the farmer and his elvish grand-daughter with the disasters; indeed, I had forgotten their very existence. "Both Selby and Carter," the manager went on, "were regular attendants at these meetings of the Germotts. Please God I am doing no injustice to the living or the dead, but I have a doubt—a very terrible doubt." He nodded to me as if to dismiss me. "You understand," he said, "that this conversation is absolutely confidential. I have spoken to you as much for your own good as for the good of the company."

I left him with my brain awhirl with suspicion and bewilderment.

The next three months were eventless. I took the "Flying 6" to London every other night, and brought her back every other morning, and with all things running smoothly, the passengers who had fallen away, and chosen slower, and as they thought safer, trains, came back to the "Londoner."

I saw nothing of the Germotts, but a month after I had been appointed, a letter came from the girl asking me if I would not come to one of the meetings. I took no notice of the letter and she wrote again. Then she called on me at my lodgings. I am a single man and rent a couple of rooms with a respectable couple, who have a cottage close to the station, and it was whilst I was taking my tea one Sunday afternoon that she walked in unannounced.

They had told me she was beautiful, but I never expected to see any human face as beautiful as hers. It might not appeal to some tastes, but to me she was the most wonderful creature I have ever seen. Her hair was as black as jet, her skin as white and as clear as ivory, there was no single touch of colour in dress or face save her lips, which were vividly red. Her eyes were big and black and shaded with long lashes, and she had a trick of looking at you from under them that gave you the curious sensation that comes to you when you know that some unseen person is observing you.

I knew her instinctively and rose to my feet. I did not for one moment regard her seriously as being a danger, but I was on my guard.

Though I was over thirty, I'd had little to do with women, so far as friendship was concerned.

Her first words were commonplace, for she smiled and said, "I am interrupting your tea-please go on, Mr. Willis."

But I stood waiting.

She took a chair by the table and rested her head on her hand easily. "Why have you not been to see us?" she asked.

I replied that I had had no time, and she nodded.

"Will you come this evening?"

She almost pleaded, but I shook my head.

"I'm afraid I'm not a go-to-meeting man."

Then she did an astounding thing, for she rose and put both hands on my shoulders. "Please come," she said, and looked me in the eyes. I shook my head again.

I was uncouth, I know—I am not a lady's man—but I took her hands from my shoulders and blushed for shame at myself when I found I was doing so.

"I can't," I muttered gruffly.

Without a word she left me.

It wasn't the last time she came. She seemed to know when the family I lodged with would be out, and she would open the latch of the cottage door and walk straight to my room.

I began to get worried for fear my superiors would get to learn of these visits, but strangely enough, the fact never seemed to reach them.

Worse than fear of discovery, I found that every time she came made it harder for me to refuse her, and that I looked forward to her visits, and even went so far as to devise means for getting my landlady out of the way.

All this may sound very weak and very foolish, but I was thirty and she was beautiful. More than this, I found the temptation to take her into my arms and kiss those scarlet lips of hers well-nigh irresistible, and whilst I cursed myself for my folly, with every recurring visit the temptation grew.

The climax came one night.

It was a Sunday—my off-day. I had spent the morning walking, and had come home to dinner dog tired. I dozed in the afternoon, and my landlady brought me my tea about five. I had finished tea, when I heard the family depart, and a few minutes later the girl's step sounded on the stair.

We talked for some time. I forget on what subject, the weather maybe, and then came the moment when she rose to depart. I heard her pleading voice, I felt her hands upon my shoulder, and the warm scent of her hair was in my nostrils.

"Won't you, won't you...?" I heard her murmur, and then she was in my arms, her white face upturned to mine, the wild splendour of her eyes fixed steadfastly on me.

I don't know what she said; I only know I kissed her again and again; that she murmured something monotonously.

I caught it.

"You have been very hard, very hard," she said in a low voice, but I was dazed and did not understand her. Then very gently she slipped from my arms and laid her hands upon my shoulder in the old way, staring at me with those eyes of hers.

"... straight—straight as an arrow," she said.

I nodded stupidly.

"It is a straight road," she said slowly, and never taking her eyes from me.

"Yes," I said dully.

"There is no Snake—it is a straight road through Barford—straight as an arrow," she repeated.

I nodded; I must have collapsed, for half an hour later, when I came to myself, I was huddled up on the fioor and she was gone.

I have no distinct recollection of what happened that night or the next day. I was numbed and stupid, but nobody seemed to be aware of my condition, and I took my engine from the shed that night as usual and coupled on to the coaches that stood at the platform. All day long I had found myself repeating the words "straight as an arrow—straight as an arrow," but without knowing why.

In a dim kind of way I knew that we had a crowded train—I think the station-master must have told me, but a matter of greater importance occupied my mind.

...The Barford road was as straight as an arrow!...and all these years we'd been deluding ourselves into the belief that there were Snake curves in and out of Barford! I could have laughed at the ridiculous mistake we had been making. Just before the starting signal was due to fall an inspector hurried up to me.

"You'll be late getting the 'right away,'" he said, "there's been an accident. Old Germott and his grand-daughter have been thrown from a trap. The old man was killed and they're taking her into Barford—to the hospital."

I nodded listlessly. I wasn't interested in Germott's grand-daughter. I saw her pass on a stretcher without emotion, her white face whiter than the pillow on which it lay.

I watched them without interest as they pushed the stretcher into the guard's van next to the engine, and the two doctors jumped in with her.

Then the starting signal fell, and we moved slowly across the points to the up road.

Dixon was very silent—even in my state of mind I noticed that much. He went about his work mechanically, not speaking a word. I thought once I saw his lips moving, and fancied he muttered the word "arrow." So he had found it out too! I remembered that he was a regular attendant at the Germott meetings, so of course he would have been told... been told...

Told what?

The last remnant of my reasoning power fought for assertion.

Told what? and by whom?

I put my hand to my forehead and tried to think.

Out of the darkness flashed a red lamp—and was gone.

A danger signal?

Well, it was natural they should put the "danger" against me, these foolish folks who did not know that the road into Barford was as straight as an arrow!

Was it, though?

I wanted to think: I wanted to sit down undisturbed by the rattle and clank of machinery, without these bothering red lights that came up out of the darkness and vanished. We passed a down express. It was the "112 Down." I used to drive that—I was on that when I passed the "Flying 6" that went to destruction on the Barford Snake...

Barford Snake? There was no Barford Snake—"Straight as an arrow—straight as an arrow."

If I could only think... not little dots of thought, but consecutive reasoning, logical thought.

Dixon was crouched down on the floor of the cab, his back against the tender-bulkhead. I could get no help from him.

Words came to my mind, a string of words—that was better: here something actual: a handle to grip reality by.

"That you have wronged me, Cassius, doth appear in this:
You have condemned and noted Lucius Pella
For taking bribes here of the Sardians."

Who was Lucius Pella?...Bribes?...There was an inspector who took bribes from a firm of carriers and was dismissed....Dick Selby wasn't dismissed, he was killed on the Barford Snake.

"Straight as an arrow—"

"I am a soldier, I,
Older in practice, abler than yourself
To make conditions."

I was younger than old Carter—Carter was killed on the Snake—seven miles an hour... regulation....

"A friend should bear his friends' infirmities, But Brutus makes mine greater than they are."

Another red light snicked past... we must be near Barford... a straight road....

Another red light. Five-mile point....

"There is my dagger,
And here my naked breast; within, a heart
Dearer than..."

I babbled the words, I shouted them. I was trying to keep down some horrible lie that was oppressing my mind. I raved with all the fervour of the tragedian and forced my leaden limbs to the regulator.

"If that thou be'st a Roman, take it forth.
I that denied thee gold will give my life!"

I shrieked the last words and threw my weight on to the lever....

Another red light.

"Strike as thou did'st at Casar!"

I brought the vacuum brake down, down, down! A thousand devils forced up my hand, but I brought it over... a child might have done it without effort, but the sweat poured from me.

I heard the brakes grip and felt the jar, and the shudder of our stopping, then ahead of me I saw the snake-like twist... and the train jolted to a standstill.

Then I awoke bathed in sweat, trembling in every limb—the horrible dream had passed.

I looked at Dixon: he was shaking as with ague.

Before us the signal stood at danger. I looked at my watch—we were nine minutes ahead of time!

We brought the "Flying 6" to Barford platform, safe.

I saw a knot of people at the guard's van, and heard the doctor's voice.

"She died when the train stopped," he said.

# The Barford "Snake" By Edgar Wallace

Every railway man knows the Barford "Snake." There isn't one of us on the road that can hear the very words without shuddering. It has brought bad luck enough to a hundred poor souls, as I well know, and might have added me to its list of dead and crippled and mad victims, but for the strange fact that down in Bymouth, where I went to school, the teacher knocked a whole chapter of Shakespeare's play, Julius Caesar, into my thick head. How I used to curse Wednesdays!—that was poetry day at our board school—when I had to stand up before the class and stammer and stutter those words, to me without sense or meaning.

When the time came for me to go into the engine shed at Trentbury and change my books for a bundle of cotton waste, and my atlas for the Manual for Firemen, I felt a great load drop from my mind, and, in my fancy, I kicked Julius Caesar from one end of the fitters' shop to the other.

I didn't know much about Barford in those days. I'd heard drivers and firemen grumble and grouse about it, but it had not earned its reputation then. What was wrong about Barford, was the road in and out! If you want to get a rough idea of what it was like, you've got to put three "s's" end to end like this  and remember that the whole distance they represent is about three-quarters of a mile, to realise what it meant to drivers. It was dead slow driving from end to end, and it spoilt the finest non-stop run in England, for it was a company order that no train should run through Barford junction.

The Barford Snake—as we called it—had a curious history. The Great Radial was one of the first roads to be built, and, at the time, there was a lot of opposition. It seems strange to us up-to-date folks that olden people should try to stop railway building, but so it was, and the bitterest enemy the rail had in the country round Barford was a chap named Germott: a regular savage fellow he was; said that railroads would ruin the country, and when the company came to him and offered to buy his land, he not only flatly refused, but induced other landowners to do the same. They tried (the company) all sorts of legal methods of making him quit, but he was protected with freeholds and every kind of ancient rights, and they couldn`t get round him. He was only a young chap at that time, full of energy, and he worked his hardest to keep the railway out of Barford. He might have succeeded, too, only one or two of the men who had promised to support him turned traitor and sold their lands, and the consequence was that the company was just able to get a road into Barford and out again; but it was a devilish road to make, for it had to twist and turn and dodge in and out to avoid Farmer Germott's lands.

He never forgave the Great Radial for outwitting him. For years and years he fought the company in the courts and out of the courts for damage to crops by fire, trespass by employees, damage to stock by fright: there wasn't a single sin that the railway company didn't commit. Sometimes he would succeed, for juries were very prejudiced against railways in those days, and it wasn't a very difficult matter to get a verdict—at least, so I've heard Mr. Dash, the Company solicitor, say.

But as often as he won, he lost, and even when he got damages against the railway, they were all swallowed up in legal expenses.

It became a perfect mania with him, fighting the company, and it was the talk of the country that he was ruining himself in his desire for revenge. He got as near ruin as he could, and that made him the more bitter. Then he took up with a girl from Ouseleigh named Lune—an elf of a wench all eyes and hair. Lune her name was, and she was well named, for there wasn't one of the Lunes that hadn't a touch of madness somewhere in them, from Cabel Lune, who became a celebrated fiddle-player in London, to Jim Lune, who did ten years' for shooting a gamekeeper. It was the worst kind of wife he could have had by all accounts, but he took her, and in course of time had three children, two of which died young; the third lived long enough to get married, then he died—killed on the railway by ill-luck, and there was an action at law, which was decided in favour of the company. Gwen Germott was born after her father's death, and lived with her mother and grandfather on the farm, this side Barford.

In course of time the mother died—old Dame Germott went to glory twenty years ago—and this old man and his grand-daughter lived together in solitude, the man teaching the child his creed, the young one feeding the fires of hatred in her very ignorance.

I mind the first time I ever saw them. It was the day I took my own engine out of the shed, and a proud day it was for me.... "97 Up" was the train, minerals and empties to Barford, but for me it was the "Flying Londoner," and I trod on air.

We pulled into Barford thirty seconds ahead of time, or rather we pulled up at the distance signal that stood at "danger," when my mate said:

"Dan, do you want to see the man who made the Barford Snake?" and pointed.

They stood by a gate of a level crossing. The old man must have been nigh on seventy then, and the girl was a lanky, thin-legged girl with the same eyes as, from what I've heard, her grandmother had, big and black and solemn. They stood hand in hand—a strange picture: for the old man had a long white beard that reached below his waistcoat, and a shaggy mane of white hair hanging over his collar. His face was pinched and scarred as though his fight with the railway had been a physical fight, and his thin hooked nose was more like the beak of a bird than a human feature. He saw us looking at him, and raised his fist passionately, and the girl followed suit, her thin little hands clenched and her small face all twisted with anger.

"Curse you!" I heard him roar above the hissing of the exhaust, and just then the signal fell with a "clack" and I took "97" into the junction.

A driver who has got his heart in his job as I had, and was as anxious to get on as I was, hadn't got much time to worry his head about the feuds of a mad old farmer and his impish grandchild, but from time to time I heard of them, though I never saw either again for five years—an eventful five years for me. I rose rapidly, passing to slow passenger work and fast mail work, till I was chosen to run the "17 Up" one of the most important passenger services of the day. "17 Up" and "112 Down" on alternate days: this was the service I was chosen for, over the heads of older, and I dare say better, men. There was only one higher step I could take and that was to run the "Flying Londoner," but it was not a step I expected for many years, for three of the best drivers in England were engaged in that run. They were all men at the top of their class, men who knew their engines as a mother knows her baby, who could hear above the roar and the thunder of their pounding machines every single part at its work, and knew instinctively the cause of every tiny ailment that affected her.

The first definite news I got of the Germotts was that they had taken a house in Trentbury—they'd driven forty miles by trap sooner than come by railway. It was Bill Sanders, a fireman on one of the locals, who told me. "They've got religion," he said, "at least the girl has."

"Starting a mission to railway men, I'll he bound," said old Carter jokingly—old Carter was one of the drivers of the "Londoner."

There's many a true word spoken in jest, and it turned out to be just as old Carter said.

She held little meetings in a disused workshop in the town and sent round handbills to the fitters and the cleaners asking them to come. A good many went out of curiosity, although the district superintendent passed the word privately that no good could come of having anything to do with the Germotts.

I did not go myself: from all accounts it wasn't so much religion the Germotts had got, as spiritualism, and there's no doubt at all about it, that, wherever she picked the jargon up, she had got it all at her fingers' ends, and folk who went to scoff at her came away half-converted. They told me she had grown into a beautiful woman, and that may have been one of the reasons our young sparks found spiritualism so attractive. But it wasn't only the young ones—the old fellows, staid sober men like Carter, were influenced.

They say she spent hours struggling with old Carter, wrestling for his astral soul, or whatever you call it, only she and him and her arguments must have been mighty powerful, for when the old man left her house, he was as white as a sheet. I could name a dozen other men, Nick Fremlin, George Willowby, Dick Selby, who took up most powerfully with this new-fangled business.

I had half made up my mind to go to the little hall one evening and see and hear for myself, when something occurred to stop me.

I pulled out of Barford one night on the down trip, went dead slow round the curves of the Snake, got "All right" from the guard, and opened up for the last spin of forty miles. It was a beautiful night. There was a young moon, and the hoar frost glittered on hedge and field, as if some mighty hand had sprinkled the world with the dust of diamonds.

We ran shrieking through Marborne and Mutwell, and struck the straight level road between the last station and Trentbury. Halfway home we saw the lights of the "Flying Londoner" ahead, and I never realised so vividly why she got her name as I did that night—for,she came past us like a flash, and with a buffet of wind that nearly made me lose my balance.

I looked hack over the side of the cab and saw her red tail lights vanish, then looked at my mate. "What's wrong with old Carter—is he late?" he asked.

I looked at my watch. I was running to time, and was due to cross the "Londoner" at a point ten miles north of Trentbury.

"He's not late," I said; "we don't usually cross him so soon." And it was not till ninety seconds later that we reached the little bridge where, day by day, year in and year otit, as regular as clockwork, the "112" and the "Flying 6" passed each other.

Nothing upsets a railway man so much as to meet a train unexpectedly, and a train that is ahead of time is always unexpected. My mate did not speak till Trentbury was in sight, then he turned his troubled face to me.

"Was there a director on board?" he asked; but I shook my head, for I knew on our line that if the greatest man in the land were on board, it would make no difference in running time.

We drew into the station, were uncoupled, and instantly got a clear road to the shed.

I had my hand on the regulator when the shed signal swung to danger and the "three siding" lamps went green, then I heard my name shouted.

I looked out of the cab.

Somebody was running along the platform toward me.

It was the district superintendent, and his face was the colour of ashes.

He sprang on to the footplate.

"Pull out!" he gasped. "Couple the breakdown. The 'Flying 6'..."

"What?" I whispered, and my heart almost stopped beating.

"She's a wreck at Barford," he said, with almost a sob.

"She took the Snake at eighty miles an hour," he groaned. "Oh, my God!"

Ten minutes later I was flying back to Barford with the breakdown train and a gang of about a hundred men. On the way I had time to mention the incident of passing the "Londoner" ninety seconds ahead of time.

"That means he'd gained three minutes in twelve miles—it's incredible, it's unthinkable!" said the superintendent. "Why, Carter is the steadiest man on the road." I was silent. The watch could not lie, and the superintendent knew it. Incredible or not, it was true.

He gave me some information about the wreck—just as much as he had been able to get through. The "Flying 6" had run past the danger signals, both the "distant off" and the "home."

"What was the engine?" I asked.

"794—she wouldn't go wrong," he said; and, indeed, I knew there wasn't an engine on the road less likely to play tricks than No. 794.

I won't describe to you the ghastly sight that met our eyes at Barford; the engine crumpled like a piece of paper, the carriages splintered as if they were so many match-boxes, the horrible, silent rows of dead that were laid on the station platform.

I was sick at heart and weary when I drew into Trentbury next morning. I had helped to draw poor old Carter from underneath his engine....

It was the sensation of the day. The newspapers were filled with speculations. Why did the accident occur? How it happened was obvious. No engine that was ever built could negotiate those damnable curves at eighty miles an hour. Even at forty it would have meant disaster. Was Carter drunk? They hinted as much, but we knew him for a staunch teetotaller. Had he gone mad? There wasn't a saner man living. Had he had a fit? Against this theory there was his mate, the fireman—it was not possible that both men should succumb at the identical moment.

If it was a mystery to the newspapers, it was doubly a mystery to us who knew the inside working of a railway. But it was a mystery which seemed as though it would never be solved.

There were inquests and Board of Trade inquiries, and a private inquiry by the company, and then we buried our dead, and the story of the Barford disaster passed into history. Dick Selby was given poor old Carter's job, and Barford became a bad memory.

Two months afterwards I steamed out of Barford at the usual hour for the home run, as I had done for a year.

It was not curious that I should have been reminded of that dreadful night when we met the "Flying 6" thundering to her doom. I never passed the little bridge to meet the oncoming rush of the "Londoner" without breathing a silent prayer of thanks. But to-night something loosened my tongue, and I turned to Dixon as we cleared Mutwell and said: "This is the worst part of the run, Ned."

He understood me and nodded.

"I've never got her out of mind. Good God!" He stared ahead, and I looked.

Right ahead of us, tearing along the up road, swaying from side to side, came the "Londoner."

"Whar-r-r-!" she roared, and was past.

We stared at each other: mechanically my hand went to my watch.

"She's two minutes ahead!" I whispered hoarsely, and there came to me a horrible premonition of disaster.

How well justified that foreboding was, all the world knows; for the tragedy of two months previous had been re-enacted. The "Flying 6" was a blazing wreck in exactly the same place where poor Carter had gone to his death.

Dick Selhy, the driver, was alive when they got him out, and they did all that they could for him, not only for humanity's sake, but because they knew that their only hope of clearing up the mystery lay in him.

Crushed and mangled and burnt, with scarcely a sound bone or organ in his body, they carried him into Barford Cottage hospital, and officials watched him through the night, trying to piece together from his mutterings some story of the disaster as he had seen it. "Straight!" he muttered all night long, "straight as an arrow—straight as an arrow!" and no other word passed his lips till he died in the early hours of the morning.

If the first wreck had caused a sensation, the second seemed to electrify all England. It was the horrible coincidence that startled everybody. On the same spot two trains had been wrecked. Both were driven by sober, competent drivers; both met their fate through a glaring breach of regulations; both drivers had ignored the company orders which prohibit a greater speed than seven miles an hour when passing the Snake, and both had been wilfully blind to signals.

One morning after the inquest I was sent for from the loco-superintendents office.

When I got there I found the general manager and the secretary of the company. They looked very grave, and the manager, a courteous, elderly gentleman whom I knew by sight, motioned me to a seat.

"We have sent for you, Willis," he said, "because we have decided to appoint you to the 'Flying 6' in place of the unfortunate man who has just met with so terrible a death."

I murmured my thanks. A year ago the appointment would have fulfilled my most ambitious hopes, but now there seemed a bitter taste to the sweet I had craved.

"I want to tell you," said the manager, "that I have made most careful inquiries into your life, and I am satisfied that you have all the advantages of the men who preceded you—and one more."

He paused, and I wondered what particular gift I had that poor Dick Selby had not. He soon enlightened me.

"You have not meddled with the Germotts," he said quietly, "and I trust you will give them a wide berth."

I gasped: I hadn't connected the farmer and his elvish grand-daughter with the disasters; indeed, I had forgotten their very existence. "Both Selby and Carter," the manager went on, "were regular attendants at these meetings of the Germotts. Please God I am doing no injustice to the living or the dead, but I have a doubt—a very terrible doubt." He nodded to me as if to dismiss me. "You understand," he said, "that this conversation is absolutely confidential. I have spoken to you as much for your own good as for the good of the company."

I left him with my brain awhirl with suspicion and bewilderment.

The next three months were eventless. I took the "Flying 6" to London every other night, and brought her back every other morning, and with all things running smoothly, the passengers who had fallen away, and chosen slower, and as they thought safer, trains, came back to the "Londoner."

I saw nothing of the Germotts, but a month after I had been appointed, a letter came from the girl asking me if I would not come to one of the meetings. I took no notice of the letter and she wrote again.

Then she called on me at my lodgings. I am a single man and rent a couple of rooms with a respectable couple, who have a cottage close to the station, and it was whilst I was taking my tea one Sunday afternoon that she walked in unannounced.

They had told me she was beautiful, but I never expected to see any human face as beautiful as hers. It might not appeal to some tastes, but to me she was the most wonderful creature I have ever seen. Her hair was as black as jet, her skin as white and as clear as ivory, there was no single touch of colour in dress or face save her lips, which were vividly red. Her eyes were big and black and shaded with long lashes, and she had a trick of looking at you from under them that gave you the curious sensation that comes to you when you know that some unseen person is observing you.

I knew her instinctively and rose to my feet. I did not for one moment regard her seriously as being a danger, but I was on my guard.

Though I was over thirty, I'd had little to do with women, so far as friendship was concerned.

Her first words were commonplace, for she smiled and said, "I am interrupting your tea-please go on, Mr. Willis."

But I stood waiting.

She took a chair by the table and rested her head on her hand easily. "Why have you not been to see us?" she asked.

I replied that I had had no time, and she nodded.

"Will you come this evening?"

She almost pleaded, but I shook my head.

"I'm afraid I'm not a go-to-meeting man."

Then she did an astounding thing, for she rose and put both hands on my shoulders. "Please come," she said, and looked me in the eyes. I shook my head again.

I was uncouth, I know—I am not a lady's man—but I took her hands from my shoulders and blushed for shame at myself when I found I was doing so.

"I can't," I muttered gruffly.

Without a word she left me.

It wasn't the last time she came. She seemed to know when the family I lodged with would be out, and she would open the latch of the cottage door and walk straight to my room.

I began to get worried for fear my superiors would get to learn of these visits, but strangely enough, the fact never seemed to reach them.

Worse than fear of discovery, I found that every time she came made it harder for me to refuse her, and that I looked forward to her visits, and even went so far as to devise means for getting my landlady out of the way.

All this may sound very weak and very foolish, but I was thirty and she was beautiful. More than this, I found the temptation to take her into my arms and kiss those scarlet lips of hers well-nigh irresistible, and whilst I cursed myself for my folly, with every recurring visit the temptation grew.

The climax came one night.

It was a Sunday—my off-day. I had spent the morning walking, and had come home to dinner dog tired. I dozed in the afternoon, and my landlady brought me my tea about five. I had finished tea, when I heard the family depart, and a few minutes later the girl's step sounded on the stair.

We talked for some time. I forget on what subject, the weather maybe, and then came the moment when she rose to depart. I heard her pleading voice, I felt her hands upon my shoulder, and the warm scent of her hair was in my nostrils.

"Won't you, won't you...?" I heard her murmur, and then she was in my arms, her white face upturned to mine, the wild splendour of her eyes fixed steadfastly on me.

I don't know what she said; I only know I kissed her again and again; that she murmured something monotonously.

I caught it.

"You have been very hard, very hard," she said in a low voice, but I was dazed and did not understand her. Then very gently she slipped from my arms and laid her hands upon my shoulder in the old way, staring at me with those eyes of hers.

"... straight—straight as an arrow," she said.

Illustration

I nodded stupidly.

"It is a straight road," she said slowly, and never taking her eyes from me.

"Yes," I said dully.

"There is no Snake—it is a straight road through Barford—straight as an arrow," she repeated.

I nodded; I must have collapsed, for half an hour later, when I came to myself, I was huddled up on the fioor and she was gone.

I have no distinct recollection of what happened that night or the next day. I was numbed and stupid, but nobody seemed to be aware of my condition, and I took my engine from the shed that night as usual and coupled on to the coaches that stood at the platform. All day long I had found myself repeating the words "straight as an arrow—straight as an arrow," but without knowing why.

In a dim kind of way I knew that we had a crowded train—I think the station-master must have told me, but a matter of greater importance occupied my mind.

...The Barford road was as straight as an arrow!...and all these years we'd been deluding ourselves into the belief that there were Snake curves in and out of Barford! I could have laughed at the ridiculous mistake we had been making. Just before the starting signal was due to fall an inspector hurried up to me.

"You'll be late getting the 'right away,'" he said, "there's been an accident. Old Germott and his grand-daughter have been thrown from a trap. The old man was killed and they're taking her into Barford—to the hospital."

I nodded listlessly. I wasn't interested in Germott's grand-daughter. I saw her pass on a stretcher without emotion, her white face whiter than the pillow on which it lay.

I watched them without interest as they pushed the stretcher into the guard's van next to the engine, and the two doctors jumped in with her.

Then the starting signal fell, and we moved slowly across the points to the up road.

Dixon was very silent—even in my state of mind I noticed that much. He went about his work mechanically, not speaking a word. I thought once I saw his lips moving, and fancied he muttered the word "arrow." So he had found it out too! I remembered that he was a regular attendant at the Germott meetings, so of course he would have been told... been told...

Told what?

The last remnant of my reasoning power fought for assertion.

Told what? and by whom?

I put my hand to my forehead and tried to think.

Out of the darkness flashed a red lamp—and was gone.

A danger signal?

Well, it was natural they should put the "danger" against me, these foolish folks who did not know that the road into Barford was as straight as an arrow!

Was it, though?

I wanted to think: I wanted to sit down undisturbed by the rattle and clank of machinery, without these bothering red lights that came up out of the darkness and vanished. We passed a down express. It was the "112 Down." I used to drive that—I was on that when I passed the "Flying 6" that went to destruction on the Barford Snake...

Barford Snake? There was no Barford Snake—"Straight as an arrow—straight as an arrow."

If I could only think... not little dots of thought, but consecutive reasoning, logical thought.

Dixon was crouched down on the floor of the cab, his back against the tender-bulkhead. I could get no help from him.

Words came to my mind, a string of words—that was better: here something actual: a handle to grip reality by.

"That you have wronged me, Cassius, doth appear in this:
You have condemned and noted Lucius Pella
For taking bribes here of the Sardians."

Who was Lucius Pella?...Bribes?...There was an inspector who took bribes from a firm of carriers and was dismissed....Dick Selby wasn't dismissed, he was killed on the Barford Snake.

"Straight as an arrow—"

"I am a soldier, I,
Older in practice, abler than yourself
To make conditions."

I was younger than old Carter—Carter was killed on the Snake—seven miles an hour... regulation....

"A friend should bear his friends' infirmities, But Brutus makes mine greater than they are."

Another red light snicked past... we must be near Barford... a straight road....

Another red light. Five-mile point....


"There is my dagger,
And here my naked breast; within, a heart
Dearer than..."

I babbled the words, I shouted them. I was trying to keep down some horrible lie that was oppressing my mind. I raved with all the fervour of the tragedian and forced my leaden limbs to the regulator.

"If that thou be'st a Roman, take it forth.
I that denied thee gold will give my life!"

I shrieked the last words and threw my weight on to the lever....

Another red light.

"Strike as thou did'st at Cæsar!"

I brought the vacuum brake down, down, down! A thousand devils forced up my hand, but I brought it over... a child might have done it without effort, but the sweat poured from me.

I heard the brakes grip and felt the jar, and the shudder of our stopping, then ahead of me I saw the snake-like twist... and the train jolted to a standstill.

Then I awoke bathed in sweat, trembling in every limb—the horrible dream had passed.

I looked at Dixon: he was shaking as with ague.

Before us the signal stood at danger. I looked at my watch—we were nine minutes ahead of time!

We brought the "Flying 6" to Barford platform, safe.

I saw a knot of people at the guard's van, and heard the doctor's voice.

"She died when the train stopped," he said.


## The Junior Reporter

If the junior reporter approached the platform with awe and reverence, it was because he was the junior reporter.

You must understand that Sir Thomas was in the chair, and Mr. Hilldry (Lord of the Manor) was prominently displayed in the front row of the platform.

Miss Cicily was there, too—they say down at Taunborough that she has half-a-million in her own right—and the canon and goodness knows what other celebrities.

The junior reporter, who was born and bred in Taunborough, looked round the crowded audience, and his heart swelled with pride that Taunborough had risen to the occasion; that Taunborough had been worthy of itself; and it may be that in this his melting mood a youthful tear glistened in his eye. He rather hoped that Sir Thomas would recognise him, but somehow Sir Thomas had no eyes for the line of young men that sat at the reporters' table sharpening their pencils.

Naturally enough, with Mr. Hilldry contesting the seat, rendered vacant by the retirement of his brother, local feeling ran high. Indeed, the junior reporter, telegraphing to his newspaper at Bristol, had said so in exactly those words. Naturally, too, the junior reporter reflected that shade of political opinion so ably represented by Mr. Hilldry.

Because it was an important by-election, there were reporters from London and from Plymouth, and between a Londoner and weary Devonian the junior reporter found himself.

They were both very pleasant young men, especially he who came from London. He had a shock of hair and wore pince-nez, and before Sir Thomas rose to open the meeting he leant across to his colleague from Devonshire and asked:

"What's it worth?"

"This?" said the Devonshire man, sharpening his pencil. "Oh, about a short half for us."

"Two sticks for us," grumbled the gentleman from town, "unless," he added, hopefully, "there's a riot."

"There'll be no riot," said the other contemptuously, "Taunborough's the slowest place on earth!"

The junior reporter listened resentfully; for his part, so far from a "short half," this meeting would be recorded in five closely-set columns.

"Who's Sir Thomas?" asked the London man.

The junior reporter would have been delighted to volunteer the necessary information, but the Devon man anticipated him.

"Oh, Sir Thomas," he said offhandedly, just as though he'd been discussing some ordinary man, "is a local person, a little tin god in his way—he'll bore your head off."

The junior gasped.

"If he speaks for an hour," the Devon man went on gloomily, "there won't be two lines you can report; but perhaps," he reflected, "he won't speak."

"What is the candidate like?"

"Shocking," said the Devon man frankly.

The junior reporter found his voice.

"Perhaps, gentlemen," he said with elaborate sarcasm, "the candidate's views do not coincide with yours."

The London man regarded him curiously.

"Speaking for myself, they don't," he confessed. "That is partly because I have no views; so far as the political colour of my paper is concerned, we are red-hot supporters of the candidate."

"Politics," said the Devonshire oracle, "means one set of rotters trying to chuck another set of rotters out—"

"Ladies and gentlemen..." (Roars of cheering).

Sir Thomas was on his feet, and the junior reporter poised his pencil over virgin pad.

"Ladies and gentlemen. I am sure—I am quite sure that you do not expect me, that you are not expecting a speech, a long speech from me tonight, this evening. We all know, most of us know, in fact we all know, we are all well acquainted with our friend and neighbour Mr. Hilldry Simes-Patrick. (Cheers.) I've known him, that is, I remember him when he was a little boy, quite a small boy in frocks. (Laughter.) I remember his father...."

"He's started," groaned the gentleman from Devonshire.

A sibilant whisper ran along the reporters' table.

"Somebody wants you," said the Devon man, and the Londoner leant forward and looked down the table.

"You taking this?" asked the whisperer hoarsely.

"No," said the London man.

"Good," said the whisperer, "I was afraid you were—how long will he talk...."

Sir Thomas had stopped speaking and was glaring at the audience.

A thin old man with big gig-lamp spectacles on his nose, and clutching a bundle of notes, was standing up, to the indignation of his scandalised neighbours.

"... I would like to ask Sir Thomas," he piped.

"I cannot answer you—wait until I have finished my speech," said Sir Thomas, very red in the face.

"... Will you explain the attitood of Mr. Chamberlain in the year 1875, when he said...."

"Sit down! Sit down, sir!"

"... Speakin' at the town 'all Birmingham on March 10th he referred to the dooty of the proletariat...."

No man cried "Sit down!" more fiercely than did the junior reporter; no partisan applauded Sir Thomas more vigorously, and certainly no journalist took so complete and copious a note of the great man's speech as did that representative of the press.

"A quarter of an hour," said the Devon man gratefully, when the chairman resumed his seat amidst loud and continued cheering. (I quote again from the script of the junior reporter.)

A burst of wild cheering: "For he's a jolly good feller" in several keys, and a smiling figure at the chairman's table.

"This," said the London man, apprehensively, "is, I presume, His Nibs!"

"That's him," said young Devonshire, ungrammatically.

Those excerpts I have been able to take from the junior reporter's book enable me to fit in the speech—as I heard it.

"... the pendulum has swung back, and the pendulum has swung true."

"A little bit mixed up in his metaphor," said the Devonshire reporter.

The junior, who thought the figure of speech beautifully apt, scowled.

"... We are going forward to a winning cause, the goal is in sight and we will not turn back—(cheers)—the prosperity of the country is in the hands of the people, let there be no...."

"What did he say after 'people,'?" asked the London man.

"I don't know," said the Devon man in despair. "Whatever he said doesn't matter much."

The junior reporter could have told them, but he spitefully covered the passage "let there be no wavering in the ranks of progress" with the palm of his hand.

The gentleman from London ran his fingers through his hair wearily.

"There were three jobs I might have taken," he said deliberately. "I might have done a memorial service, or the opening of the Oyster Fishery Exhibition, or the Brixton murder; and to think," he soliloquised bitterly, "to think that I chose this!"

"... whatever might be the opinion of a few self-seeking politicians with axes to grind—(cheers)—the vast majority of the electorate is in favour of...."

"I rather like funerals," mused the Devon man, "you get such a splendid opportunity of ringing the changes on 'sombre magnificence' and 'gloomy grandeur'—why didn't you take the memorial service?"

The London man yawned and shook his head wearily.

"... we cannot put back the clock—(cheers)—we cannot—er—identify ourselves with an anachronism...."

The junior reporter, with a rapt frown, scribbled down the burning words, faithfully, religiously, literally.

"....if you send me to the House of Commons—"

Above the speaker's monotonous voice rose a shrill cry. A cry that sent an indignant flush to the junior reporter's cheek, that brought a bright light to the eye of the London man, that jerked a dozen bored metropolitan journalists to their feet seeking the face of the interrupting member of the audience.

Again the thin voice.

"Votes for wimmin!"

"Madam," muttered the London man under his breath, as the uproar began, "from the bottom of my heart I thank you!"

"So" (I quote the junior reporter again) "the meeting concluded in great disorder, owing to the unseemly conduct of two ladies." And after "ladies" the junior reporter put marks like this: (?), but his all-wise editor cut them out.

## The Linchela Rebellion

As a variation of the tag that nothing new comes out of Africa I commend the saying of His Excellency the Governor-General of Manica and Sofala that "In Africa, all things are possible."

This is partly a story of Africa, and partly a story of journalism, and partly a biographical sketch of the rise of William James Gill, that eminent explorer and man of letters.

There is a great blob of country that lies between the Congo basin and German South-West Africa. Its exports are slaves tor the cocoa fields, its imports are mainly gin, and it is referred to in all the learned geographies in the chapters on "The Civilisation of Africa." Some say that there are parts of that wild country that have never been tamed, and certainly from time to time Portugal sends a few thousand soldiers who land at Mossamedes and march into the interior. I have never heard that any of them returned.

Because of this perpetual unsettlement, the Linchela Rebellion was always possible, and, if William James Gill had not exploited it, I do not doubt but that somebody else would have done so.

William James Gill, being accepted as the fool of the family, set his heart upon being a pirate; his father, being the bigger fool, chose the Church for his son. By some misadventure William James found to his unbounded surprise that he had passed the necessary examination that took him to the Ecclesiastical Schools at Wells. When he recovered from his astonishment he ran away. He had outgrown his early desire for piracy, but in a letter written from Plymouth to his outraged parent, he expressed (inter alia) his intention of making a fortune in the wilds of Africa. His father hastened to inform him that he had cut him out of his will, and out of his heart, but this trite, theatrical, and pompous pronouncement was returned through the Dead Letter Office, William James having sailed by an Elder-Dempster boat for the Coast.

The conversation between William and the Elder-Dempster agent is a sad commentary on the ignorance of the modern young man, and the value of a University education.

"I want to go to Africa," said William James, with the high light of resolve in his nice blue eyes.

"Yes, sir?" said the agent, and waited.

"Africa," repeated William, with an air of finality.

"Dahka, Sierra Leone, Flagstaff, Bassam, Lagos, Boma, St. Paul de Lonanda, Benguella, Mossamedes?" recited the agent patiently. He was getting perilously near to the end of the Elder-Dempster itinerary.

"St. Paul de Lonanda," hesitated William, "that sounds all right." So he took his ticket.

The Cape Verde Islands, no less than the Grand Canaries, were exactly as William James had pictured them, but Sierra Leone came as a shock. He had thought of this place conventionally as "the white man's grave"—a stretch of yellow sand under a hot sun, with palm trees and things. Instead, there rose out of the sea, to his astounded gaze, a great mountain covered with verdure, with tiny white houses on its slopes, and a prosperous little city at its base.

"This can't be Sierra Leone?" he said in amazement.

Then somebody explained that "Leone" meant "lion" and "Sierra" stood for mountain in the Spanish tongue, and that "Sierra Leone" meant the "Mountain of the Lion."

William James was tremendously impressed, and made a note of the interesting fact in his diary. Little Bassam was more like the coast of his dreams. The ship landed forty huge barrels. They were roped together and made a monstrous string of beads as a panting tug boat hauled them to the shore.

"What might they contain?" asked William, and his informant said tersely, "Rum," and added, "for the natives."

This was the beginning of the boy's education. It was continued at Lonanda, where he went to make his fortune, and found that whilst a fortune might be made in the course of time, the hotels charged at the rate of 10/- a day during the period of waiting.

Life would be very pleasant if the unhappy patches could be ...'d, and it is infinitely more simple to write of the education of W.J. than it would be to experience. He found a job at £12 a month transport-riding to the Katanga... When he recovered from his fever he went with a Portuguese half-breed down on to the Kalahari edge of Angola... fortunately he was found in time by a patrol of the B.B.P.

He explained to the corporal that the Portuguese gentlemen had deserted him, carrying away his supplies, his rifle and ammunition and the rest of his visible means of support.

So he had wandered on and on, living on the charity of natives (there was a palaver at one village, did be but know it, and the question of "chopping" W.J. was vigorously debated). So he came to the edge of the Kalahari and foolishly essayed the crossing ... stands for a torturing thirst, a maddening hell of misery, a sun that blistered, and everlasting Dust Devils.

"How you got out of that dam' streak alive beats me," said the admiring N.C.O. of the Bechuanaland Border Police.

"He's born to be hung, Gus," said his familiar... At Cape Town W.J. found work in an Adderley Street store.

This was twelve months later and he had come to the Cape via Taung, Klerksdorp, Johannesburg, Klerksdorp again, Kimberley and De Aar. At De Aar, weary of walking, he found shelter in an empty railway wagon. He was wakened in the night by some very unpleasant shunting operations, went to sleep again, and woke up to find himself travelling at 30 miles an hour on route for Cape Town... Men were wanted for the new railway from Lobito Bay to Katanga, so he drew his month's salary, took a ticket for Lobito Bay (he knew all the ports by heart now), and left Cape Town on a floundering tramp steamer with a light heart.

Ernest Frederick Gill, W.J.'s father, never referred to his son; Millicent Mary Gill, W.J.'s mother, used to weep in secret, and had sundry premonitions that her son was dead. She had these on an average twice monthly. She knew nothing of W.J.'s adventures, because the only letters he ever wrote were posted at Lonanda, where their bulky appearance attracted the attention of a postal official at that port and were opened. Finding no tightly-packed banknotes, as he had expected, he put the letters in his fire. So W.J.'s mother knew nothing of the doings of Lonanda.

Naturally, she did not know of the trip to Lobito Bay, and how, not finding work, W.J. started to tramp across country to Rhodesia, of how W.J. came upon his friend, the half-breed Portuguese.

She knew nothing of the explanations and voluble excuses the Portuguese offered, or of how W.J. jerked out a revolver and shot Senhor Saumarez through the stomach. Even the Angola authorities knew nothing of this.

W, J. struck a Rhodesian town somewhere near the Angola border. I will not disclose the name of the town, because the citizens might not like it. I will call it Umtambo, and tell you it was a township which had grown up around a rich little reef, that boasted a Zeederberg coach service, an hotel, a court-house, a newspaper, and a gaol.

W.J. wandered all round the reef looking for work, but he'd arrived in an evil hour, when the Rhodesian Government over in Salisbury was debating the question of the new gold law, and work had been suspended until the question of Retrospective Taxation had been finally settled.

Sitting in the shadow of the courthouse, wondering where his dinner was coming from, and gazing pensively at the big toe that peeped through his dilapidated right boot (this would have shocked Millicent Mary Gill almost as much as the shooting of Saumarez), he was beckoned by a young man, who was sitting astride a restless horse and was unable to get any closer to him than the middle of the ramshackle street.

"Hi!" said the young man.

"Go to blazes!" said W.J. sourly.

"You have just come through Linchela's country?" shouted the youth. W.J.'s form of address brought no sense of novelty.

"Yas," drawled W.J.

"Hear anything about the fightin'?"

"Ya-as!" said W.J.

"Then you're the man!" said the youth, and recklessly dismounted. He introduced himself as the editor and part proprietor of the Umtambo Message, and seating himself by W.J.'s side prepared to make a note.

"Hold hard," said the young man from the Theological School at Wells. "Where do I come in?"

"If your stuff is worth printing, I'll stand you a drink," said the young man magnificently, and W.J. guffawed.

"I'll see you in the hot watertight bulkheads of steaming Hades," said W.J. picturesquely, "before I let you suck my brains for a three-real drink. I'll see you saggin'."

"Let us talk business," said the young man earnestly, and explained that in addition to being editor and part proprietor of the Umtambo Message, he was the Umtambo correspondent of most of the papers that are issued from Fleet Street, and not a few of those that live in the provinces.

Whereupon W.J. struck a bargain, and for two pounds sterling, a week's board and lodging, and a new pair of boots, he told the thrilling story of the Linchela Rebellion, of the turmoil, then burnings, killings, raids, massacres, that had been a feature of the outbreak. It was dead easy.

"This is my forte," said W.J. to himself. "I can live on—what did he call the brute?—Linchela, for months."

So the editor of the Umtambo Message sent a wire to his various London newspapers that began, "Intrepid Explorer, William James Gill arrived from Linchela country, tells thrilling story of massacre..."

"And who the dickens is William James Gill?" asked thirty-five foreign editors simultaneously.

Ernest Frederick Gill, reading his morning newspaper the following morning, said, "Ha!" and folded his paper to read more comfortably, and the family of Gills that sat round the breakfast table preserved a respectful silence, as was its wont when E. F. Gill condescended to read things aloud from his newspaper.

"Ha!" said E. F. Gill again.

"There is some news about that African trouble at last." He mumbled through an introductory paragraph, and began:

"Our special correspondent at Umtambo wires: 'The intrepid and famous traveller, William James Gill—'"

He stopped.

"William James Gill?" he repeated, like a man in a dream.

"It's not Willie?" fluttered Millicent Mary, on the verge of tears.

"William James Gill?" repeated the head of the family slowly. "That's very curious—I've never heard of any other William James Gill."

(Which was exactly what thirty-five foreign editors had said, only they omitted the word "other.")

"If it is Willie?" said Mr. Gill, senior, "and then I don't see why it shouldn't be, the boy has any amount of grit, determination, initiative. He comes," said E. F. modestly, "from a stock which has given, time after time, its best work to the service of the State."

(E. F.'s grandfather had held a post of honour in the Inland Revenue Department.)

It was Willie, of course. William James, sitting in Umtambo's best hotel, was famous without realising it. Numerous foreign editors wired furiously to the editor of the Umtambo Message, and their messages were to this effect:

"Send Gill back to Linchela country; get good exclusive story for us."

The Government at Lisbon wired to the Governor at Benguella to the following effect:—

"What is this yarn about rising in Linchela country? Thought it was squashed."

To which the Governor replied that it was squashed, and that any statement to the contrary was "a lie."

This Lisbon published broadcast, but the wily foreign editors in London said, "Oh, yes," and "I know," and "We've had these official denials before." By this time W.J. was on his way back to the Linchela country with strict instructions to get exclusive stories for The Daily Times, The Telegram, The Standard News, The Evening Post, The Morning Mail, and several other papers.

W.J., never having been in the Linchela country before, never having heard of it, until the devil put it into his heart to invent grisly scenes for the edification of a young editor and part proprietor, found some difficulty in reaching his objective.

When he did, he discovered Linchela in the innocent pursuit of domestic happiness, and the warriors, on whose ferocity he had erected the fabric of his story, peaceably engaged in the Central African equivalent for marbles.

"This will never do," said the shocked W.J., and saw the chief, the great Linchela himself.

"War?" said the chief. "Master, there is peace in the land. Linchela's heart is soft toward the Portuguese, his hand is outstretched in friendship, his feet turn—-"

"When you've finished this anatomical palaver," said W.J. coldly, "will you be good enough to listen to reason?" And W.J. spoke eloquently of the valour of the chief's people, of how their enemy's hearts turned to water at the sight of them, and what a wicked waste of talent it was possessing all these qualifications for riotous living, Linchela let his people stagnate.

The chief listened in silence. "Master," he said, when W.J. had finished, "I am for peace; I love the Portuguese—"

"That is not only a lie but an unnatural one," said W.J., and went off in a huff.

He returned to Umtambo with six separate and distinct stories of assaults, repulses, heroisms, barbarities, and desolations, and the editor and part proprietor fell on his neck and advanced him £70 on account of expenses.

For three years he kept the Linchela country in a state of uproar. Sometimes whole districts would be devastated, sometimes the natives would storm a Portuguese fort, sometimes (when he was in a generous mood) they would be repulsed with slaughter. After a while he'd earned enough money from his correspondence to buy a half-share in the Umtambo Message, also he bought a gold watch and chain and a house. Best of all, one night he bought the bank in a hot game of baccarat and took £6,300 out of the citizens of Umtambo... and the war with Linchela nearly came to an abrupt end, there being no further occasion to continue same.

"My son?" said E. F. Gill proudly, "yes, William James Gill, the great explorer and correspondent, is my son." He was being interviewed by a representative of the Stayboro' Herald, which was a sort of civilised Umtambo Message. "He was originally intended for the Church, but his mind running upon adventure I sent him to the Cape, where, after holding a Government appointment, he set out on behalf of the Government to make a report on the minerals of Rhodesia..."

You will observe that there are certain qualities that all the Gills possess in common.

Now the Linchela Rebellion was an important rebellion without being a serious one—I am speaking from the point of view of the newspapers—and when editors and their satellites met together with the object of planning the next day's newspapers some conversation like the following would ensue:

Editor: "Anything startling?"

Satellite (humbly): "No, sir. Fire at Bermondsey."

Editor: "Huh?"

Satellite: "Bye-election."

Editor: "Bah! What about the Linchela Rebellion? Send a wire to William James Gill and ask him for the latest developments."

By this will be seen the value of W.J.'s little war.

By-and-by it took on a new aspect. On the back pages of popular weeklies would appear such useful information as:

The Wars of the Roses lasted forty-seven years.
The Linchela Rebellion has lasted three years and is not yet suppressed.
The tallest soldier in the British Army is Captain Ames, who is 6 ft. 7 1/2 in.

It was in vain that Portugal protested that there was no war. In vain that they brought home Linchela himself to prove it. (W.J.'s scathing exposure of that trick was a notable contribution to the literature of the subject.)

In vain that independent investigators penetrated to the Linchela country, and wrote fluent and special articles in the Diário de Lisboa on the peaceful condition of the land.

"Hireling pens," said W.J. scornfully, and sent a column news letter descriptive of a raid made upon the Portuguese camp and the annihilation of the European force.

"In my ears," wrote W.J., "still ring the fierce shouts of the painted warriors, the boom of the tom-tom as it led them to the attack. I hear again the shrill cries for mercy..."

In the end Portugal sent out to Angola a special commissioner with unlimited powers. This Senhor de Silva was an intelligent and amiable gentleman, and he did not attempt to go to the Linchela country. Rather he went straight to Umtambo and found William James Gill in the act of writing a leader for the Message on "Government Morality."

Senhor de Silva asked W.J. if he would come outside, and the editor and proprietor (as he now was) accepted the invitation.

"The fact of the matter is, Mr. Gill," said the special commissioner, "we are getting rather tired in Lisbon of this war of yours."

"Not mine, I assure you," W.J. hastened to remark.

"Yours," said the commissioner firmly. "The description of the Portuguese attack on Linchela's village could only have been written by a man who knows as much about military tactics as a cow does of painting china."

W.J. got very red.

"But we are not amused," Senhor de Silva went on, "and what is worse than all, our Republican papers are taking your war seriously and are attacking the Government for hushing it up."

"Well?" said W.J.

"Well," said the special commissioner, "we regard you as a gentleman of infinite tact and judgment. You know the country, you know Linchela, you know the cause of the war."

"Naturally," said W.J., and coughed.

"What I want you to do," said the commissioner, "is to go down into the Linchela country and settle the war. Settle it for good and I will pay you a fee of £3,000—we will throw in a couple of decorations if they have any fascination for you."

"But," said W.J., "on what basis do you fix my remuneration at £3,000?"

Senhor de Silva shrugged his shoulders.

"We regard this as your war, we will give you three years' purchase—is it a bet?"

"It's a bet," said W.J., and shook hands on the bargain.

W.J. now lives in England. The local flyman will point out his house to you.

"That's William James Gill's house, sir," he will say, "the great war correspondent, him that settled the war in Africa."

It was suggested by Gill, senior, in a letter signed "Lover of Justice," which appeared in the Times newspaper, that for his services in the interest of Peace, W.J. was entitled to the consideration of the Nobel trustees; but somehow the Nobel Prize never came to Stayboro', and W.J. bore the neglect philosophically. "He cherished much higher," he said (speaking at a garden party given in his honour), "the embroidered motto worked and presented to him by the Young Ladies' Guild of Stayboro', 'Blessed are the Peacemakers.'"

But then, of course, W.J. had been intended for the Church.


## Halley's Comet, the Cowboy and Lord Dorrington

Lord Dorrington was a middle-aged man. He showed no evidence of mental decrepitude, and the alienist who was invited on one occasion to dine with his lordship—the invitation came from anxious relatives, who feared that, unless the poor dear fellow was placed under proper control, he would dissipate the fortunes of the Dorrington family—this alienist wrote so cheery a report upon Dorrington's health that the question of the payment of his fifty-guinea fee was seriously debated. It was felt by a select committee, composed of the beneficiaries under Dorrington's will, that the alienist had not done his duty. They called him (the alienist), disrespectfully, the 'mad doctor', and decided that his report upon Dorrington's sanity was a remarkable proof of the generally-accepted theory that all alienists become mad themselves—in time.

The reason for their fears for Lord Dorrington's reason is understandable. He was an enthusiastic seeker after light. He was a spiritualist, a student of thaumaturgy, theurgy, electro-biology, and something of a Shamanist in an amateur kind of way. He believed that unlikely things happened.

It must be understood that he was, in many ways, a practical man. He once had a butler who neglected the silver horribly. The butler's somewhat ingenious excuse that he also was given to occult studies, and was, moreover, a cadet in the practice of demonology, was received coldly. Further, explained the butler, the silver was cleaned every day, but by night there came a little devil who smeared his dirty paws all over the polished surface of the plate. 'A little devil named 'Erbert, me lord,' said the butler pathetically, 'who cursed me when I was born.'

'You have been reading German fairy tales,' said his lordship, with chilly hauteur, 'and your impudent excuses decide me: I shall not give you a character.'

It was obviously absurd and unthinkable that even a little devil should condescend to consort with a mere butler, and Lord Dorrington very properly resented the assumption of his servant.

Dorrington was a rich man and a shrewd man. The Dorrington belt was the eighth wonder of the world, as any guide-book to the castle will tell you. It was the belt presented by an English king to a lady who was the founder of the family. It was six inches broad, and made of diamonds—not large diamonds, but very saleable diamonds. The Dorrington strong-room was the strongest strong-room in England, for many people desired those gems, the market value being somewhere in the neighbourhood of £80,000.

Lord Dorrington, as I say, was very practical in such matters, and where many a less fanciful man might have contented himself with phylacteries, his lordship, though a student of phylacteries, pinned his faith to doors of chilled steel and Chubb locks.

It would occupy a great deal too much space to give at any length the number of attempts which were made upon those strong-rooms at Dorrington Castle.

There was the still-room maid, who came with forged credentials from an eminent domestic agency, whose box contained diamond drills and a portable axe. There was the groom of the chambers, so suave and polite, with a hundred-pound 'kit' of well-tempered, safe-breaking tools. There was the Swiss valet, who was so very satisfactory until he was discovered one sad night walking cautiously in his stockinged feet in the direction of the strong-room. His explanation that, as a connoisseur of paintings, he desired an uninterrupted study of his lordship's 'Ribera Espanolito' in the east gallery was not accepted by a sceptical bench of magistrates, who gently pointed out that the skeleton keys found in his possession were not consistent with his statement.

These and many others I could name.

Whatever views his relatives might have concerning his mental balance, I am happy to say that in select criminal circles the acumen and intelligence of Lord Dorrington was held in the greatest respect.

'Not that he's so wonderfully clever,' said Billy the Boy (sometimes called Willie the Nut), 'for, in spite of his electric bells and alarms, three men working together could open the safe—only the devil of it is that it's as much as we can do to get one man inside.'

His companions in crime—they were dining at Figgioli's, in Conduit Street, and were beautifully arrayed—nodded their heads in approval.

'They tell me,' said Augustus (nobody knew his other name), 'that a New York crowd are thinkin' about—'

'Let 'em think,' said Billy contemptuously. 'If we can't do the job, they can't.'

There was some justification for such arrogance, for Billy the Boy was a master of his craft, and one remarks, with a glow of national pride, that for scientific burglary England's old supremacy stands unassailed.

I record this conversation that you may have a true appreciation of Lord Dorrington's contadictory qualities, and because he occupied a position of some fame a month or so later, and every scrap of information concerning him is of interest. He was, too, something of a biologist, but that has nothing whatever to do with this story.

You may remember that the year 1910 was chiefly remarkable for the visitation of Halley's comet, and for the fact that the world passed through the tail of our celestial visitor. Now, in spite of lucid articles appearing over the signatures of eminent astronomers, and set forth prominently in the popular organs of public opinion, proving beyond doubt that you might take the tail of Halley's comet and fold the whole of it into a grip sack, there were hundreds of thousands of people who shook in their shoes at the mere thought of the phenomenon they were to witness. As one pseudo-scientific writer querulously pointed out, nobody had ever packed the tail into a portmanteau, so that it was ridiculous to say that such a thing could be done without creasing the tail and ruining it beyond repair. But the most important contribution to the literature on the subject was a letter signed 'Dorrington', which appeared in The Times. It began: 'There is something more than a material aspect to the approaching comet...' and went on to deal with the extraordinary happenings which had coincided with its appearance in former years.

For my own part, (concluded Lord Dorrington soberly) I anticipate remarkable results from the visitation. For the first time in the world's history we have the scientific equipment to register and convey simultaneously the observations of psychists the world over....

There were gross and sordid writers in Fleet Street who guffawed loudly on reading this; worse, they wrote sarcastic paragraphs and little poems, and generally shocked the psychic world by their levity.

But their confusion came quickly.

The comet came, growing brighter and brighter nightly, and, as the superb spectacle increased in splendour, the world began to take the comet more and more seriously.

The earth entered the comet's tail on May 18th, and quite a number of people sat up all night destroying so much of their correspondence as, being recovered from the week of the world, might tend to make them look ridiculous.

But nothing happened on the night of the 18th, and the sun rose on the 19th in very much the same way as usual.

The busy world awoke, and went about its work. Factory horns hooted the toiling millions to labour, trim maids knocked at innumerable doors with tea and buttered toast, and the charwoman reigned supreme in the City of London.

At 7.15, PC Albert Parker, of the City Police, came leisurely out of Shoe Lane into Wine Office Court. He turned the corner of the court, and came to a narrow stretch which leads into Fleet Street. On the left is the white-bricked wall of the Daily Telegraph paper store, on the right is the dingy facade of the Press Club. Lying between the Press Club and the far end of the court was the body of a man. 'Lying' is hardly the word, for he sprawled face downward, with arms and legs outstretched in spread-eagle fashion.

PC Parker hastened his steps, and came up to the prostrate figure.

It was clad in the most extraordinary garments. The trousers were of undressed sheepskin, with the woolly side outermost; a dark blue shirt was on his back, and round his neck was a gaudy neckcloth of great size. Under his baggy trousers he wore top-boots, and two large silver spurs stuck up, sparkling in the sunlight. Add to this a broad-brimmed hat, which lay at some distance from the figure, and a huge revolver at his side.

The constable knelt down and felt the man's face; it was quite warm. He turned the figure over on its back. The man was breathing regularly, his heart was strong and normal; he appeared to be in a deep sleep.

PC Parker frowned, and smelt his breath. No, he was not drunk, and the policeman shook the man by the shoulder.

'Come along,' he said sternly; 'you can't sleep here.'

The man drew a long breath, sighed, and opened his eyes, blinking at the light. He stared at the policeman, and the policeman stared at him. The stranger was about thirty years of age; he was unshaven, and his face was covered with a faint coating of white dust.

'Gee!' he said, and sat up, scratching his head. Then he yawned, stretched himself, and rose a little shakily. 'Whar's that all fired hoss of mine?' he demanded sleepily.

'Look here,' said the policeman, 'what's this—a circus performance?'

The stranger stared coolly at the officer of the law.

'Say,' he repeated, 'whar's that old greaser of mine?'

Then he seemed of a sudden to realise that something had happened.

He looked up and down the deserted court curiously. He allowed his eyes to wander along the buildings, then they came back to the policeman with a scared look.

Then he passed his hand over his forehead wearily.

'I was goin' out to brand a steer,' he said, in a dreamy voice, 'an' that old light, she came prancin' over the prairie—she was a sure enough comet's tail, an' she hit me good. Where am I?' he asked suddenly.

'You're in the City of London,' said the police constable; 'and I'm going to take you along to the station.'

The strange sleeper staggered back.

'City of hell!' he roared. 'I'm in Colefax, Texas. Whar's my horse?'

Four policemen, hastily summoned by a shrill whistle, hustled the cowboy—for such he evidently was—to the Bridewell, and two hours later, charged with being 'a suspected person' the man in the sheepskin chapperos came up at Guildhall before the alderman.

That he told the same story, only more coherently, of the 'sure enough comet which came prancing over the plains about Colefax, Tex.,' is evidenced by the fact that at noon there was not a newspaper bill in London which was not screaming the news of the extraordinary occurrence. I give you the headlines of one of the more sedate of the evening newspapers:

AMAZING DISCOVERY IN THE CITY
COWBOY CAUGHT UP BY THE COMET'S TAIL
DEPOSITED IN LONDON
ASTRONOMER-GENERAL SAYS IT IS IMPOSSIBLE.

It was the one great splash of news of the day—nay, it was the most amazing happening of the century. Astronomers became apoplectic in their attempt that the whole thing was impossible. Yet—but let me quote The Evening Advertiser:

...Another extraordinary fact is that when the man was taken to Bridewell his face and hair were covered with thin, white powder. The City surgeon, who was called to examine the man, took the trouble to brush some of this powder off, and submit it to analysis. It proved to be a fine alkaline matter, such as a man might accumulate in a ride across the alkali plains which abound in that part of the world from which the man said he came. Moreover, on being searched, he was found to be in possession of ten five-dollar bills, a Mexican five-dollar piece, some loose American money, and, most remarkable of all, a receipted hotel bill. The bill was for 'one night bed' at Golden South Hotel, in a town in Texas, and was dated May 17th, 1910. There was also a note of some laundry work done on the same date, and some thin hide laces, wrapped up in an American newspaper, which, although the title was undecipherable or torn off, has the date fairly legible, and that date is May 18th.

This, and other evidence of the extraordinary character of the visitor, may be found in The Psychical Magazine, if it is not destroyed—but I rather fancy that that particular number of the publication in question has been burnt.

It is no exaggeration to say that England talked of nothing else but 'the man the comet brought', and that there was not a psychical society in the world but hastily assembled to gather data upon the remarkable visitation.

Excitement was at its height, when a new and even more sensational discovery was made.

The particulars may be given in the words of The Sussex Times:

A sensational affair has happened at Eastergate, which has caused great local excitement. It appears that a number of horses from Mr Alfred Knight's training establishment were proceeding along the road in the direction of the downs, when the leading horse, Master Hopmoon, shied at the figure of a man lying by the side of the road. It is by no means a strange thing to observe tramps sleeping out at this time of the year, but the remarkable fact about the present case was that the figure was that of a Chinaman. The boy cantered back to where Mr Knight and his head lad were riding, behind the exercising horses, and informed his master. Mr Knight immediately rode forward and, dismounting, examined the man. Apparently the Chinaman was sleeping. He was dressed in the costume of his country, and Mr Knight informed our representative that the man was evidently one of the labouring class of China.

As might be expected, the newcomer did not speak a word of English. He seemed dazed and terrified, and was with difficulty persuaded to accompany Mr Knight to the Eastergate Drill Hall, where temporary accommodation was found for him until the police were communicated with. Much greater difficulty was found in persuading him to get into the train at Barnham Junction, to accompany the police to Arundel. The man was in a condition of abject fright, jabbering and gesticulating as though he had never seen a railway train in his life. Fortunately, there lives in Arundel the Rev J. Wiggs, who has, until recently, been a missionary in China, and the rev. gentleman had no difficulty in conversing with the Celestial.

So much for The Sussex Times. It was after that memorable conversation with the Rev J. Wiggs that the story of the Chinaman acquired a larger value. No man in England read that interview with greater interest than Lord Dorrington. He read it in the The Morning News, and straightway took a train for London, and thence to Arundel.

'It is quite true, my lord,' said the Rev J. Wiggs, a little bewildered by the extraordinary experience of the previous day. 'I saw him as soon as he arrived. He is a Chinaman from the province of Yste-Yang; so far as I can make out he is a boatman. His story is so remarkable that my head whirls with it.'

'What is it?' demanded Lord Dorrington, not unprepared for the answer.

'Virtually he tells the same story as was told by the cowboy who was, as your lordship may know, discovered two days ago in the City of London.'

Lord Dorrington nodded.

'He says,' continued the returned missionary, 'that in the cool of the morning he was walking through a rice-field, in the direction of the village of Lung-tsi-lang, where he had made an appointment to meet a moneylender, who wished to marry his daughter. He had noticed, with fear, the apparition of the comet, and as he walked he faced that portion of the sky where the tail of the comet showed dimly. If anything, as he says, the comet was less brilliant than it had been. But on the horizon he observed a curious light. According to his account, it was a 'great wall of silver dust', which rose higher and higher, and became more and more brilliant, until, terrified by the apparition and by the almost blinding dazzle of the vision, he stopped, covering his face with his hands. He heard a whistling roar and lost consciousness, and the next thing that he knew was that he was lying on a soft, grass bank, and a foreign devil was talking to him in a strange tongue.'

Later, Dorrington saw the Chinaman, very sullen, and showing as much evidence of his fear as his natural imperturbability of countenance allowed.

Lord Dorrington returned to London to find a small crowd of reporters awaiting him at Victoria, to face innumerable cameras, and to answer a hundred questions.

'No,' he said, shaking his head, when questioned by the special representative of The Morning News, 'I am not in a position to give my theories as to the remarkable happenings of the past two days. I have my own ideas concerning them, but they are not sufficiently definite to give to the world. I intend bringing both men to Dorrington Castle, and, through an interpreter as far as the Chinaman is concerned, collect as much data as possible before these victims of astral phenomena are returned to their homes.'

'Do you think that these comet translations have occurred elsewhere?' demanded the reporter.

'I do,' replied his lordship. 'In a day or so, in a few hours perhaps, we shall have further manifestations of the comet's power.'

The newspapers had, by this time, reversed their attitude of amused scepticism, and awarded Lord Dorrington's statement the dignity of leaded type.

His prophecy, and the story of its fulfilment, appeared side by side, for, whilst his lordship had stood in the centre of the interrogating pressmen, the third, and, so far as can be ascertained, the last of the strange visitations, came.

The third was even more dramatic in its circumstances than were the others.

Dorrington had arrived at Victoria at 10 o'clock on the night of the 20th, which fell on a Saturday, and whilst he was giving his views on the phenomena with which all England was ringing, a curious scene was being enacted in one of the theatres.

The curtain had just gone up for the second act of Our Miss Gibbs, at the Gaiety, and the stage was filled with beautiful women, picturesquely grouped, when there entered from one of the wings a figure which brought the play to an immediate standstill, which left the very conductor petrified with upraised baton.

The figure was that of a man, of medium height and enormously stout. He was in evening dress, stained and dusty. His shirt front, in which glittered a huge diamond, was crumpled and grimy, and as he came waddling down the stage, rubbing his eyes and yawning, the immaculate chorus fell back on either side.

He looked around with a puzzled frown, and then addressed a question to the actor nearest to him.

'Señor,' said he, in the dialect of the Estremadura, 'will you, in the names of the blessed saints, inform me where I am?'

The actor, who did not understand a word of Spanish, shook his head, and glanced appealingly to the wings, and the curtain was rung down amidst some excitement.

This, indeed, was the third visitant!

José Sebastian Lopez, to give him the name by which he described himself, was a Brazilian, on a holiday visit to Spain. His story, inscribed in Lord Dorrington's neat handwriting, is not the least interesting of the memoranda on the men who were hit by the comet:

I am (says this document) a native of Brazil, although I cannot tell you what part of Brazil, for the time being, for I seem to have lost my memory. I arrived in Madrid on the night of the 16th, and stayed at the Hotel de Paris, on the Puerta del Sol. On the 17th, I believe, though I am not certain in my mind, I saw a man with whom I had some business relations. Who he was, or what was the nature of his business, I forget, but probably, when my head is less clouded, I shall recall the matter. The next day I spent in walking about Madrid. I have a dim idea that I went to the Prado, and that I spent some time admiring the old Spanish masters. In the evening I know that I dressed for dinner, and, the evening being a warm one, I went out without my overcoat, to the Casino. I left the Casino late. It must have been in the early hours of the morning but there were a number of people about and most of the cafés were open. I went up to my room and sat by the open window, smoking a cigar. It was then that over the houses, to the west side of the Puerta del Sol, I noticed a strange white light in the sky, resembling a pillar of white fire, which expanded in breadth visibly as I watched it. It grew broader and broader, and I pinched myself, thinking I must be dreaming. I sat with open mouth, paralysed, and the light grew fiercer and fiercer, till I felt it envelop me. I had no sensation of warmth, only a strange feeling of lightness, as though I could step through the window into the street below without hurt—and that was all I remember. When I awoke I found myself in a strange building. There was above me a skylight, which was open, and through which I must have fallen. I knew that I was in a theatre, for the curtain was raised, and the seats were all shrouded in holland, but I had no feeling of curiosity. All I wanted to do was sleep, sleep, sleep. I climbed over the orchestra on to the stage and wandered around, looking for a place in which to lie, for I was like a man drunk with sleep.

Lord Dorrington steadfastly refused to receive any reporters, although some of the best men journeyed down to High Dorrington to secure his views.

'The only thing I can say is this,' said his lordship to a select deputation, whose persistence had secured for themselves a short interview. 'I have, as you know, the three men here at Dorrington Castle. We are, through the instrumentality of interpreters, collecting and comparing everything they say bearing upon their transmigration. I can tell you this much, that their stories tally in every respect, but the full account of my investigations will be published at a very early date. The cowboy seems to have the most vivid recollection of all that happened, and I am certain that we have at last a manifestation of an occult mystery which will convince the most sceptical.'

Saying this, his lordship ushered the Pressmen from the room, and returned to his strange investigations.

We have not, unfortunately, the minutes of that inquisition, although it has been stated on most reliable authority that they covered reams of foolscap. We may guess that an irritated cowboy, a wondering but impassive Chinaman, and a most voluble gentleman from Mexico sat and suffered as Lord Dorrington, with the cold persistence of the enthusiast, extracted from them the particulars of their varying sensations.

It was the night of the reporters' visit that the fourth and the most inexplicable of the comet's vagaries was recorded. The three men, after a lengthy examination, had retired to their separate bedrooms, and Lord Dorrington sat alone in his study, revising the notes he had made.

Engrossed in his labours, he did not regard time, and time, utterly independent of Lord Dorrington's patronage, moved ruthlessly forward.

Looking up, in a passionate attempt to find a synonym for 'extraordinary' and 'remarkable', his lordship was astounded to observe that the hands of the clock pointed to half-past two.

He put away his papers, locked them in his desk, lit his bedroom candle, and extinguished the light in the study. Then he made his way along the silent hall toward the big stairway that led to his sleeping suite.

Then, of a sudden, when he was half-way along the broad passage, there came a blinding white flash of flame. It leapt to him, and, as he staggered back, something struck him on the head, and he went to the floor like a log.

Some say that he was stunned, but others aver that it was blue funk that kept his lordship lying on the floor of the hall until an early-rising servant discovered him, and assisted him back to the study.

His first act—and here he showed the soul of the true scientist—was to send for the three men to compare their sensations with his.

There came no answer to the knockings of Lord Dorrington's hired servants. An examination of the rooms led to the discovery that the men were gone. Their beds had not been slept in; there was no sign of their presence.

Lord Dorrington stood before the door of the cowboy's room, a water compress about his head, wrapped in deep thought. The tremendous character of the new phenomenon impressed even him.

He returned to his study, and sent thirty-six telegrams to thirty-six different newspapers, but the wire was in every case the same.

THREE ASTRAL VISITORS AGAIN TRANSMIGRATED. I MYSELF HAVE EXPERIENCED POWER OF COMET. SEND REPORTER.—DORRINGTON.

Long before the reporters could possibly respond to the invitation, a tall, clean-shaven man, with bushy eyebrows, came flying up to the great door of the Dorrington demesne, and demanded imperiously to see his lordship.

He spoke with a strong American accent, and, when ushered into Dorrington's presence, nodded curtly.

'You have come,' began my lord, 'to ask about the men—'

'One was a Chink,' interrupted the other rudely, 'one a Spanish fellow, one a tough from our side, I think?'

'That is so,' said Lord Dorrington gravely, 'but a phenomenon which—'

'Phenomenon nothing,' said the brusque stranger. 'They are the Denver three—the cleverest devils that ever held up a bank. Where are they?'

'Gone,' said his lordship, staring at the man.

'Gone!' roared the other. 'Oh, steaming Hades! Gone! See here,' he went on rapidly, 'I'm Torken, of Pinkerton's. I've got a warrant for the lot; they're bank robbers. We've been after them for a year. They're the people who impersonated the Chinese delegation last fall, and got away with the British ambassador's jewels—'

'Jewels?' repeated his lordship faintly.

'Jewels,' said the vigorous American.

Lord Dorrington, supported on the arm of the detective, led the way to the strongest strong-room in England.

Outwardly it appeared as though nothing unusual had occurred, but when his lordship had inserted his key he found the operation was unnecessary, for the door was unlocked and the Dorrington belt was gone

## Uncle Dick

Mr. Agnew, magnate, gave the children of Illingham, Saxby, Taunton-Newbery, and the villages about a Christmas treat at his "seat," Illingham Park; the barn and outbuildings were transformed, there were marquees and lemonade, tents and buns, a hired conjurer, and a superior Punch and Judy show, where all the characters of that disreputable drama were respectably arrayed in the newest of clothes.

Mr. Agnew entertained because he was fond of children and because he was a magnate, and a magnate should be associated with some hobby or other. So Mr. Agnew was known throughout the length and breadth of the county as "the children's friend," in which capacity his portrait appeared in the Saxby Chronicle on more than one occasion.

The amusing part of this present situation was Uncle Dick.

Not Mr. Agnew's Uncle Dick, I hasten to assure you, nor Mary Agnew's Uncle Dick. Mr. Agnew's only uncle's name was, of course, Reginald, and he was popularly supposed to be in heaven.

It was Clara Smith's Uncle Dick who was the cause of all the amusement.

Clara Smith's father—if you will excuse this genealogical digression—had been coachman to a great lord, and a widower. One day he drove a pair of restive horses—and little Harry Boyne was making interesting experiments with a kite on the high road—the carriage was smashed, and so was one of the restive horses. The great lord picked himself out of the debris of the wrecked brougham, and used shocking language to Coachman Smith, calling him dolt, idiot, ass, ploughboy, and the like. Coachman Smith took not the slightest potice, and offered no apology, because he happened to be lying in a ditch with his neck broken.

Whether or not Coachman Smith went to heaven like Uncle Reginald, is conjectural. He drank beer at the Coach and Horses, and had been known to make bets.

The great lord, who was a mean, stingy great lord, was all for sending the orphan, Clara, aged two years, to the workhouse; for, argued the great lord, what the devil do I pay rates and taxes for?

Despite the indignant protests of his Honourable son, there was little doubt whatever that the noble lord—his name was Fallingham of Fallingham and St. James—would have carried his threat into execution but for the intervention of Uncle Dick.

This providential uncle wrote from London offering to provide the child with a home, and that is how Clara Smith came to be the adopted child of Mrs. Jane Fairbridge, a pleasant widow of Saxby.

A ten-shilling postal order came punctually to the widow every Saturday morning. Toys, dolls, and dolls'-houses came to Clara at ecstatic intervals.

Once or twice "Uncle Dick" had run down to see her, and to tell her stories, and these visits were precious memories.

It happened, unfortunately, that he had timed one of these rare excursions at Christmas; so that it synchronised with Mr. Agnew's children's fête, to which Clara had been invited.

Here was a tragic problem!

To miss Uncle Dick would be unthinkable; to miss the treat unbearable.

Widow Jane Fairbridge suggested a remedy and a solution. Why not, she asked in the innocence of her heart, write a little letter and ask if Uncle Dick could come to the party?

So Clara laboriously wrote and re-wrote, her little pink tongue sticking out, and following the painful contortions of her penmanship.

Mary Agnew smiled, Mr. Agnew laughed. Of course it was unusual. Only the mothers of the children or their female relatives were invited, but he would stretch a point, yes—yes, he would stretch a point.

Mary knew something of Clara's history, and her generous heart had rebelled against the cynical indifference of the great lord and the wicked callousness of the great lord's son—now the Lord Fallingham of' Fallingham himself. For the old great lord had died, and most certainly had gone to heaven, for he drank port, and had never been known to bet in any less sum than a "pony."

So that Mary welcomed the opportunity of expressing, in a few well-chosen words, her appreciation of Uncle Dick's generosity in providing for his little niece so handsomely.

The day of the great fête dawned in quite an ordinary manner, the wintry sun came up over Wylie Copse as usual, and went about its business as if Mr. Agnew had never existed.

None the less, the magnate, who in some subtle fashion took credit alike for natural phenomena and solar activity, pronounced the weather suitable, and, with the coming of two hundred happy little ones, shrill or shy as the fit took them, the fête began.

"This," said Mary to herself, "is Uncle Dick."

He was dressed more decently than she expected for a man of his class. He was better looking, too, than she had anticipated; clean-shaven, with grey, thoughtful eyes, and a thin, tanned face.

"So you are Uncle Dick," she greeted him, with the exact tincture of patronage in her voice.

This manner of hers had, under normal circumstances, the effect of hypnotising and confusing the lower classes.

"I'm Uncle Dick," he said with a quiet smile.

"This," thought Mary rapidly, "is a forward young man who will have to be kept in his place." Aloud she went on, less warmly: "My father, I know, wishes to thank you for your generous care of Clara; we are very much interested in her, and think you have acted splendidly."

"I think I have," said the young man gravely, and Mary gasped at the smugness of the man.

"Naturally," she went on, with a touch of hauteur, "you couldn't very well do less than you have done for your brother's child."

"Naturally," he agreed.

Something in the solid ease of the man annoyed Mary.

"I am afraid you arc missing the children's games," she said coldly.

"I don't mind in the least," he replied with great earnestness.

"If you find them dull, any one of the gardeners will direct you to the servants' hall," she went on. "There will be a cold luncheon at one o'clock, but if you require refresh—"

"Beer?" he interrupted eagerly. "Can I get beer now?"

She regarded him with icy disfavour.

"It Is rather early, for beer, Mr. Smith, is it not?" she asked severely.

"I always drink beer after breakfast," said the young man with relish. "It's a fine old English custom; look at our forefathers—"

She arrested his rhapsody with a raised hand.

"I'm sorry I haven't the time to go into the question," she said with increasing coldness.

She voted him a priggish specimen of the educated working man, and avoided him the greater part of the day.

When she again came into contact with him she was with her father.

Uncle Dick was hot and tired, having been initiated into the mysteries of blind man's buff.

He was lying on a bundle of straw in a secluded part of the great barn when Mr. Agnew found him.

Mr. Agnew, being a magnate, and, moreover, a member of Parliament for a manufacturing town, had a way with the British workman.

"Ha! there you are, Uncle Dick," he said, as the perspiring young man rose at his approach; "did you get your beer all right?"

Uncle Dick cast if reproachful glance at the girl—a glance which in itself (said Mary) was a gross piece of impertinence.

"Yes, thank you," said Uncle Dick.

"Had much—jolly good tuck out—what?" asked the jocose Mr. Agnew.

"I should hardly call it that," said Uncle Dick thoughtfully, "although it was very satisfying and very nicely cooked."

"Um!" said the magnate dubiously, "I'm afraid you're rather a sybarite, Mr.—er—Smith!" He added beneath his breath, "Ungrateful beggar!"

"Not a bit," said the young man. "But—oh, I beg your pardon. You think I am referring to the lunch at the Hall? I am speaking of the lunch the good Mrs. Fairbndge provided me with. You see I had no idea that you were doing us so well: we—er—parents and guardians, I mean."

Slightly mollified, the magnate was preparing a suitable pronouncement on plain fare for plain people, with a few remarks on the simple life, when a servant brought him a telegram. With a courteous apology (Mr. Agnew's patronage of the working man took the form of treating him as an equal) he opened the buff envelope, read the message with a gathering smile, looked at Uncle Dick benevolently, and said, "Excellent!"

"What is it, father?" asked the girl.

"Lord Tupping," said Mr. Agnew impressively. "Our friend Lord Tupping has telegraphed to say we may expect him." He looked at Uncle Dick with an arch smile. "I'll be bound that Undc Dick is a Radical, a Socialist, 'Down with the House of Lords!' and that sort of thing, eh?" He beamed jovially. "It will be a lesson for you." He wagged his forefinger at the proletarian. "You shall see the House of Lords in its most—"

Mary did not seem to share her father's enthusiasm.

"Indeed," thought Uncle Dick, "she appeared to be annoyed."

She interrupted her parent.

"Why on earth is he coming?" she asked in a tone of dismay.

"My dear," said Mr. Agnew, magnate, severely, "Lord Tupping is not only a personal friend, and a fellow director, but I have reasons to hope—"

Seeing the flush on the girl's face, Uncle Dick wisely turned to stare at the decorations of the barn.

He rather fancied he heard a tiny wrangle, just such a wrangle as a magnate would permit himself to engage in within hearing of a third party—and such a third party as Uncle Dick.

As is very well known to all those who mix in good society, there are two classes of wrangles—those the servants may hear, and those they may not hear.

The patient servitor may listen unchecked whilst my lord damns the tough chicken, but when it comes to "Mildred, I have had a bill from your milliner this morning—now what the—" it is a case of "Jane, go out, and shut the door after you."

Uncle Dick was wondering in which class the present disagreement lay, when the sound of retreating footsteps caused him to look up from his artistic criticism, to find himself alone with the girl.

She was rather pink, and rather angry, and Uncle Dick was a little tactless, because he laughed softly but heartily.

"I think you are a most abominably rude man," she flamed, and would have gone, but the protesting young man, thoroughly alarmed, barred her way.

"Please, please don't go," he Implored. "I was only laughing at my thoughts."

He was so earnest that she hesitated.

"Poor old Uncle Dick," he wheedled. "Don't be hard on Uncle Dick. It's Tuppy," he went on, with outrageous familiarity; "it's the thought of Tuppy that amuses me. Poor dear, he does so dislike Christmas festivities."

She felt that it was high time that she asserted herself.

"Mr. Smith," she said gravely, "I hardly think you realise how exceptionally impertinent you are. I pass over your unmannerly request for beer—that is a natural requirement of your class. I will not dwell upon the familiarity that was implied in your—your look when my father referred to your refreshment, but this reference to our guest is one that I cannot overlook."

"Poor Uncle Dick!" he murmured.

A voice hailed her; her father was coming into the barn, and behind him walked a young man upon whose round, good-natured face was the impression of boredom,

"Here's Lord Tupping," said Mr. Agnew boisterously. "Mary, here's—oh, here you are."

Mary held out her hand.

"How de do, Miss Agnew; your governor wants me to play skip-in-the-ring, at my time of life! I say—" He stared at Uncle Dick. "Why, it's the Fallin' bird!" he chortled, and Mr. Agnew looked round for the curiously-named fowl.

Lord Tupping seized the hand of Uncle Dick.

"Fancy, old feller," he begged, "skip-in-the-ring at my time of life! Go an' play it, old friend; be a true Fallin'ham of Fallin'ham, an' step into the breach."

Mr. Agnew was fairly bewildered, but before Mary's accusing gaze Uncle Dick dropped his eyes.

"Lord Fallingham," she said sternly, "you are neglecting your niece."

"It was very nice of you, of course," she said later.

The little guests had all departed, and they sat in the drawing-room, drinking grown-ups' tea.

"I am sorry I said such horrid things about your father."

"It was his idea," lied the young man eagerly; "it was part of the dear old man's pose, unbending severity, and that sort of thing, and when the child was left an orphan he suggested that a relation should be found, so he wrote through my lawyers."

What the old lord had said was: "Why the devil hasn't the little brat got relations;—the improvidence of the working classes is too appalling!"

"But I think," reproved Mary, "you ought to have told us. Shall you tell the child?"

"No," said the young man thoughtfully. "I'll still be Uncle Dick. It sounds nice," he mused. "Uncle Dick—and Aunt Mary."

The girl changed the subject a little incoherently.


The Murder at the 'Port Helm'

My name is Thomas Carlyle Smith, but my professional name is Carlyle Thorn, and I am a crime-investigator. My father named me after the Sage of Chelsea, whom he intensely admired but imperfectly understood, and I adopted my second name and an abbreviation of my first, because it is very necessary in my business to secure a nom de guerre which is at once unusual and consonant with the accepted view on private detectives, namely, that preternatural genius invariably runs hand in hand with eccentricity of nomenclature.

I have always had a natural bent for investigation, my childish curiosity, coupled with a nasal organ of an emphatic type, having earned for me an offensive nick-name which I often recall with a smile.

From the first my entry into the realms of detection was crowned with success, with much of which, I must frankly confess, my own ability had little to do. Thus, I discovered the diamonds of Lady Sathell of Sarum by a fluke; I tracked down George Cutville by the luckiest of accidents; and, with the aid of my friend Trufill, of the firm of Trufill, Colebrook, and Porter (solicitors), I was able to check what might easily have been the most stupendous of blackmailing schemes known to history.

I cite these few out of thousands of very ordinary and fairly uninteresting cases. A detective's life is made up of little things, but, since the main consideration of life is life itself, and since, moreover, the object of my engaging myself in my profession is the securing of an income sufficiently large to make life supportable, I have even welcomed the fifty-guinea fee which accompanies the enquiries of the jealous husband.

Yet there are moments when the artist in me awakens to life, when my whole being thirsts for adventures more poignant than those incidental to watching the suspected bourgeoisie.

Such an adventure came in the Port Helm mystery. The story of the crime which startled England may be familiar to my readers, but I will tell it as briefly as possible.

On August 9, 1904, a gentlemanly man, whose dusty clothing and hot appearance suggested that he had come from some distance by road, arrived at the Port Helm, towards the evening, and asked for a room. The "Port Helm" is a tumble-down hostelry between Seaport and Colehaven, on the Kentish coast. There was a time when extensive slate quarries in the neighbourhood had justified the existence of this solitary little inn, and when it had enjoyed a thriving trade, but the slate had proved difficult to work, and had, moreover deteriorated in quality as the working progressed, and at the time of which I am speaking the quarries were deserted, the Port Helm depending upon the infrequent travellers who passed along the road between the two towns. It stood on the cliff road, the only building within sight. Two hundred yards before it, the cliff fell four hundred feet sheer to the rocky shore below, and only a crazy hand-rail, doubtlessly erected by the quarry proprietors, protected the night wanderer from instant and terrible death.

At this time the inn was kept by a young man named Hilker, whose character, unfortunately, was not of the best. I say "unfortunately," because it was on his behalf that I was engaged.

It is indisputable that he drank; it is as well established a fact that he had been in trouble with the police over a sheep which had disappeared from a neighbouring farm, the fleece of which was afterwards found in an outhouse of the inn. Hilker, however, strenuously and indignantly denied that he had ever seen the sheep, protested that the circumstance of the fleece being found in his tool-house was explained by the machinations of an enemy, and spoke vaguely of a dark man whose enmity he had earned when he was in Gibraltar (he had been in the army, and had been discharged for striking a non-commissioned officer), and in the end, owing to a flaw in the chain of evidence, the charge of sheep-stealing was dropped.

Hilker lived by himself with one manservant, whose duty it was to "tidy up," so that the evidence I required to prove his innocence on the greater charge was of the unpromising kind. Indeed, never have I gone into a case where first appearances were so black against the accused.

The dusty stranger who had arrived on the evening of August 9 was Belmont Trair, an eccentric millionaire who spent his life in walking tours. Many extraordinary stories have been told of this gentleman—that he would associate with tramps, live and sleep happily in their company, and willingly undergo all manner of unwholesome privations; but the truth, so far as I have been able to ascertain, is that he had a passion for walking, was something of a nature-lover, and found more joy in his healthy recreation than in more artificial forms of amusement. I think it is a convincing refutation of the tramp and casual-ward story, that he invariably carried a large sum of money on his person, was extremely fastidious as to his fare, and was exceedingly talkative.

The testimony of Hilker is that the traveller arrived at sunset, and ordered-tea and ham. In this he was supported by the evidence of the old man, George Wish, who was, as I have said, general factotum to Hilker.

The landlord further said—and here we have no corroborative evidence—that Mr. Trair complained that he had been shadowed in the last two miles of his walk by "two dark men—one Spanish-looking," and, a rain storm coming up, together with the fear of these men in his mind, he decided to stay the night.

So far the story has corroboration, except in one essential particular. What happened after that is a matter for surmise.

The old attendant went home to his cottage, three miles along the road, at 8.50, at which hour it was raining heavily, and the stranger had expressed in his hearing his intention of staying the night. According to Hilker's statement to the police, Mr. Trail—who was a man of fifty, of very small physique—went up to his room at 10.15. Hilker remembered, he said, looking up at the clock as his guest left the room. At eleven o'clock, when the landlord was preparing to retire for the night, Mr. Trair came hurriedly down the stairs, fully dressed, and in a very agitated condition.

"I must go on," he said, incoherently. (I am giving the purport of Hilker's signed statement.) "I cannot stay another minute here," and with that he put down a sovereign on the table (the conversation described was supposed to have taken place in the landlord's private room behind the bar), and, in spite of the landlord's urging, who pointed out that the rain was still heavily falling, he hurriedly left the house.

Nothing more was seen of him until the following morning, when his body was discovered by the coastguards at the foot of the cliff, with a knife thrust through his heart, the body being terribly battered by the fall.

The police were immediately summoned, and county detectives were on the spot within two hours. When searched, it was discovered that the unfortunate man's watch and diamond ring were intact, and that in the pockets were two sovereigns, nine shillings and sixpence in silver, and a few coppers, but that the notes (some £140, as it afterwards transpired) were missing. A careful examination of the ground was made, but there was no evidence of a struggle, although the guard rail at the edge of the cliff was broken.

A search was made of the inn, and here was discovered a piece of evidence sufficient to hang any man—a large stain of blood recently shed on the floor of the living-room.

Hilker was immediately arrested, charged with the murder, and brought into Seaport.

At this time my name was fairly well known. I had appeared in a few criminal trials on behalf of the accused, and I had been instrumental in one case at least in proving the police at fault.

At the same time, I was both astonished and flattered to receive a summons on behalf of Hilker.

It came on the evening of the arrest.

I was preparing to leave my office for the evening, when the telephone bell rang.

I answered it myself.

"Is that Carlyle Smith?" said the voice; and when I answered that it was, the caller, speaking somewhat peremptorily, said:—

"Come at once to 942, Cambridge Gardens."

Before I could answer, I was rung off.

A little annoyed by the brusqueness of the demand, I was in two minds whether or not I should take any notice of the request, but something within me urged me to accept the invitation, and, jumping into a taxi-cab, I was driven off to the address.

I found it was a house of somewhat imposing exterior. A neat maid-servant opened the door to me, and, without enquiry as to my business, I was ushered straight into a study. It was furnished in excellent taste. I had time to notice that there were two maps of Spain on the walls—a circumstance which struck me as curious at the time—when the door opened and a gentleman came in. He was past middle age, his hair was iron grey, his face white and forbidding. He had the facial lines of a man of chronic bad humour.

He looked at me discontentedly—I can find no other words to describe his attitude—and nodded curtly.

"My name is Hilker," he said, motioning me to a chair, "and I am the uncle of the unfortunate young man who, as you may have seen from the evening newspapers, has been arrested for a murder in the South of England."

I nodded, and he paced up and down the room, his chin on his breast, before he spoke again.

"I do not doubt for one moment but that he is guilty," he said, suddenly, and shot a sharp glance at me, "and that the story he tells about the dark, Spanish-looking gentlemen is false."

He must have seen my eyes wandering to the maps of Spain, for he added hastily:—

"I am interested in Spanish mines, and he himself has been in Spain; it was one of the chances I gave him when I found he was going wrong."

He stopped before me.

"I want you to go down to Seaport and investigate this matter. I will pay you a fee of £600 if you prove his innocence, and £100 if your investigations are futile. Do you agree?"

I nodded again and, with no other word, he sat at his desk and wrote me a cheque for £50.

"This will cover your expenses," he said, and struck a bell.

In twenty seconds I found myself in the street, with the cheque in my pocket.

I drove straight to my lodgings, packed a few necessary articles of toilet, and arrived at Victoria in time to catch the 7.5 for Seaport. It was after nine when I walked into the Blue Lion at that port.

I knew it would be impossible for me to see the prisoner that night; indeed, knowing how strict the police are in all such matters, I did not expect to see him at all, but the following morning, by reason of my acquaintance with the inspector in charge, I had the briefest interview.

I must confess that my first impression of him was by no means a happy one. He was a largely built young man of a florid kind; his face told me by unmistakable signs that he was a heavy drinker. He was big, loose-lipped, brutal, and his eyes were of that peculiar shade of light blue to be found in men of an utterly callous and cold-blooded nature.

He was greatly depressed, but vehemently protested his innocence, and repeated the story of the "Spanish-looking" men, but I learnt nothing that I did not already know.

Before leaving the police station I interviewed Detective-Inspector Cass, who had charge of the case.

He was a typical police officer, dull and dogmatic, ready to jump at the obvious, having no mind for the subtle possibilities of such a case as this.

"He did it all right," he said, complacently. "You take my tip, Carlyle, and back out of this case; it will do your reputation no good. Why, isn't the evidence clear? A rich and eccentric man stops at Hilker's Inn, Hilker is in financial difficulties—as he always has been, since I can remember—he murders his guest; and chucks him over the cliff, hoping that the tide will wash away the body and all evidence of his guilt: It's as clear as daylight."

Strangely enough, it was not as clear to me, and I left the station house unimpressed by the self-satisfaction of the inspector.

It was whilst walking back to my hotel that chance threw in my way a remarkable clue. I have previously said that the detection of crime is as much a matter of luck as anything else, and here was proof, if proof be needed, of that fact.

In the old-fashioned High Street of Seaport is a gunsmith's, and I was passing this, when the door of the shop opened quickly, and a man stepped out.

He was tall and swarthy, with a complexion like old ivory, and one didn't need to be especially knowledgeable to recognize that he was a foreigner.

An inspiration came to me.

"Buenos días," I said.

"Buenos días," he replied, and looked confused.

I watched him hurrying from the gunsmith's.

The old proprietor, spectacles on nose, was behind the counter, which was strewn with revolvers of every conceivable type, from the heavy army Webley to the pocket Browning. It was evident that the Spaniard had been making a purchase.

I asked to see some cleaning brushes, and whilst examining these I managed to start a conversation with the old man.

He was, fortunately, of a garrulous disposition.

"I was afraid you wanted to buy a revolver," he said.

"Why afraid?"

"Well, not exactly afraid, but I've lost a good customer in that gentleman that just went out. He'd chosen one of the best arms I have in the shop, when I asked him for the licence that was necessary before I could serve him. He tried to persuade me that, as he's a member of the Spanish Embassy, a licence wasn't required, but that yarn didn't satisfy me."

I had learnt all that I wanted.

In a few minutes I was in pursuit of the Spaniard. I had no difficulty in tracing him. He was living at the best hotel—the Marine, facing the sea—and, to my surprise, the story he told about his being attached to the Embassy staff proved to be true. He was at Seaport for his health, and had been there three weeks.

I saw my friend, the inspector, and told him about the revolver, but he did not seem impressed.

"Very likely," he said, carelessly; "After, a murder, there's usually a scare that drives timid people to the purchase of firearms."

For myself, however, I was not prepared to dismiss the matter so lightly.

Was it not more than a coincidence that Spain came into this case, so insistently? A sudden thought struck me, and I sent an inquiry wire to my assistant in London.

Without waiting for an answer, I drove out to the Port Helm. It has been described as "lonely," but that inadequately describes its isolation. It stands back from the cliff road, a gaunt, unlovely building, angular of design, uninviting of aspect. The police were in possession of the house, but again fortune was with me. Had Scotland Yard men been in charge, I could have done nothing; as it happened, the local police were quite willing to oblige the "gentleman from London."

I made a careful examination of the premises.

They were simple in their arrangement.

There was a bar, a bar parlour, a little sitting-room, and, connected by a long dark passage, a kitchen at the back. There was a small cellar, where Hilker kept his stock of coals, and this comprised the ground floor.

The only other rooms in the house were three upstairs, a large, untidy bedroom, which was Hilker's own, a lumber-room, and a room which was a sort of store-room. I returned to the ground floor.

"This is where the murder was committed," said the stolid policeman, and showed me the stain on the floor.

"This is where you think the murder was committed," I said, sharply, and the policeman smiled.

"He did it all right," he said, with a self-satisfied leer; "anybody who thinks he didn't must be mad."

Since I might want to visit the house again, I did not attempt to argue with the man, but, giving him half-a-sovereign for the trouble I had put him to, I went out.

From the door of the Port Helm to the edge of the cliff was about a hundred yards. I spent over an hour making a thorough survey of the ground, and found nothing—or rather, found nothing until I had given up my search in despair.

From the edge of the road to the edge of the cliff was a "border" of grass, and I was walking back-to the road to enter the carriage I had hired to bring me out to the Port Helm when I saw something glittering amongst the green. I stooped and picked up a tiny ornament. It was in the form of a six-pointed star, and was attached to a ribbon. One glance at it, and my heart leapt with excitement. It was the miniature of the Order of Charles III. of Spain!

I went back to Seaport elated. Here, at any rate, was the beginning of a clue.

When one has a line to work upon half one's difficulties vanish. I determined to call upon the Spaniard, and that night, after dinner, I made my way to the Marine Hotel.

Yes, Senor Don Alberto Fuentes was in, and he would see me.

A dark young man rose to greet me.

He was calm, inscrutable, very polite, and motioned me to a seat.

"What can I do for you, sir?" he asked. .

He spoke English perfectly.

"I am a detective," I said, "a private detective, and I am investigating a crime which has been committed in the neighbourhood."

He nodded, keeping his eyes fixed on my face.

"You mean the murder committed by Hilker?" he said.

"I mean the murder with which Hilker is charged," I corrected. Then, as a thought struck me, I asked, quickly, "Do you know him?"

He hesitated.

"I know him slightly," he admitted. "I come to Seaport every year. It is the one place in England that is good for my chest."

"And you have met him?"

Again he hesitated.

"Yes," he said. Then, hurriedly, "You observe I hesitate. That is natural, is it not? A member of the Embassy does not care to admit that he knows a man charged with murder."

"Very natural," I said, drily. "Did you know the murdered man?"

"No."

The answer came quickly, emphatically, loudly.

"Do you know of him?"

He shrugged his shoulders.

"As much as anybody knows who reads the papers."

I took from my breast pocket the little decoration and held it in the palm of my hand.

"Do you know this?" I asked.

He looked at it with a frown.

"Yes," he said, "it is a miniature; it was stolen from me."

I met his eye, but he did not quail.

"You might like to know the circumstances," he went on. "I was motoring to London to attend a dinner—it was the King of Spain's birthday, and I carried my kit in the tonneau behind. A few miles out of Seaport I punctured a tyre. I had no mechanician with me, but fortunately, or unfortunately, I was near the Port Helm, and it was Hilker who helped me to patch the tyre. When I got to London I found my suitcase had disappeared."

Again our eyes met.

"You suggest that Hilker stole it?" I said.

"I suggest nothing," he replied, shortly.

He rose to his feet as though to bring the interview to an end.

"One more question, Senor," I said, "and I am finished. Have you purchased a revolver lately?"

"I refuse to answer any more questions," he said, and opened the door.

I returned to London by the last train that night and drove straight to Cambridge Gardens.

Though the hour was late old Hilker was at work in his study and I was shown in.

He gave me a frowning welcome. "Well," he said, "what have you discovered?"

I gave him an account of my work. I told him of the Spaniard, the miniature decoration, and the purchase of the revolver.

"And what does all that prove?" he demanded. "What is your theory?"

"I think your nephew is innocent," I replied. "I am as certain that the Spaniard knows something about the matter."

"What is his name again?"

"Fuentes," I replied.

"'Fuentes'—nonsense," he said testily. "I know Senor Fuentes—it is ridiculous to suppose that he knows anything whatever about it."

"But the decoration?"

"I'd accept his explanation. Don't I know that my nephew is the biggest villain un—"

He checked himself suddenly.

"What do the police think?" he asked, and I smiled.

"You know what the police are: they jump at the obvious conclusion."

"And quite right!" said old Hilker, violently thumping the desk with his clenched fist; "quite right! It is the obvious that requires detection. You've no more to tell me?"

All the time I had been in the room my eyes had been busy.

I had wondered when I came in what had been the business of such importance to keep a man like old Hilker out of bed at twelve o'clock at night. I had caught a glimpse of the document which had been before him when I was announced. He had swept it aside, but the words "Will and Testament," boldly engrossed, were too prominent to escape my eye.

He had been making his will. Why?

Let me piece together the scraps of information I had secured.

1. Hilker was accused of a brutal murder.

2. He denied his guilt, and talked of a dark man, a Spaniard, who sought his life.

3. A Spaniard, Fuentes, admits that he knows Hilker. Moreover, a decoration belonging to Fuentes is found on the actual scene of the crime.

4. The uncle of the accused man also knows Fuentes, is vehement in protesting the innocence of the Spaniard of any guilty knowledge, and his faith in his nephew's guilt.

5. Fuentes purchases a revolver and refuses to discuss the purchase.

I have said that the murdered man was an eccentric, who had spent a great deal of his time on walking tours. By dint of enquiry I discovered that he, too, had lived in Spain; more remarkable still, he had occupied a house in the Calle de Recolletos exactly opposite that in which Fuentes had lived.

At about this time Mensikoff, that brilliant head of the Russian secret police, was in London. I had been of service to him in the collection of evidence against the infamous Spilotski gang, and he had told me that if ever I was in a difficulty I was to go to him.

If ever there was an occasion where such advice should be followed it was surely now, and that night, after leaving the old man, I drove straight to the Russian's hotel.

"Well?" he said, as he gave me a smiling welcome, "What brings you at this hour? Some badness. Yes?"

He spoke English with a little accent, but his diction was mainly remarkable for its curious misuse of words.

In as few words as possible I detailed, the case, and he sat, nodding his great head, as I brought out each feature of the case.

When I had finished he said:

"It looks like Hilk—what you call him?—Hilker."

"But what of this Spanish clue?" I protested.

"There is no remarkable, in that, my frien'; he has been in Spain, so all foreigners are Spaniards to him. If he imagines a foreigner, he imagines a Spaniard, hein? The old man have been in Spain, so he knows Fuentes, who is a prominent man in Madrid. The murdered man, he have also been in Spain—but then he have been everywhere, all over the shop; eh?"

"But the revolver?" I persisted, and he shrugged his shoulders.

"Over 50,000 revolvers are sold every year in England, yet every man who buys is not a murderer."

"And you think?" I suggested, irritably.

"I think Hilker stabbed Belmont Trair and threw him over cliff. Yes, it seems simple."

He must have seen the look of blank disappointment which came into my face, for he laughed.

"I am police officer—eh?" He wagged his forefinger at me. "I deal with actual, not fantastic—eh? I see a man, with his han's in another fellow's pocket. I say. 'This is a thief'—you, au contraire, say, 'Is this a thief?' an' try to find reasons extraordinary for his strange conduct—obvious, my frien', obvious—he is the little god of the secret service."

Descending the stairs I cursed Mensikoff and his infernal "obvious."

We were getting near the day of the trial, which was to take place at Canterton, the county town, and, hard as I had worked I had not succeeded in getting any nearer the solution of the mystery.

I returned to my fiat dispirited.

A telegram and a letter were waiting for me. It was from my assistant, who had taken charge of the London end of the case. It was brief.

"FUENTES LEFT SUDDENLY FOR SPAIN BY THE NINE O'CLOCK BOAT TRAIN."

So he had cleared. "Suddenly," said the telegram, which meant unexpectedly. I took up the letter and opened it. It was from old Hilker, and had evidently been written after I had left that night.

"Dear Mr. Smith" (it ran). "I am enclosing herewith a cheque for a hundred pounds, the fee I promised you in the event of your failure to establish my nephew's interest. I am so satisfied of his guilt that I have this night struck all reference to him out of my will. I am leaving to-morrow morning for Spain, and as I do not intend returning to England until this grisly business is over, I am settling our account."

So he was going to Spain, too.

I made no further attempt to see him. The next morning he left London. There was nothing for me to do but to sit down and wait. I was refused any further opportunity of seeing my client, and even the solicitor who had charge of the case did not seem disposed to help me in the matter.

By careful inquiry I discovered that the revolver Fuentes could not purchase in Seaport he had secured from London. Through a friend who had the entrée to most of the embassies I found that Fuentes was a man of nervous temperament, but that was the sum total of my discoveries. There was nothing to do but sit tight and learn what the trial revealed.

And it revealed nothing.

It was tried before Mr. Justice Cadbury, and the evidence was the most ordinary I have ever listened to.

The man in the dock sat through it all unmoved. Now and again his eyes would stray to where I sat in the well of the court, and the ghost of a smile would hang about the corners of his loose mouth, then his eyes would go back to the judge, and the jury, and the witness, whichever object of interest held him for the moment.

It was all over in four hours. The jury, without retiring, returned a verdict of guilty, and Hilker stood up with his hands in his pockets, to hear the dread sentence of the law. His face retained its colour, there was not so much as a tremor to indicate his perturbation as he listened to the sentence.

Then, turning on his heels as the last words were spoken, he went down the stairs, out of the sight of men. I was leaving the court when I heard my name called. It was the solicitor who had defended the man.

"Hilker wants to see you," he said. "Inspector Cass, who has had charge of the case, will take you to him."

I found Cass waiting for me in the corridor beneath the court.

He nodded a kindly greeting.

"He wants you," he said, and led the way.

There was a large reception-room, and in this I found my man.

He was sitting on a form, a warder at each side.

Would he give me the clue?

My heart leapt at the thought.

Now that he was face to face with death, would he drop some hint that would lead me to the right track? I felt, and had felt all along, that he could tell me more than he had done.

He looked up as I entered, and smiled wryly.

"You'll be seeing my uncle, I suppose?" he said.

"Yes," I replied.

"Well, tell him from me," he went on, "that I'm much obliged to him for the trouble he has taken; he's been a mean old dog all his life, but he's played the game at the end."

"Have you any message for Fuentes?" I asked, quietly.

He frowned.

"Fuentes? Who the devil is Fuentes? Oh, I know. The Spanish fellow. No. What message can I have for him?"

A wild fear suddenly seized me.

"But—but," I stammered, "you are not guilty?"

There was scornful amusement in his glance.

"Guilty? Of course, I'm guilty. Any fool could see that!"

Inspector Cass led the way out. I was dazed, upset.

"Look here, Mr. Smith," said Cass, with a note of irony in his tone, "you ought to write an account of this murder, it would be the most extraordinary crime story ever known."

"Why?" I asked, in astonishment.

"Why?" he repeated, "because the obvious man committed it, and the average policeman detected it."


## Edgar Wallace – A Short Biography

Richard Horatio Edgar Wallace was born on the 1st April 1875 at 7 Ashburnham Grove, Greenwich. His mother, Mary Jane "Polly" Richards was born into an Irish Catholic family in Liverpool in 1843 and had worked in theatres, both as an actress in bit-parts and as a stagehand and usherette, until she married a Merchant Navy Captain, Joseph Richards, in 1867. He too had been born into an Irish Catholic family in Liverpool. His father had also been a Captain in the Merchant Navy, and his mother's family had a marine background. Mary was eight months pregnant with Joseph's child when he died at sea, and it was once the child had been born that she first turned to the stage, taking the stage name Polly Richards.

She joined the Marriott family theatre troupe in 1872. It was managed by Mrs. Alice Edgar, Richard Edgar, Grace Edgar, Adeline Edgar and Richard Horatio Edgar, Wallace's father. In late 1874 Mary and Richard Horatio Edgar had a brief sexual encounter at the party following a successful show, and she fell pregnant. Worried about the scandal which would ensue and fearing that she might forever lose her job at the troupe, she fabricated an obligation in Greenwich would detain her there for at least six months. She lived in a room in the boarding house on Ashburnham Grove until her son, Edgar, was born. She had already made preparations through her midwife for a couple to foster the child, and when Edgar was born the midwife presented her with Mrs Freeman. Her husband was a fishmonger at Billingsgate market and she already had ten children. She was happy to foster the child and for Polly to make frequent visits to see him in exchange for a small sum of money which Polly made from her work in the theatre troupe.

Wallace was now known as Richard Horatio Edgar Freeman, taking his father's forenames and his foster family's surname. Broadly speaking his childhood was a happy one. The Freemans looked after him lovingly and he had good friendships with his foster siblings, particularly Clara Freeman, twenty years his senior, who often looked after him as a child. After a few years Polly's finances tightened and she was no longer in a position to afford the fee she had been paying the Freemans. However, they had grown to love the young Wallace and opted to adopt him in order to keep him out of the workhouse. Polly could no longer visit him. George Freeman was keen to ensure that he had equal opportunities and did all he could to secure him an education at St. Alfege with St. Peter's, a Peckham boarding school. Despite his adoptive father's efforts, though, Wallace left the school aged twelve for truancy.

Instead he went to work and by the time he was fourteen or fifteen he had experience selling newspapers at Ludgate Circus, near Fleet Street, as a worker in a rubber factory, as a shoe shop assistant, as a milk delivery boy and as a ship's cook. He stole from the milk company which resulted in his dismissal, and in 1894 was engaged to a local girl from Deptford named Edith Anstree, though he broke this off and instead joined the Infantry. He adopted the name Edgar Wallace which he took from Lew Wallace, the author of *Ben-Hur*, and his medical record records a diminutive 33" chest and a stunted growth. his first posting was with the West Kent Regiment in South Africa in 1896, though he did not enjoy military life, arranging to be transferred to the Royal Army Medical Corps. Though this was a less strenuous job, it was also significantly less pleasant and so he again transferred to the Press Corps, which he found suited him far better.

He was in Cape Town in 1898 where he met Rudyard Kipling and was inspired to begin writing and publishing poetry and songs. His first collection of ballads, *The Mission that Failed!* and was enough of a success that in 1899 he paid his way out of the armed forces in order to turn to writing full time. His first work was as a war correspondent for Reuters who kept him in Africa to cover the Boer War, and then for the Daily Mail in 1900 and various other periodicals after that. It was while he was in South Africa that he met and married Ivy Maude Caldecott, who was 21 when they married in 1901, despite her Wesleyan missionary father's strong opposition to the union, for several reasons, one of which was that Wallace's writing was not turning quite the profit he had expected it would. *War and Other Poems* and *Writ in Barracks,* both published in 1900, had not proved as popular as his first collection. Eleanor Clare Hellier Wallace, their first child, died of meningitis in 1903 and, in rather deep debt, they returned to London. Wallace used his contacts with the Daily Mail to get work with them in London, electing to write detective novels as a means of making quick money.

Wallace met Polly, his birth mother, in 1903. He didn't remember her from his childhood as he had been too young when she became unable to visit, so it was as though they were meeting for the first time. She was sixty years old and terminally ill, living in abject poverty. She had come to Wallace seeking financial support, but he turned her away. She died in the Bradford Infirmary later that year. In 1904 he and Ivy had a son, Bryan. He was still writing and had completed his first thriller, *The Four Just Men*. Since nobody would publish it he resorted to setting up his own publishing company which he called Tallis Press and he published a serialised version of *The Four Just Men* in 1905. He received promotional assistance from the Daily Mail in which he ran a competition for entrants to guess the method of murder in the final chapter, with a prize of £1,000 for a correct guess. Although the paper's proprietor, Lord Alfred Harmsworth, refused Wallace the £1,000 prize money, Wallace persisted and went ahead with the competition, recklessly advertising on billboards and buses all over the country, hoping to expand his advertisements across the Empire. His worried colleagues at the Daily Mail managed to convince him to lower the prize money to £500, split into a first prize of £250, a second prize of £200 and a third of £50, but with the total cost of his advertisements nearing £2,000 he would need to sell £2,500 worth of copies before he could see any profit. He was confident that this could be achieved in just three months.

Though he had remarkable enthusiasm, it became clear that his managerial skills left a lot to be desired. It soon emerged that nowhere in the competition terms and conditions had he included a clause limiting the competition to one single winner; instead, any entrant with a winning answer was entitled to their corresponding prize money. Thus, if ten entrants guessed the first prize answer, the competition was obliged to pay each entrant £250. This error was only noticed after the competition had been closed and the solution had been printed in the final installment of the novel, meaning that not only was there no opportunity to write his way out of enormous financial obligation, but the entrants who had guessed correctly would by now have read the final chapter and know they had done so. £250 was an enormous amount of money to the average Edwardian family and those entitled to it were likely to make a lot of noise if they didn't receive their money. Despite this, Wallace's fist instinct was to attempt to ignore the issue entirely, even as he discovered that he initial calculations had been dramatically over-enthusiastic and it would take nearer to two years of continuous sales to break even at the initial cost of £2,500, let alone the new figure which included every correct guesser. Compounding the problem even further was the awful realisation that as sales continued throughout the initial three month period and Wallace approached the £2,500 break-even figure, new readers were still eligible to enter and guess correctly. Though it is unknown how much he eventually owed his readers, Lord Harmsworth found himself having to loan over £5,000 in order to protect the reputation of the newspaper, since 1906 had come around and there still hadn't been a list printed of all prize-winners. It was less a charitable act than one of a man anxious that the failure would reflect ill on his own paper. Wallace filed for bankruptcy shortly thereafter and as a token gesture to his creditors sold the rights to the novel to Sir George Newnes, a publisher and editor, for £75. In the midst of this chaos though, Wallace managed to write and published *Smithy*, which would become the first of a series of *Smithy* novels.

Following this fiascos Wallace was dismissed from the Daily Mail in 1907 when inaccuracies which were found in his reporting, resulting in libel cases being brought against the paper. That year he became the first reporter to be fired from the Daily Mail and was his awful reputation prevented him from finding work at any other papers. Despite all this, though, he travelled to the Congo Free State later that year and reported on the criminal treatment of the Congolese people by King Leopold II of Belgium and the Belgian rubber companies. Up to fifteen million Congolese were killed in various atrocities, and Wallace was asked to serialise stories based on his experiences for her penny magazine *Weekly Tale-Teller*. He and Ivy had another daughter, named Patricia, in 1908. Though his new work for *Weekly Tale-Teller* was bringing in some money, their financial situation was still dire and Ivy was occasionally forced to sell off her jewellery and possessions in order to pay for food. In 1911 his Congolese stories were published in a collection called *Sanders of the River*, which quickly became a bestseller. He would publish eleven more such collections featuring a total of 102 stories of adventure and tribal life set on the river Congo.

From 1908 he started to enjoy a revival of both his success and his reputation. The majority of his initial writing he sold outright in order to make money as quickly as possible and placate his creditors in the United Kingdom and South Africa, but as his success saw the reestablishment of his reputation he began to find work once again as a journalist, beginning in horse racing for the *Week-End*, the *Evening News* and then as an editor for the *Week-End Racing Supplement*. Following this success he started his own racing papers, *Bibury's* and *R. E. Walton's Weekly*, eventually buying his own racehorses and losing thousands gambling. His success was insufficient to support his newly extravagant lifestyle and his marriage began to fail in the light of his financial irresponsibility. He and Ivy had their last child together, Michael Blair Wallace, in 1916, and she filed for divorce in 1918 moving to Tunbridge Wells with her children.

Wallace began to fall for his secretary Ethel Violet King and they married in 1921, having a child, Penelope Wallace, in 1923, who would herself go on to become a successful crime writer. Wallace now began to take his career as a fiction writer more seriously, signing with Hodder and Stoughton in 1921. He now began to organize his contracts more carefully, arranging for royalties and properly organized promotions, run by people more business-minded than himself. He was marketed as the 'King of Thrillers' and they gave him the trademark image of a trilby, a cigarette holder and a yellow Rolls Royce. He was truly prolific, capable not only of producing a 70,000 word novel in three days but of doing three novels in a row in such a manner. His publishers signed off on almost everything he wrote as soon as he turned it in, estimating that by 1928 one in four books being read at any time was written by Wallace, for alongside his famous thrillers he wrote variously in other genres, including but not limited to science fiction, non-fiction accounts of WWI which amounted to ten volumes and screen plays. Eventually he would reach the remarkable total of 170 novels, 18 stage plays and 957 short stories.

Wallace became chairman of the Press Club which to this day holds an annual Edgar Wallace Award, rewarding 'excellence in writing'. In 1923 he broadcasted a report on the Epsom Derby horse race for the British Broadcasting Company, making him the first ever radio sports correspondent. His ex-wife Ivy had suffered from breast cancer between 1923-1924, and it eventually killed her in 1926 despite a successful operation to remove a tumour the year before. He wrote the essay "The Canker in our Midst" in 1926 which dealt, aggressively and controversially, with the problem of paedophilia in show business, describing how children were unwittingly left open to sexual abuse, and linking paedophilia with homosexuality. Its tone has been described as "intolerant, blustering, kick-the-blighters-down-the-stairs". He was appointed chairman of the British Lion Film Corporation on the back of the success of *The Ringer* and on the agreement that he give British Lion first choice on all his future work. This contract gave him an annual salary and a large amount of stock with the company, along with a stipend on all British Lion production of his work and 10% of their annual profits. This extraordinary contract gave him annual earnings by 1929 of almost £50,000, or almost £2 million in 2014.

He now became an active figure in politics, entering the 1931 general election as a Liberal contestant in Blackpool, rejecting the current government in favour of free trade. He lost the election by over 33,000 votes and went to America in late 1931, once again deeply in debt after buying the *Sunday News* which closed six months later. In America he quickly found work as a script doctor for RKO Pictures, enjoying early success with the 1932 adaptation of *The Hound of the Baskervilles*. This success, along with that of the play *The Green Pack*, established his reputation in America and he was able to see his own work adapted for film, beginning with *The Four Just Men*. His most successful theatrical work, *On The Spot*, which explores the life of Al Capone, has been described as "arguably, in construction, dialogue, action, plot and resolution, still one of the finest and purest of 20th-century melodramas". These successes led to his assignation on RKO's "gorilla picture" which would become famous as King Kong in 1933.

He worked on the first draft though he was beginning to experience severe headaches which brought about a diagnosis of diabetes. Despite taking medication to address his condition, it deteriorated in a matter of days. His wife booked him passage home but soon heard that he had entered a coma and died of his condition and double pneumonia on the 7th of February 1932 in North Maple Drive, Beverly Hills. In his honour the bell at St. Bride's church on Fleet Street tolled for the duration of the morning while the flags flew at half-mast. He was buried near his home in England at Chalklands, Bourne End, in Buckinghamshire. Once again, at the time of his death he was in severe debt, mostly to racing bookkeepers, though these debts were settled within two years thanks to the enormous royalties his estate continued to receive from his contracts. His writing has been translated into 29 languages, and is considered one of the most important bodies of Colonial writing.

Edgar Wallace – A Concise Bibliography

African Novels
Sanders of the River (1911)
The People of the River (1911)
The River of Stars (1913)
Bosambo of the River (1914)
Bones (1915)
The Keepers of the King's Peace (1917)
Lieutenant Bones (1918)
Bones in London (1921)
Sandi the Kingmaker (1922)
Bones of the River (1923)
Sanders (1926)
Again Sanders (1928)

Four Just Men (Series)
The Four Just Men (1905)
The Council of Justice (1908)
The Just Men of Cordova (1917)
The Law of the Four Just Men (US title: Again the Three Just Men) (1921)
The Three Just Men (1926)
Again the Three Just Men (US title: The Law of the Three Just Men) (1929) a.k.a. Again the Three

Mr. J. G. Reeder (Series)
Room 13 (1924)
The Mind of Mr. J. G. Reeder (US title: The Murder Book of Mr. J. G. Reeder) (1925)
Terror Keep (1927)
Red Aces (1929)
The Guv'nor and Other Short Stories (US title: Mr. Reeder Returns) (1932)

Detective Sgt. (Inspector) Elk series
The Nine Bears or The Other Man or The Cheaters (1910)
revised as Silinski - Master Criminal (1930)
The Fellowship of the Frog (1925)
The Joker or The Colossus (1926)
The Twister (1928)
The India-Rubber Men (1929)
White Face (1930)

Educated Evans (Series)

Educated Evans (1924)
More Educated Evans (1926)
Good Evans (1927)

Smithy (1905)
Smithy Abroad (1909)
Smithy and The Hun (1915)
Nobby or Smithy's Friend Nobby (1916)

Angel Esquire (1908)
The Fourth Plague or Red Hand (1913)
Grey Timothy or Pallard the Punter (1913)
The Man Who Bought London (1915)
The Melody of Death (1915)
A Debt Discharged (1916)
The Tomb of T'Sin (1916)
The Secret House (1917)
The Clue of the Twisted Candle (1918)
Down under Donovan (1918)
The Man Who Knew (1918)
The Strange Lapses of Larry Loman (1918)
The Green Rust (1919)
Kate Plus Ten (1919)
The Daffodil Mystery or The Daffodil Murder (1920)
Jack O' Judgment (1920)
The Angel of Terror or The Destroying Angel (1922)
The Crimson Circle (1922)
Mr. Justice Maxwell or Take-A-Chance Anderson (1922)
The Valley of Ghosts (1922)
Captains of Souls (1923)
The Clue of the New Pin (1923)
The Green Archer (1923)
The Missing Million (1923)
The Dark Eyes of London or The Croakers (1924)
Double Dan or Diana of Kara-Kara (US Title) (1924)
The Face in the Night or The Diamond Men or The Ragged Princess (1924)
The Sinister Man (1924)
The Three Oak Mystery (1924)
The Blue Hand or Beyond Recall (1925)
The Daughters of the Night (1925)
The Gaunt Stranger or Police Work (1925) revised as The Ringer (1926)
A King by Night (1925)
The Strange Countess (1925)
The Avenger or The Hairy Arm (1926)
The Black Abbot (1926)
The Day of Uniting (1926)

The Door with Seven Locks (1926)
The Man from Morocco or Souls In Shadows or The Black (US Title) (1926)
The Million Dollar Story (1926)
The Northing Tramp or The Tramp (1926)
Penelope of the Polyantha (1926)
The Square Emerald or The Woman (1926)
The Terrible People or The Gallows' Hand (1926)
We Shall See! or The Gaol-Breakers (US Title) (1926)
The Yellow Snake or The Black Tenth (1926)
Big Foot (1927)
The Feathered Serpent or Inspector Wade or Inspector Wade and the Feathered Serpent (1927)
Flat 2 (1927)
The Forger or The Counterfeiter (1927)
Terror Keep (1927)
The Hand of Power or The Proud Sons of Ragusa (1927)
The Man Who Was Nobody (1927)
Number Six (1927)
The Squeaker or The Sign of the Leopard or The Squealer (US Title) (1927)
The Traitor's Gate (1927)
The Double (1928)
The Flying Squad (1928)
The Gunner or Gunman's Bluff (US Title) (1928)
Four Square Jane or The Fourth Square (1929)
The Golden Hades or Stamped In Gold or The Sinister Yellow Sign (1929)
The Green Ribbon (1929)
The Calendar (1930)
The Clue of the Silver Key or The Silver Key (1930)
The Lady of Ascot (1930)
The Devil Man or Sinister Street or Silver Steel
or The Life and Death of Charles Peace (1931)
The Man at the Carlton or The Mystery of Mary Grier (1931)
The Coat of Arms or The Arranways Mystery (1931)
On the Spot: Violence and Murder in Chicago (1931)
When the Gangs Came to London or Scotland Yard's Yankee Dick
or The Gangsters Come To London (1932)
The Frightened Lady or The Case of the Frightened Lady or Criminal At Large (1933)
The Green Pack (1933)
The Man Who Changed His Name (1935)
The Mouthpiece (1935)
Smoky Cell (1935)
The Table (1936)
Sanctuary Island (1936)

Other Novels
Captain Tatham of Tatham Island or Eve's Island or The Island of Galloping Gold (1909)
The Duke in the Suburbs (1909)
Private Selby (1912)

1925 - The Story of a Fatal Peace (1915)
Those Folk of Bulboro (1918)
The Book of all Power (1921)
Flying Fifty-five (1922)
The Books of Bart (1923)
Barbara on Her Own (1926)

## Poetry Collections
The Mission That Failed (1898)
War and Other Poems (1900)
Writ In Barracks (1900)

## Non-Fiction
Unofficial Despatches of the Anglo-Boer War (1901)
Famous Scottish Regiments (1914)
Field Marshal Sir John French (1914)
Heroes All: Gallant Deeds of the War (1914)
The Standard History of the War – Volumes 1 – 4 (1914)
Kitchener's Army and the Territorial Forces:
The Full Story of a Great Achievement (1915)
Vol. 2-4. War of the Nations (1915)
Vol. 5-7. War of the Nations (1916)
Vol. 8-9. War of the Nations (1917)
Famous Men and Battles of the British Empire (1917)
Tam of the Scouts (1918)
The Real Shell-Man: The Story of Chetwynd of Chilwell (1919)
People or Edgar Wallace by Himself (1926)
The Trial of Patrick Herbert Mahon (1928)
My Hollywood Diary (1932)

## Screenplays
King Kong (1932, first draft of original screenplay, 110 pages) While the script was not used in its entirety, much of it was retained for the final screenplay.
The Hound of the Baskervilles (1932, British film)
The Squeaker (1930, British film)
Prince Gabby (1929, British film)
Mark of the Frog (1928, American film)
The Valley of Ghosts (192

## Short Story Collections
The Admirable Carfew (1914)
The Adventure of Heine (1917)
Tam O' the Scouts (1918)
The Fighting Scouts (1919)
Chick (1923)
The Black Avons (1925)
The Brigand (1927)
The Mixer (1927)

This England (1927)
The Orator (1928)
The Thief in the Night (1928)
Elegant Edward (1928)
The Lone House Mystery and Other Stories (1929)
The Governor of Chi-Foo (1929)
Again the Ringer The Ringer Returns (US Title) (1929)
The Big Four or Crooks of Society (1929)
The Black or Blackmailers I Have Foiled (1929)
The Cat-Burglar (1929)
Circumstantial Evidence (1929)
Fighting Snub Reilly (1929)
For Information Received (1929)
Forty-Eight Short Stories (1929)
Planetoid 127 and The Sweizer Pump (1929)
The Ghost of Down Hill & The Queen of Sheba's Belt (1929)
The Iron Grip (1929)
The Lady of Little Hell (1929)
The Little Green Man (1929)
The Prison-Breakers (1929)
The Reporter (1929)
Killer Kay (1930)
Mrs William Jones and Bill (1930)
Forty Eight Short Stories (George Newnes Limited ca. 1930)
The Stretelli Case and Other Mystery Stories (1930)
The Terror (1930)
The Lady Called Nita (1930)
Sergeant Sir Peter or Sergeant Dunn, C.I.D. (1932)
The Scotland Yard Book of Edgar Wallace (1932)
The Steward (1932)
Nig-Nog and other humorous stories (1934)
The Last Adventure (1934)
The Woman From the East (1934) Co-written By Robert George Curtis
The Edgar Wallace Reader of Mystery and Adventure (1943)
The Undisclosed Client (1963)

Other
King Kong, with Draycott M. Dell, (1933), 28 October 1933 Cinema Weekly

Plays
An African Millionaire (1904)
The Forest of Happy Dreams (1910)
Dolly Cutting Herself (1911)
The Manager's Dream (1914)
M'Lady (1921)
Double Dan (1926)
The Mystery of room 45 (1926)
A Perfect Gentleman (1927)

The Terror (1927)
Traitors Gate (1927)
The Lad (1928)
The Man Who Changed His Name (1928)
The Squeaker (1928)
The Calendar (1929)
Persons Unknown (1929)
The Ringer (1929)
The Mouthpiece (1930)
On the Spot (1930)
Smoky Cell (1930)
The Squeaker (1930)
To Oblige A Lady (1930)
The Case of the Frightened Lady (1931)
The Old Man (1931)
The Green Pack (1932)
The Table (1932)

www.ingramcontent.com/pod-product-compliance
Lightning Source LLC
Chambersburg PA
CBHW071943170626
46813CB00005B/1815